The

Manipulators

Book One

Anthony Tacheny

"I'D LIKE TO GET AWAY FROM EARTH FOR AWHILE

AND THEN COME BACK TO IT AND BEGIN OVER."

-ROBERT FROST

CONTENTS

DEDICATION

This book is dedicated to those that have supported me while I wrote it. I know that I was crazy, obsessive, passionate, and often times relentless about this book. Thank you for reading and encouraging. I hope you're able to find your own story throughout the white spaces.

Prologue

Everything happened so slow it felt like nothing happened at all. She was a slow swelling wave that pushed everyone away. She cut the strings that linked her to the outside world until they snapped; outside her hospital bed, outside the house, outside her own hell. It was inescapable, we all knew, but it didn't make it better.

Neither did the pre-made dinners or the pretentious phone calls from people that didn't matter. All I had left were my step-father and step-brother; my mother left everyone else when she escaped the world within ours. She left everything except for me. This was the last tale she told me.

She didn't tell me why she left years ago; she didn't tell me who she ran from, but she fled a world where people like us exist. My small hands wrapped around her cold ones. My entire world rested between my palms, and her world was falling apart.

Every good thing that happened with her flashed through my mind: the long drives to school every day, the late nights we sat in my room under an orange glow, and watching the sun dissolve behind the horizon every single Sunday night. My mother was patient, and caring, and kind, and strong. She was everything I craved to be and everything I wasn't. She listened to the best music, had the brightest laugh, and had the most piercing blue eyes in the universe.

"I'm sending someone," my mother said. Her voice was silk wrapped around me in layers until it felt warm. "Someone to get you. Someone to take you back where you belong."

That was a promise and all she left me with. I stepped out of the room to let my step-dad say his last words. My eyes became glossy and my head spun as I walked through the blank white walls of the hospital. My step-brother wrapped his arms around me and held me close. I didn't hold him at all.

My step-father opened the door and called us back a few minutes later. I tiptoed to my mom who looked weaker than ever. Her eyes sealed closed, and her face void of all color. I held her hands, but she didn't hold mine back.

"I love you," I tried to say. My voice shook more than my hands, faster than my heart, and more deliberately than her death.

I squeezed her hands tighter, hoping that she would feel something, anything. Hoping that I would feel anything, but she didn't say a word back. All I've known rested in the palms of my hands, dissolving into darkness in front of me.

And in that fleeting silence, I heard the muffled voices of a dead world begging me to bring it back to life, to bring flames to the dark ashes. And I will.

CHAPTER ONE
FROM FLAMES AND STARS

The days I didn't have to think about it were the only good ones, but those days hardly came around. Today lined up to be one of those stumbled upon days where my life seemed to be just like anyone else's, but it wasn't.

It was the last night my step-brother, Jeremy, was in town before he left for college. He had it all figured out, he always has. Tomorrow, he leaves to play football at a big school down in Los Angeles on scholarship.

I applied to the same school, but I won't find out if I got in until January. College was never a part of my plan though. My abilities made me dangerous. My mom told me about a place I could learn how to control it, but I had to wait to get brought there.

It has only been me, Jeremy, and his father, Jim, for the last two years. My mom got sick and spent the last year of her life hooked up to IV's and in and out of hospitals. It was hard when she died, but seeing the slow deterioration of everything became excruciating. If my mom had never married Jim - if I hadn't had him and Jeremy in my life - I would've deteriorated too.

We went to the beach all day today. Jim was better at surfing than Jeremy and I combined. He grew up right on the beach in central California, so he had a slight advantage over us already. Although he had tried to teach me for years, I still stumbled when I stood.

The beach was a sanctuary for me, just water for miles and miles. The second we stepped on the beach they put their wetsuits on and sprinted to the water, but I liked the cool temperatures. I kept only a swimsuit on, paddled out past the waves, and let the water surround me. The rhythmic waves tilted my body back and forth with a fluid and constant repetition. My left hand grazed the surface of the water, just like it did years ago.

My mother used to stream water over our heads and all throughout the living room. Never ending rivers came from the sink and kept a constant speed, whatever speed she wanted them to. She would pull me onto the couch with her and make the water dance around us. She seemed happiest whenever water followed her command.

"Finn," I heard my step-dad shout.

A wave swelled high above my head.

"Take it in," Jeremy said.

I panicked as I paddled with the wave. I had never taken a wave this big, but I began synching with the water. The wave curled over itself. I pushed myself up on my forearms and then straightened my left leg in front of my right. The wave crashed, mist rose, and I stood tall above it.

My pride took ahold of me, and I tried to cut the board back up the wave like Jim does. Almost immediately, I lost balance on the board and tumbled through the water. The leash pulled at my foot, and I kicked up to the surface. Jim and Jeremy laughed as I got back on the board and swam towards the shore.

"You aren't supposed to tail whip after the wave has already crashed," Jim said, "but I like the effort."

Jeremy pushed me back into the water when I stood off the board. I grabbed a handful of wet sand and threw it at his back.

"You don't want to start this." He dug both of his hands in the sand and formed a dense ball.

"It's already began," I laughed as my step-father dropped a handful of sand on top of Jeremy's head.

Soon enough, all three of us were running around the beach throwing balls of sand at each other. This was our beach. Even though other people were there, no one else seemed to matter. If only we could've stayed there all day, if only we had our whole lives ahead of us.

Before long, the sun set behind the thick clouds piled on the horizon allowing the cold air to overtake the heat of the day.

"It's getting cold, we could use some of our old wood and build a fire," Jeremy said.

"No," I blurted. "We have to pick up Kate for the show."

"Oh shoot, I forgot about that," Jeremy said.

We grabbed the boards and walked up the white stairs to the bridge. My mother was the only one who knew about my abilities, much like I was the only one who knew she controlled water. A big part of me that wanted to tell Jeremy, but I promised her I wouldn't show anyone.

Kate was my girlfriend. She lived a couple blocks away from me, but she used to live right across the street. She, Jeremy and I were going to a concert in a couple of hours.

When we got home, I jumped in the shower first. I wanted to take a hot shower for once. I wanted ribbons of steam to dance around me and meet somewhere on the mirror or the window that leaked light just above me, but I didn't. The lukewarm waters had to be enough for me. The temperature was perfect if the dial creaked to about two o'clock.

I always took too long to shower. The water led me to think as it washed the salt off of my skin and the sand out of my hair. Something about the water gave me the desire to leave and find my own way back to the place my mother ran from years ago, but I never left.

Kate was in my room by the time I got out. I grabbed the outfit she picked out for me and changed in the closet. She pulled her long brown hair into a ponytail as she stood in front of the mirror. We sat on my small bed, and she laid her head on my lap. A pale blue light reflecting off of a David Bowie poster onto her face made her look like someone else. I combed my fingers through her messy hair.

"Are you getting sad about Jeremy?"

"Getting sad," I laughed. "I haven't stopped thinking about this for a month. Everything will change."

"Does that scare you?" She put her hand on my chest.

"Terrifies me." I slid my fingers out of her hair and moved my hand over her stomach.

"Life is change. That's all it is. The moments where everything is constant are the ones you won't remember."

It's hard to believe she's same age as me. "I'm worried I won't be able to keep up."

She said nothing else. She moved out of my lap and sat on her knees in front of me. She wore shirts covering her shoulders most days, but tonight she didn't. I saw the pale scar traveling down the left side of her body, the thing she so often tried to hide.

But everyone desperately tries to hide something.

Three years ago, her kitchen caught fire late at night. I was still up looking at the stars - I used to do that a lot - and panicked as the flames from across the street took over the light of the sky. I tried to run over, but Jim pulled me back into the house while he ran to help.

Everyone made it outside except Kate's sister. Kate sprinted into the house to find her, but it was far too late. Kate burned herself and found nothing. After that, the stars didn't seem so cathartic.

"Have I ever shown you all of it?" She looked up at me.

"No." I realized our hands still circled around each other.

She took off her shirt, and I followed the scar down her chest. It was an enchanting part of her body. It showed a lot of pain but just as much beauty. My hand traced down the rough history of her family's tragedy.

"Think about how much has changed since then," she whispered.

Static circulated between the small space between our lips. She pulled her hair in front of her shoulder, and I grabbed her face as she leaned towards me. I laid down, and she fell over me like a morning fog covering the cold ground below.

"Come on lovebirds, we're gonna be late," Jeremy said while hammering the door with his fist.

Kate sprung up and threw her shirt back on.

"Yeah, we're coming," I said.

She put her denim jacket on and opened the door. Jeremy leaned against the wall looking as cool as ever in his leather coat. Kate walked to the bathroom and made sure her makeup looked all right.

"You dog," Jeremy whispered.

"Shut up." I threw a pillow at him and stood up.

"You're gonna miss me." He put me in a choke hold. "Admit it."

"I never denied it," I laughed. I grabbed his arm and twisted it behind his back. "I won't have anyone to beat up."

He rolled his shoulder around once I let go of his arm. "Maybe one day little bro. Maybe one day."

Kate walked out of the bathroom and the three of us headed towards the front door. I grabbed my keys and yelled goodbye to Jim although he was probably asleep by now. I opened the passenger door and closed it for Kate while Jeremy pushed himself over the rails and into my Jeep.

"Why can't you just use the door?" I laughed.

"It's a good night. That's how you start a good night."

I shook my head and started the car. Kate fiddled with the radio, but signal hardly existed in the hills. She grabbed the *Rumours* cd from the glove box and turned the volume all the way up. We couldn't afford to get actual Fleetwood Mac tickets, so we found a decent cover band instead.

When we reached the highway, she stuck her head out of the open roof of my Jeep. *Don't Stop* blasted through the speakers, but it wasn't loud enough to block out our pitchy singing. Jeremy followed Kate's lead and screamed out into the night. Usually I would make them buckle their seatbelts, but I wanted tonight to be special for them.

On the right side of the road, a figure stood still in the darkness like a living shadow. I slowed down and noticed an unsettling white mask painted with dull shades of red and orange. My car crept down the road now. The mask had a dark red color over the eyes that faded into scarlets and yellows. The bottom reached no lower than where a mouth would be, but the top of the mask seemed to have no end. It stretched all around the head and down the back until it became two stretched out wings.

"Are you looking at the stars too?" Kate tucked back into the car. "They look so beautiful tonight, so light."

I looked in my rearview mirror, but the being - whatever it was - was gone. "Yeah, they're beautiful," I said.

They seemed oblivious to the eerie creature that stood frozen in the road. I tried to forget the creepy image but as tall trees surrounded us, it was hard not to imagine the shadow lurking somewhere in the woods.

I drove again, trying to get whatever I saw out of my head. Where I lived was rather odd compared to anywhere else in California. One second we're at beaches surrounded by rocks structured by some divine sculptor, and the next we're driving through a road curving up and down a mountain covered with tall trees.

We only got through a couple more songs before we reached the top of a hill where the venue was. It was at an old church called the Tabernacle that should've been demolished years ago. A lot more people flooded through the large wooden doors than I expected, so we had to park near the woods because the lot was already full.

I turned the car off, but we didn't step out. I leaned on the wheel and looked at Jeremy. Things would be different for both of us next year. Today was the last of what I had grown accustomed to, and I might not adapt to what came next.

"I don't know what I'll do next year without you," I said.

"Everything'll be all right." He slapped my arm. "You still have Kate, and I'm only a couple hours away."

"But things will be so different."

"Nothing will change. Yes, we will be in different places, but you can come up on weekends without football, and I will be back here for your birthday."

"But what about every other day?"

"Hey. We can get all sentimental about this later. Tonight, I want to have an unforgettable night with you guys." He opened the door. "Let's go dance."

I looked at Kate, and her infectious smile took hold of me. She opened the door and hopped out of the car. I followed. I noticed the same dark figure, standing off to the side of the building staring at me. It stood unmoving.

"Do you guys see that?" I pointed towards the shadow.

"What?" Kate scanned the building. "I don't see anything."

"The dude with the mask. It's creeping me out."

People walked right through the shadow as if it weren't there. It faded into the walls of the building until it vanished.

"Finn, you're losing it buddy." Jeremy kept walking towards the church.

I grabbed Kate's hand and scanned behind us to make sure we weren't being followed. I know I wasn't just seeing things this time.

"It's just some weird kid," she said. "Don't worry about it, it's gone now."

When we walked into the church, I made sure the shadow wasn't on the walls. I must've looked insane, but I knew what I saw. It wasn't in here.

"There's a space close to the stage," Jeremy said. He towered over the girls that occupied most of the floor.

Kate looked back at me and pulled me forward. The venue took the pews out to create standing room. Tall candles at the front of the stage and a mosaic behind it were all that remained from the church. The band waited on stage, ready to start their set.

They introduced themselves as Thursday Night Dilemma, which wasn't the worst band name but certainly wasn't good. The lead singer had long, greasy hair and crooked teeth, but the second he sang, his looks didn't matter. The girls in the crowd fawned as he opened with a Pet Shop Boys song and continued to scream as he took off his jacket.

"They're good," Kate said.

"They're incredible," Jeremy yelled while he danced to the heavy drum beats.

Dancing was just about the only thing he wasn't good at. He tried to make his large arms flow to the music, but it looked awkward and offbeat. I wasn't much of a dancer either, but that's why I had Kate. She was hypnotic. She grabbed my arms, and we swirled around each other until a group of people surrounded us.

I spun her around my body and pulled her through my legs. We crossed arms, and she flipped off of my back to stare at me again. She forced me to go to dance practices with her for the musical she did at our school, so it was all muscle memory.

"Looks like we have dancers over here," the singer said. "Don't steal the spotlight too much," he laughed.

I kissed Kate, and the surrounding teenagers clapped. When I turned back to the band, the masked figure stood in front of me. I jumped back as everything crashed into stillness. The creature was a foot away. Its mouth and sharp yellow teeth peeked through the bottom of the mask. The muscle bulged from the tight flesh.

It charged towards me and knocked me to the ground. I became dizzy and saw swirling figures of Kate and Jeremy above me. They tried pushing people away from me to give me space, but the shadow didn't move. They screamed that I was seizing, or I fainted, but they were the only ones in real danger. The thing standing behind Kate began enveloping her with shadows. I tried to close my eyes and wake up, but this was real and she couldn't see it.

"Watch out," I yelled.

I jumped to my feet and when I went to push the shadow off of Kate, flames came from my palms. The creature strung together by darkness caught flame and dissolved into nothing but ash. I had never been more powerful, but this was the potential I always had.

Kate looked at me like an animal far too small for my cage. She pushed her way through the crowd and away from me before everyone else tried their hardest to escape.

The fire from the candles rose and set the maroon curtains ablaze. Fire climbed the walls of the church and surrounded us. I felt it. The flames. The heat. It was inside of me, breathing and growing with the intense emotions I felt. I couldn't stop it.

Kate looked at me with wide eyes as I stumbled to catch my breath. The more I tried to concentrate, the stronger the fire became. My mother told me to control my emotions, but I couldn't control something I'd never experienced before. My chest was burning. It wasn't coming from the heat of the fire, but somewhere deep within me. The flames caught the wood at the top of the building. I felt powerful. I felt terrified.

The fire rose quicker than it should've. As the crowd scrambled and screamed, my anxiety and fear only made the flames spread larger and faster. No one stopped to pull anyone up from the ground, or helped move my still body from the engulfing flames. Wooden structures holding up the building fell down, and the people inside were sprinting out in a panic. My heart was burning, and now an orange glow shrouded the entire building with light.

A girl laid on the ground near one of the exit doors. I scurried to pick her up and run out the emergency exit doors. I laid her on a patch of grass away from the flames, and then I ran back towards the church. The large, colorful mosaic cracked. I looked around and saw Jeremy mouth something, but I couldn't hear him. He pointed to the church, and I looked back at the mosaic. Glass came crashing all around me and the floor shimmered with different colors.

I drifted closer to the burning remains of the building. Fire danced right around me, but I didn't get burned. I looked down into a thick piece of red glass and stared at it while the orange glow flooded the bottom of my face. For the first time, in this tainting light, I didn't recognize myself.

My blue eyes looked black, and the shadow cast below me made me look cynical. The flames still erupted while Kate and Jeremy tried helping people out of the church. I tried to control the growing fire, but it wouldn't extinguish. I gave the car keys to Jeremy and stared at him with bloodshot eyes.

"I have to -" I didn't know what to say, so I ran.

As I ran through the warm colored trees, I heard the sirens of a fire truck. My head spun faster than I could move. I was too dizzy to continue, so I laid down on the dirt. I caught my breath and wept.

Through the trees the only thing I saw was the cross rising high above the church. It hadn't caught fire yet, but it seemed like everything else already had. It seemed as if I had already corrupted this world with flames.

There was no one to blame but myself and my lack of control, but I would give anything to control those flames again. It was stronger and brighter than anything I had ever seen. It was just as tainting as my mother said, I was just as tainting as I thought I would be. Just like the fire, I was vibrant and extraordinary.

Now everyone knew; I can control fire, destruction by its very core, *and this fire will control me.*

CHAPTER TWO
AN UNFORSEEN WORLD

I tossed and turned in bed all night expecting Jeremy or Kate to barge in with a load of questions. Often, on these late nights, I ignited a small flame in my room. It was not out of control, or too big, just a small light that rested in the palm of my hand creating an orange glow. My mother used to walk into my room at two or three in the morning and say the glow peeked underneath the door. She said my flame was tainting, and that showing my manipulation would corrupt the naïve world with our power.

One of the last good nights I can remember with my mom was another late night while the bright orange glow highlighted my walls. We sat underneath my sheet and the dimmest flame, one smaller than a match, lit up our faces.

"Flames lie deep in your emotions," she said. "Anger, embarrassment, sadness, joy; these will be reasons you will be able to manipulate fire." She cupped my hands, like she wanted to hold the timid glow. "But the strongest flames, the purest ones are when you can understand those emotions and examine why you are feeling a certain way."

I was never able to control, much less examine, my emotions. I felt things more than most people did, like my emotions were hyperactive. The littlest of things excited or depressed me for days, but as I grew older, I learned how to hide what I felt. I bottled things in so that no one else would get hurt. My mother understood; that's why she wanted me to leave.

She said someone would come to take me to the place we're from, where manipulation existed. Once she died, I looked forward to casting the light of my flame in public. After a year, I stopped hoping for change.

Tonight was the first time in years that someone interrupted my flames. It wasn't by Jim or Jeremy, but by several rocks being thrown at my window. A large silhouetted figure catching only the dim light of the moon stood still in the night staring at me.

"Finley." A voice echoed in my head.

I looked behind me, but the only person was the man outside my window. His mouth didn't move as he spoke. I heard what he needed me to hear in my mind.

"I need to talk to you. Your mother sent me," the voice inside me spoke again.

The immediacy of a dozen different emotions left me confused. It felt like one of my dreams. I threw on my jacket and crept through the halls. I opened the door, and he leaned against a wooden frame on my porch. When he stepped into the light, the large white scar that curved down his right eye was the first thing I noticed.

"Finley, right?" His voice sounded strained although he didn't look older than forty.

"You can just call me Finn," I whispered. "Did you know my

mother?"

"I did not, but we have heard stories about her escape. She seemed fearless. There are only a couple people have tried to come to the common." He continuously looked behind him to make sure nothing was there. *"We need to go."* His voice returned to my head. *"If you want to go to Centure, to the world where you can control fire and learn how to tame it, we must go."*

This man asking me to leave was a stranger, but more than ever I wanted to go. My small cross necklace dangled between my fingers. *I can't stay here.* I can't lose control again. My eyes fluttered back to the man, a native to the world I belonged.

"All right," I said.

"All right?" He looked at me and I nodded my head. "That was a lot easier than it usually is. Toss me your keys. Forgot to mention my name is Sylvic."

My Jeep sat in the driveway. Jeremy and Kate were already back, but they said nothing about the concert when they got home.

"They don't remember what happened," he said. "They remember the fire, but no one will remember you controlling it. I made sure of that."

"How did you-"

"It's been my job to watch you for a while. To wait for the right time, and this was it." He stood straight and rolled his long sleeves up. "It's now or never."

I was ready. I've been ready for years. A part of me wanted to say goodbye, but that would only lead to questions unanswered. "Do I need to grab anything?"

"No," he blurted. He took a deep breath trying to stay calm. "Just your keys. We'll have clothes and your other needs at Centure."

I walked inside and grabbed the keys from the hook on the wall. I closed the wooden door and held my hand on the doorknob for a couple seconds too long; it was colder than the copper usually was.

I've been waiting for this day for years, but I thought it would be different. I thought I would say goodbye to Jeremy and show him the fire I control. Jim would know the truth about what my mother and I could do, but knowledge like that didn't belong here. I didn't belong here. This day was destined to come, and I'd never been more ready.

Sylvic snapped his fingers, and I turned and threw the keys to him. He unlocked the car and sat in the driver's seat.

"I can drive us you know."

He laughed, but I wasn't kidding. He turned on the car and looked five years younger gesturing me to come in. I stood outside the car staring at my home.

"Look, I'm sure you have a lot of questions, but we need to go." His voice gathered sincerity it hadn't before. "I'm not the only person who knows what you're capable of. And believe me, you're glad I found you before they did."

I hopped over the door and into the seat. I didn't understand why I trusted this guy, especially this guy, but he knew more about me then maybe I did. He pulled out of my driveway, hitting a trash can while reversing.

"Have you driven one of these before?" I clutched onto the

handle just above me.

"Yes." He sped through my neighborhood, without stopping at any of the signs or slowing down for speed bumps. "I'm known to be a bit reckless, but we'll probably get there in one piece."

He opened the glove box and shuffled through all the albums I had. A Bowie disc sat between his fingers, and he closed the glove box again. He held the disc in his hand instead of putting it in the car.

Scars and blisters covered his arm. Large pale lines zigzagged across the back of his hand with an intricate pattern stitched together by someone. He flipped his hand around so I wouldn't stare at it any longer.

We reached the bridge that stretched over the coastline. "I always forget how beautiful it is," he said.

He looked at the ocean reflecting the half-moon. For a minute we were on top of the world with crystallized water pushing and pulling beneath us, and then he made a sharp turn off the bridge.

The cement railing broke, and I lifted out of my seat as we plummeted towards the white beach below us. It was only a matter of time until we slammed into the ground. Sylvic lifted his hands off the wheel and pulled sand from the beach up and around us. The sand became denser as Sylvic used it to cradle our fall until we stopped. Light dwindled back into the car as sand sunk back onto the beach and we rested on top.

He sat there, natural as if this were an everyday thing, and then laughed as sand sifted back into place.

"Are you out of your mind?" I said while wiping the tears from my eyes. "How the hell did you do that?" My chest stretched by the heavy beating of my heart.

Sand poured out of the door as it opened. "I can control stuff just like you can. We're manipulators." He walked towards the ocean, and I followed behind him after I caught my breath.

I pushed hard on the door, but had to crawl out of the window to get out. The car didn't have a scratch on it.

"What are you doing with the car?" I asked.

"There are people from our world that will take care of it," he said. He walked even faster towards the water, and I ran to catch up with him.

"Where exactly are we going?" I looked out at the miles of water in front of me.

"Why don't I show you?" He stepped on the sand, and stretched out his arms, pulling the sand open underneath him.

I dragged my feet towards the hole and tilted my head over it. A bright, white light shined about ten feet below us. Sylvic nodded his head towards the ditch. I pinched my wrist, but I still could not wake up.

"Am I going to come back?"

"You can, but you probably won't want to leave where we are going." He looked at me as if he knew what I would say next. "You'll have another family there. With people as extraordinary as you."

As a wave crashed, I looked up at the stars. I let the flames I saw in them dissipate to darkness. *Life is change.* This was my chance to meet the potential I always had.

I jumped, falling into an abyss. Light passed me every couple of seconds, then every second. The walls and wind became cold as I sped towards the metal ground, and then there was no wind. I wasn't moving at all. Some unknown power held me still in the air for three seconds. I didn't know how to think in those three seconds. I was amazed, and scared, and confused, and finally hurt as I landed on my stomach.

I pushed myself to my feet and Sylvic reached for the floor. His foot stretched out as far as possible, but he didn't reach the ground until the force let him.

We ended up in an underground room with clear walls separating us and the ocean. It reminded me of the subway stations underneath New York. When the wall between us and the sea opened, one man wearing an all navy uniform pushed his hands forward to keep the water out. A silver subway car came out of the water and onto the platform tracks.

The train was dry and empty except for a strange fox like creature walking out on two legs. It crept towards me and tilted his face up, revealing an unsettling white mask with two sharp ears, like the one the dark figure wore yesterday. It stood up and made direct eye contact with me.

I reached my hand out towards the creature. It lowered its head toward me until the soft brown fur behind the mask grazed my fingertips.

Sand came from above it and knocked the creature back to the ground. It let out a piercing cry and ran to the wall.

"Back up Finn. This is not a friendly creature." Sylvic stood in front of me and pushed it back using a big wall of sand. "We need to go."

We tiptoed back into the subway car. The door closed with the blank faced creature keeping a constant glare through the glass window.

"What was that?" I asked.

"That was an alokrite. They were once foxes until seirons took over their bodies. They can't possess you like seirons can, but they desire to take the light out of you. And they want people like you more than anyone."

The inside of the train no longer looked like a subway. White lights covered the silver walls, and light blue doors led to small rooms on each side. I followed Sylvic down a silver hall with empty rooms on each side.

"What do you mean 'people like me', and what are seirons?" I asked.

He stood in front of the door with a 13 on it and pressed numbers on a keypad until it opened. Two marble benches with a small white table filled most the small car.

"Seirons are beings of the shadows; the first things created by the Keeper of Dark. They wear the same masks the alokrites wear. If you ever see one, think as happy as you can, or they will take over any ounce of darkness they find in your soul and inhabit your body." He stopped talking.

That's what followed me yesterday. That's what tried to hurt

Kate. The more I learned about this world, the less I wanted to be here.

"What are you going to do with that one?"

"Guards will throw it in the water. Kill it. It doesn't matter what they do, but it will get taken care of."

Sylvic pressed the side of the table, and a screen unfolded showing a map of the California coast and a place off the coast called Centure. He moved a hollow triangle to a bay and pushed it into the map.

The weight from the other cars separated from ours. The white walls around our car folded down revealing a transparent wall. Everything except for a few blinking red lights from the other trains were too dark to see.

"How are we moving?" I asked.

"Metal manipulators are propelling us along." Sylvic nodded to tinted walls behind me with vague shadows of a person moving behind.

"Can everyone manipulate where we are going?" I stared at the map of Centure. It was shaped like an askew letter "j" with large coves and small islands.

"Yes. Everyone specializes in one of the different branches."

All of my questions annoyed him, but I asked another. "How can you control two; sand and minds?"

"You will control two substances one day. All the Craved can."

"What's a-" he cut me off before I asked another question.

"The Craved are the rare few who at birth aren't for light or darkness. All the Craved will, at some point, be chosen. We are taking you somewhere you can stay safe."

"Safe from what?"

"Anything. Everything. A lot of people view our ability to control two different substances as a threat."

He looked at me expecting me to ask something else, but I sat silently. I leaned on the curved doors and tried to sleep through the rest of the trip, but it was hard to let my mind sit still.

I leaned on the wall as a loud yawn forced its way out of me. It had to be pushing midnight already, and my eyes started pulling down on themselves. My head spun with thoughts as I tried to fall asleep: I was a Craved, I needed protection, this is the world I belong to.

At first light, the sun reflected into my eyes. Bright colored fish swarmed around us and the reefs not too far under us. The water was much clearer here, wherever we were. I looked down to a city with spiraling towers sparkling under the water. We stopped and floated up towards the land.

Sand here was dark black, but shining like crystal. The top of the subway opened, and I climbed the ladder to the roof. A crisp breeze rolling off the waves harmonized with the warm summer sun.

The water matched the color of the sky, and the sunlight reflected off the water with the same speed as me. The wind pushed my wavy hair all over the place, and the mist from the water kept me cool. I reached the shore and drew circles in the warm sand with my finger. I grabbed a handful and let the wind carry it away. My arms rose under the salty breeze. My eyes shuttered close.

I sat in the sand and played with flames. I controlled them without worrying who watched. It was the first time I had manipulated during the day. Heat rolled through my hands as I torched the black sand in front of me.

"Kid." Sylvic gripped my arm. "You can't just do that. I will go over rules in a second, but rule number one is no open manipulation outside class."

He walked away from the beach and into the jungle. I wasn't ready to leave yet, but I followed him through the trees, anyway. We walked through tall oak trees that were still a bright green color, not like they were at home.

When we reached a river and a splintering bridge he stopped, but I began to walk across it. Sylvic's strong hand pulled me back.

"Woah kid, slow down," Sylvic said still pulling my shoulder. "This bridge is a mentibus."

I looked at him with a blank stare.

"It's an object that can manipulate something. This bridge can glimpse through time. The first time you cross it, you will see a vision that will affect your near future. Remember what you see."

I looked at the plain, brown bridge stretching over the greenish waters. I took one step onto the bridge and saw nothing. When I was about halfway across the bridge, something sinister took over.

My hands shook as shadows crept from every direction imaginable. They crawled up my arms, twisting around me. They tried to penetrate me, but it was like a butter knife that couldn't quite make it through my skin. I looked for Sylvic, but saw nothing past a dense, gray fog.

Soon, even the fog became overpowered by an unstoppable darkness that poured into my throat. The pain was too much to handle without falling onto my knees. Darkness coursed through my veins, I felt despicable and sick to my stomach. I screamed as loud as I could and expelled all the demons conquering my skin.

Just as quickly as it began, it ended. I stood, but my knees were shackled. Sylvic looked at me and raised his eyebrows. He walked across the bridge and didn't say a word, but I needed to know what I felt.

"I saw this. . ."

"Darkness," he interrupted.

"What does it mean?" I stuttered as my heart tried to slow down.

"Don't worry about it yet," he assured me. "I still haven't seen what I saw when I crossed this thirty-something years ago."

"What did you see?"

"You," he said under his breath.

"What do you mean?" I jogged towards him as he continued to walk faster.

"You'll find out soon enough," he laughed. "Don't be all antsy it's a good thing not anything bad. Come on we have a lot to do today."

I kicked a small rock through the dirt path until it thudded across a tan cobblestone. A single yellow leaf fell onto the unexpecting ground. Right before my eyes, the green leaves of summer changed one by one into a bright yellow. It started as something unnoticeable, then the phenomenon overwhelmed me.

"Looks like Erra's changing her mind already," he laughed as he picked the yellow leaf from the tree. "Erra's the Keeper of the seasons. Hope you never have to see her during winter."

I laughed instead of asking the obvious question of what a Keeper was. I thought my mother had told me a good majority about his world, but it was clear I still knew so little. We approached the top of the hill and just ahead was a large white brick building with a marble clock and a bronze bell standing high above the trees.

We walked into the building, and an unpleasant old woman with yellow teeth and gray hair welcomed us. Sylvic told me to sit down and then had me sit on a chair near the wall. He left with the woman, and I had to wait.

My heart raced with anxiety. I sat here for an hour waiting for something in silence. There was no one else, no music, no pictures to look at; it was just me and my thoughts. And my thoughts were wild.

I kept thinking about what I saw on the bridge, and the coldness overwhelming me; or how I was a Craved, and that made me unique and powerful. I was here. Finally, after having potential but never letting it show, after being an unstruck match my entire life, I was here. Anything seemed possible, except for me to get out of this waiting room.

An hour or more passed before Sylvic came back and called me towards the hall. I walked through the beige hallways and into a small room with a single table. I sat across from him and he sighed that this is the boring part of my arrival.

We sat in there for another hour while he and the old woman told me everything I can and cannot do. I can't manipulate outside class, I can't be out past eight, I can't leave Anador or Domister unless I was taken by someone. Maybe I couldn't do *anything*.

I had to sign about fifteen pages of paper I tried to read before getting bored and skimming through. It stated the same rules they told me and a few pages about needing to pass certain exams to move onto the next year. The woman placed a large blank paper on top of her desk and pulled ink from a bottle. She spread her hands to draw a map of the campus all in one stroke.

"The dark building is where you're staying." She filled in a small rectangular building in the middle of the page.

"Thank you," I said grabbing the map.

Sylvic said a quick goodbye to the old woman, and then we walked out of the office. Six bells struck above me. It was six o'clock already, and the sun was settling around us.

Behind the tower, a marble courtyard scattered with pillars holding together tan roofs stood above the woods. A fountain with an older woman and a dragon in the center of the courtyard captivated the view over everything else.

"Welcome to Domister," Sylvic said with a wide-open arm. "This is where teenagers from Anador come to learn how to control their branch."

No one was here. The cobblestone pathway continuing past tall buildings scattered with a couple kids rushing to get inside.

"Where are the other students?" I asked.

"Domister is the only unrefined school in Centure, so because kids claimed for dark have a curfew, everyone here has to be inside at the same time."

"Why do people claimed for darkness have curfews?"

"You can just call them Alturus." He looked at the painted sky and inhaled a deep breath. "Some things don't change. No matter how much we try to bring the two classes together, someone pushes back."

"Are you one? An Alturus?" The foreign word rolled off my tongue as if it were something I wasn't supposed to say.

The sound of the bell tower echoed in the round stadium. "We have to get back before curfew."

The surrounding buildings illuminated with the light of a small candle. Gold patterns shined over the white marble that most of the buildings were made of, and all of them were named after people I've never heard of like Vatius Velanius or Camben Layler.

A large grass field rolled past the buildings. We walked through a dirt path in the middle of the field with only flames lighting it up. The sky here was intriguing, the stars were brighter than the moon, and white streaks of light covered the dark sheet above us. A small metal shack stood alone in the middle of the grass.

"This is your dorm," Sylvic said.

Of course it was.

"I know it's not special, but it has the most protection for you guys we can give." Sylvic gave me a key to the room. "Goodnight

Finn. I'm looking forward to seeing you tomorrow."

I walked down to the small shack. Today was the longest day in my entire life. Just yesterday, I lost control of myself, I left. Now, for the first time, I'm in a world full of people like me. I wanted to make assumptions of what this place held for me, but there was no point in second guessing myself. I was here for now and I needed to make the most of it. I looked up at the cold steel walls and accepted it as my new home, *for now at least.*

CHAPTER THREE

SPARKS

I knocked on the cold steel door in front of me and different murmurs became silent as footsteps echoed through the walls. Bright blue eyes illuminated as light shined through a small hole that slid open in the door.

A girl with dirty blonde hair covering her face peeled open the door.

"You must be the new kid?" Her voice was low, but still held a pleasant sound. She pulled her hair out of her face, and I couldn't help but stare at her. She had a skinny face with a defined structure and grayish-blue eyes, like a wolf.

"Yeah, I'm Finn." I held my hand out and waited for her to shake it.

"I'm Keegan," she laughed. She cautiously grabbed my hand and shook it.

"Nice to meet you," I said, and she laughed again. "What's so funny?"

She looked down at my hand entangled in hers. "No one's shaken my hand in years, it's strange."

Her hand was warm without being humid. The bones just past her cheeks stuck out, but a smile covered the strong accents on her face. I held on for far too long. Her other hand came towards my bicep as she told me I could let go of her hand.

"Sorry it's been kinda a crazy day."

She said nothing but shook her head and walked through the hall. The room was a lot bigger than it looked on the outside. There were five bunk beds, a decent sized bathroom, and a small open area in the middle of the room with four chairs and a small square table. There were only two other people in the room: a tall guy with copper hair and a broad girl with dark brown, almost black hair reading a book on the floor.

The guy hopped off of the bunk bed and towered over me. He gave me a quick hand wave.

"I'm Miller." He had an enormous mouth and white teeth. "This is cool." He grabbed my necklace. "What does it mean?"

"It's just a cross. My step-dad gave it to me for my sixteenth birthday."

"That's sweet." He pushed his curly hair back and drifted to his bunk.

Silence scattered through the room like it does when trying to meet new people. Miller talked at the same time as I did, and then we both told each other to go first.

"What do you manipulate?" Keegan said over us.

"Yeah, show us what you got," Miller said pulling his hands towards his body.

I closed my eyes and tried to create a small flame, like the ones I used to create under my sheets, but nothing was happening. My hands weren't warm enough to create a flame. I tried to pretend that no one was watching me, but I could hear their whispers. I rubbed my hands together to generate heat, and a flame finally sat just over my palms.

"You still need friction to start a flame," Keegan snarked. "You're out of luck, none of us specialize in fire."

"What do you guys-"

She was not the best listener.

"I control water, Miller controls rock, and the bookworm plants." She snapped her fingers in between the girl and the book. "Hey Hadlee, you've been reading that thing for months. We have a new kid."

"I'm almost done." We all waited for her to finish the chapter, and she slammed the book closed. "How's it going? I'm Hadlee." She spoke with an almost unnoticeable lisp. "And you are?"

"I'm Finn Lynch."

Her white teeth contrasted her dark skin as she laughed. "We haven't used last names throughout the past century unless you're a Vestrin, which you are not."

"What's a Vestrin?" I asked.

"Anyone claimed for light," Hadlee said staring at her book.

I looked at her book. Symbols that looked like skewed letters of our alphabet containing dots underneath and dashes through the letters covered the back of the book. "What's your book called?"

She picked it up and showed me the front. *Outworldly Tales of the Awestruck Man* stretched down the light brown book surrounded with constellations and flowers.

"It's super interesting, and it's believed to be written over three-hundred years ago, when Centure became colonized. Most of the stories are fantasies and hyperbolized allegories, like the ignorance of death, but others are actually historic."

Sounded like something I needed to read so I had the slightest clue about this place. "What do you mean the ignorance of Death?" I sat down on the floor next to her.

"You guys are riveting," Keegan said as she crawled to her top bunk.

"Well, in this story - every chapter is different - Death is a child in a wheat field. He meanders around waiting for the wheat to shake. When it shakes, he cuts it with his sickle. Every wheat is attached to a life, and Death doesn't know who he killed. He was doing it based off of the fate of the winds. It turns out that someone had been manipulating the winds, to kill who he wanted to. Death felt cheated and killed the man with the blade of the sickle. After he killed the man, he was ashamed of what he had done so he ran away from the wheat field. Some say the blade is still somewhere and wields great power."

"That's a load of grink," Miller shouted.

"That's interesting," I said, laughing at Miller.

A bag of clothes covered every bed. "Which bed is mine?" I sat on one without a bag resting on it. The large steel door screeched open.

"Here it comes," Hadlee groaned as the door slid open.

"That's not why it's called altercation, Foster." A short girl with black hair and small brown eyes laughed as she nudged a tan guy pushing his chest as far forward as possible.

"Is so. Ask Nax, I helped him come up with the classes a couple years ago." He walked up behind me and clutched his hands around my shoulders. "Hey, you must be the new guy, Finn."

I looked up at him from the bed. "Yeah, it's nice to meet you. Foster, right?"

"Yeah," he said with a boosting confidence. Without warning, a strong current of wind pushed hard on my back and knocked me to the ground. "That was my bed," he laughed.

When I stood up, he backed away a few inches, realizing how much bigger I was than him. It wasn't so hard to create a flame anymore. My fist glowed with a small flame held just inches away from my knuckles.

"Finn, I wouldn't," Miller said.

I leaned in closer to Foster while he carried the same stupid grin. I opened my hand and let the flame disintegrate. "Which bed is mine?" I asked.

"That one, with the black backpack on it," Hadlee said, pointing to the bunk just below Miller.

I jumped on my bed, unzipped the heavy black backpack, and pulled out books and clothes. All the clothes were black, and what I was wearing now wasn't much better. Even worse news was that one of my books was a math book. The other book was *History of Centure* and weighed about twenty pounds.

The girl with Foster walked up to me. "Hi. I'm Jin. Sorry about before, Foster can be very-"

"Completely full of himself?" I interrupted.

"Confident," she laughed. "Don't let it get to you, he gets better with time."

I couldn't see that being true at all, but I nodded my head anyway. Foster walked to the bathroom, followed by Keegan and Miller. They came out a few minutes later wearing comfortable looking clothes.

The lights turned off, and everyone scuffled to their beds. No one spoke as the persistent ruffling of blankets and flipping of pillows kept me awake. It was my first night in a place I had dreamed of, and a tiny box trapped me inside.

It seemed like before I even fell asleep, the sound of scraping steel over the dorm woke everyone up. The lights turned on, and my eyes were burning.

"Morning'," I yawned.

Hadlee, Jin, and Miller were the only ones left in the room. I threw on black pants that hugged my waist and a black shirt. A *D* inside of a *U* written in white covered the shirt, most likely standing for Domister University. Under the logo was a small circle that was half white and half black.

"How'd you sleep?" Hadlee asked still glued to her book. Her feet bumped into each other with a steady beat.

"All right. Have you slept at all?"

"She's trying to find anything about the Craved, but there's nothing in there," Miller moaned. "She keeps talking about it. I don't know how you've been asleep."

"You remember that story about the Mallux?" Hadlee asked.

"Hadlee, I'm from Kordia, we were *raised* on that story. We based a whole equality movement off of it," he laughed.

"I'm saying that the story is about the Craved and about the ability to choose whether we are light or dark." She kept flipping through the pages, looking for this story but couldn't find it.

"It's a dumb children's book. And it got everyone in a lot of trouble because our Sovereign Lady knows how dangerous ideas like that are."

"Is this in the Outworldy Tales book?" I asked.

"Yes. And Hadlee conveniently forgot to mention we aren't supposed to be reading that book anymore." Miller stood up and pulled the book away from Hadlee. "We don't have class for two hours, let's show Finn some of Domister while we have time."

"How much of Centure have you seen?" Jin asked.

"This is it," I said.

Hadlee and Jin looked at each other and screamed *Atlas Atrium* in perfect synch. They grabbed my hand and pulled me out the door. Miller walked behind us shaking his head while mumbling that they always drag him there.

We walked through the marble courtyard and past a couple more light-bricked buildings before we got to a central lawn with a tall brown building sitting at the end. The main building had a tall tower with a gold emblem perched at the top. Two more buildings sat perpendicular to the first on each side.

The doors were large, glass doors that required strength to open. A long spiral staircase hugged the walls of the room and circled around a thirty-foot-long glass sculpture until it reached the top. We kept walking through without giving me any time to appreciate the details of the walls or paint on the ceilings, but the atrium was something different.

In the middle of the three buildings was a peaceful, empty area resting beneath intricate steel and glass structures connected to the walls. Jin turned around and walked on top of a large map painted on the ground.

Wow was all I could say as I glided over the world.

Everything was painted using a dull green, a tannish yellow, a pastel blue, and white. The colors smudged together instead of being bordered by mountains or the sea. It was an askew *J* shape with lots of little coves and a few islands on the western side.

"This is the Atlas Atrium," Jin said. "It's mine and Hadlee's go to place."

"And I always get dragged here," Miller said.

I bumped into Jin as I scanned the different cities all over the map.

"Sorry," we both muttered.

She pulled her short black hair behind her ear and looked down at her small feet.

"Do you want us to give you the tour?" she smiled.

I nodded. She grabbed my hand and pulled me into the blue

shaded region marked The Pacific. Domister was the most southeast region on the map and labeled with a tiny font.

"There's eight major cities," Hadlee walked up next to us. "Each one has a Keeper to take care of the city, meet with council members, and ensure the laws are maintained."

"How are Keepers chosen?" I asked.

"We don't choose. Animals were the first manipulators, and when the spirit of a beast decides to link with a human, they become a Keeper," Hadlee said.

"The Keeper of Darkness has the spirit of a dragon," Miller exclaimed.

"Anador is where the Keeper of the Sea lives. He makes sure the storm is raging, and the border is secured," Jin said.

Hadlee walked north into Caltus, which was one of the largest cities on the map. "Caltus is run by the Keeper of Youth, and they export steel and technology around Centure."

Jin hopped over a large mountain range that circled around Misula. "Most of the people here live in the mountains and hunt wild game," Jin said. "The Keeper of Seasons live here and I think one of our mentors, Kira, grew up with the hunters."

She walked just to the edge of a large city in the most northwest portion of the map, but didn't cross into the thin line. "This is Umbrous. The Keeper of Dark lives here almost in complete isolation."

"You can't step in the border or its four years of bad luck," Miller whispered.

I didn't believe in that kind of stuff, but I was careful not to step in that territory.

"This is the most vital city." Hadlee drifted into Emor, the largest city on the map.

"Hey, way to leave me out," Miller pulled me back over towards Umbrous. "This is Kordia, it's where I was from, but there's not much left of it now." Just as I was about to ask him what happened, he pushed us back towards Emor. "This is the City of Light."

"Me, and Foster are from here," Jin said. "Well, he's from the city. I lived just outside."

"The Keeper of Light, Vatius, lives here," Hadlee said.

"She has ultimate authority over everything and everyone. If you hear people talking about Our Sovereign Lady, or Our Pureness, or anything that sounds like someone canonized, it's Vatius," Jin said.

"*Our Pureness,*" Miller mocked.

The girls became silent as they walked to the city between Domister and Emor. It was a small city called Pravon that had a long river cutting through the middle.

"This is where the Keeper of the forest lives," Jin said cutting through the silence. "She keeps the animals and plants safe from our world and determines where we can expand."

There were only two more cities labeled on the map. Just west of Pravon was a city surrounded by tall stone walls and intricate caves called Molaris. In the furthest stretch away from everyone else in the southwest region was a city called Fremaine.

"Fremaine is a silent city," Hadlee said. "They cut off trade and communication with the rest of Centure once the genocide started."

"Genocide? What genocide?" I asked.

"It had to be thirteen–fourteen years ago now," Jin said. "There were uprisings all over the place: Kordia, Caltus, Pravon." She listed the cities one by one as if she was walking on glass with them. "Innocent people continued to die and Vestrins demonstrated their authority by killing off the Alturus with no consequence."

"Those who didn't die got shipped to prisons even if they were just affiliated with the rebels. It made everyone remember how important order is," Hadlee said.

"A brief introduction of *Our Pureness*," Miller scoffed. "That's why we can't be talking about the Mallux, it doesn't fit with Vatius's agenda."

"Vatius didn't kill the Alturus. She didn't know about the orders until it was far too late," Hadlee said. "If she was in charge of that, no one would support her."

"Whatever," Miller shrugged. "I don't want to be in a sour mood the rest of the day. Should we head over to class?"

He was talking to me, but I didn't know I had a class today.

"All the Craved have manipulation classes together, even though we're in different years. It is supposed to keep us protected," Miller said. "Come on its back in the Confines."

We all walked together, but we walked in silence. Tension filled the air as Hadlee and Jin walked far in front of us.

"Why do they keep the Craved together?" I asked. "What are they keeping us from?"

"A lot of people have a problem with us," he said. "Domister houses Craved our age, and then there's younger Craved in Pravon and that's it. We are rare, and people think having a choice between light and dark is unfair."

"Do we have a choice?" I asked. "When I crossed the bridge, I saw and felt something—something sinister take over. Sylvic said he saw it too."

"Light and dark live in the Craved. My mom used to say the beast you feed more will come out victorious." He looked up at the clouds above us. "Our actions say something about who we are and ultimately what we're claimed for."

Darkness overtook the light when I crossed the bridge, and I hated it. If we had a choice, I wanted to make sure I didn't fall victim to my fate.

The Confines were steel buildings at the edge of Domister placed with no obvious pattern or reason. A small fence stood in front of the trees marking where the school ended. The room was only lit by a large glass ceiling and filled with a block of stone, a slab of steel, and a pool of water. Plants climbing the walls of the room contrasted the cold silver color.

Keegan and Foster walked in a couple minutes after us and stood near the middle of the room. He looked back at me and smirked before turning back toward Keegan.

A tall, muscular, red-headed girl maybe ten years older than us walked into the room without saying a word. She stomped over to the pool. As she stepped on the water, it froze. Plates of ice spiraled towards us one after another with little hesitation between each.

Keegan laughed as she ducked beneath the speeding slabs of ice and directed a thin river through the oncoming ones. Foster looped his arm in a large circle until a wheel of air caught the ice just to redirect it into the steel wall. Hadlee ripped long vines off the wall and whipped them through the ice before the red-head could even project them into the air.

"Whew!" she laughed as she stepped off the frozen pool. "I can't keep up with you three. Jin, I understand why you didn't step up but what about you two guys?"

"I tried," Miller said, "but they were too fast."

"It's Finn, right?" She walked over to me. She had beautiful green eyes and a couple freckles running across her nose.

I couldn't quite catch my tongue, so I nodded.

"I'm Kira," she said. "One of your mentors." She walked back towards the front of the room. "There is not one substance that is stronger or better than the other. Every branch of manipulation has different pros and cons and techniques. One of the universal techniques is being quick-thinking, not impulsive."

She grabbed my hand and pulled me up to the front. "Finn, what do you branch in?"

"Fire," I stuttered.

She pushed my shoulders back, forcing my chest out. "Fire is wild," she said kicking my feet further apart. "Fire requires someone to control it. Be louder and bolder than it. Say it again, this time with some confidence."

"Fire," I boasted.

"Let's see it," she applauded.

This was one of the first times I could command fire in public, and I was ready. I brought my arms back towards my body and punched the space in front of me, but only a few sparks came flaring from my hands.

A laugh spurred from Foster, but Keegan told him to shut up.

"What happened?" Kira asked.

"I–I don't know."

I let my shoulders fall back over my chest. Kira put her arm around my back and pulled me up. She grabbed my shoulder and turned me until I was just facing her.

"What was your goal while manipulating just then?"

"I guess I was just excited to do it publically and see what I am capable of."

"You should already know you can do unbelievable things. Fire is a very proud branch, you need to understand how delicate and reliant it is. Your other mentor, Nax, branches in fire, so he will be a big help to these fundamentals."

I tried to feel the overwhelming heat I felt at the church. Heat was inside of everyone at the church, especially myself. There was still warmth inside of me, but no one else seemed to discharge the same heat.

"Watch Keegan." Kira grabbed Keegan's hand and pulled her up to her feet. "Water is quite the opposite of fire. You need to be flexible and become one with water, not any stronger than it. try to study how Keegan moves with it."

She stood up and took long, slow breaths. The glass pool became empty as Keegan pulled the water out. She spun in circles, and like ribbons attached to a string, the water followed. It orbited around her, blocking the view from everything except a musky silhouette.

Keegan walked through the wall of water without a single drop hitting her body. She sprinted towards me and slid across the floor a foot in front of me. The rivers of water soon followed as they split around me without getting me wet. She lifted her hands up, and the streams curled above me and back towards her. She let the water crawl across her arm as she spun back towards the pool.

In the moment of her freedom and ecstasy, heat was evident deep in her stomach. She seemed passionate and connected to the water she controlled, and she let the water control her just as much.

The water poured back into the pool, and Kira told Keegan how beautiful it was. Keegan looked at me and smirked before turning back towards the front of the room and sitting down.

"Finn, what did you notice?" Kira asked.

"How she didn't just move the water, she kept moving with it," I said.

"Exactly," she said. "And if water is the opposite, you should. . ."

"Be unmoving."

Kira nodded and gestured me to come back towards her. I stood with my shoulders back and head high. Kira pulled my right arm towards my chest.

"Remember what you felt when you found out you controlled

fire," she whispered. "Nax always talks about a heat inside of him and creating that heat just to let it out."

Kira took a few steps away from me and gave a warm smile. I always knew when my mom was coming towards my room. She had an overwhelming warmth somewhere inside her head. There was a comfort with it. I knew she was safe, and that I wasn't alone.

Heat ascended into my chest, but it didn't feel the same as what I felt at the church. At the church, it propelled all around the room with a warlike chaos. Here, it was peaceful and familiar to what my mom exuded. I brought my hands back towards my chest and directed the heat out of my body.

A long, single stream of fire poured out from just beyond my fist. I kept releasing it, but the bright fire became fleeting sparks, and then it became nothing at all. Kira applauded me, and soon the rest of the Craved did too. While I was taking a second to catch my breath, my chest fluttered with heat again.

CHAPTER FOUR

OXYGEN

Classes were scheduled a lot differently than they were back home. There aren't weekdays or weekends because the seasons depend on Erra, the Keeper of Seasons, and what she thinks the animals and forest need the most. I had two sets of classes that met on alternating days, and then every fourth day we didn't have a class at all.

Day one: Tangible Manipulation with Kira, History 300, and Statistical Analysis.

Day two: Health, and Altercation Practices with Nax.

Day three: same as day one.

Day four: no classes meet.

Day five: same as day two.

And so on.

Keegan was the only person who was the same year in school as me, so we shared almost the same schedule. We didn't have to take *Ethics and Essences* at eight A.M., so we could spend most mornings together if we weren't sleeping in.

"Finn." I woke up to her tapping my arm. "I was about to meet everyone for lunch if you wanted to join us." She pulled her shoe over her heel and stomped into it. "Do you want to go get a bite?"

We had Health in the next hour, but we've already missed two of the four classes without punishment. "Yes," I groaned.

She smiled and caressed the side of my forearm. "We're going to The Seadragon," she said.

"Yeah, let me change really quick." I ripped the sheets off of me and rolled out of the bed. It was strange sleeping in a room with a girl that wasn't Kate, but everyone was comfortable with each other. *Too comfortable.*

I threw on the University shirt and some black pants. We walked down the path Sylvic and I walked that first day. The leaves fell and danced around us as we walked through the golden path. She was something contagious to watch. Her hands would rise with the wind, and her eyes would shutter close. Her blonde hair flew in her face, and she wouldn't move it out of the way. She was captivating.

We reached the old brown bridge I haven't crossed again since I first arrived and a coldness shuttered through me. I've had a few nightmares about what I saw and what I felt, but Hadlee assured me I had nothing to worry about.

"So, do you remember what you saw when you first crossed this?" I asked.

"I do," she went into a soft whisper, "but if I told you I'd have to kill you." She jumped up on the arm of the bridge and tiptoed across.

Her arms stretched like the wings of a plane to keep her balance. The stream of water below followed the line her hand was creating. She jumped off the bridge and back onto the path, and then she nodded her head signaling me to follow.

"Do you miss it?" she asked to break the silence. "California."

"It doesn't seem like I've gone anywhere, I mean it's a couple hours away," I said.

"How can you say that when we're in a different universe?" She laughed. "It might be the same planet, but everything here is so different." Once we reached the black sand, she took off her brown sandals and buried her toes under the warm grains.

"Have you been there?" I asked.

"I used to live there too, a few years back," she said. "I was twelve when I came here."

"How'd you find out," I said, "that you can manipulate?"

"It was at my birthday party." She stopped walking. "A ton of my friends came over for a swim party. I had a crush on this boy that my best friend liked and she told him. I was so embarrassed. Next thing you know, something dragged her to the bottom of the pool, and she passed out. She never woke up."

Her facial expressions didn't change as she told me this as if it had no lasting effect on her.

"I knew I was pulling her down. I came inside to tell my mom, and Sylvic was already waiting inside to take me here."

"Sorry, Keegan."

"Don't be. I'm stronger here."

I wanted to ask her how she moved on, or how she got over the guilt of her power, but she wasn't interested in talking about that. She smiled and grabbed my hands as we reached the sand bridge between us and the island.

The volcano covered half of the island but instead of the fresh blue lava that slid down the mountain yesterday, it cooled to a purple color. The path was lit with torches even though it was light outside. A small wooden arch rose above the sand. It was twisted with light and dark brown bark with a vine spiraling throughout. On the top, coal carrying traces of red and orange flames spelt "Anador".

"What's Anador?" I asked.

"That's the island," she said. "This has to be my favorite city I've been to." She slapped the sign above us as we walked through.

We walked down the torch lit path with the clear sea next to us. A palace stood tall and submerged in the water underneath us. We reached the bottom of the massive mountain and instead of going towards the small village in the distance, Keegan walked towards a green lagoon. A man wearing a tight green shirt and scaly blue pants walked toward Keegan.

Heard you have a new one," he said with a feminine voice. He looked over at me. "He's cute don't you think," he whispered to her.

"I'm literally standing right next to you, I can hear everything you're saying," I said.

"He is cute,' she laughed. She looked over at me and mouthed the word sorry.

"You showin' him around?" he asked while pulling stray hairs out of Keegan's face.

"Yeah, we're meeting everyone at the Seadragon," she said.

"Ugh, how are you not over that place yet?" he asked as if the restaurant made him sick to think about. "I'm Brav." He grabbed my hand and brought it to his heart. He took my hand off of his chest, but continued to hold it as he pulled us towards the lagoon.

A sharp metal fin rose out of the greenish water. It only kept rising. Copper colored steel dragged from the corners of the ship to the same point in the middle. I followed the different pieces of copper to the front of the ship where it created an eight-rayed star. Underneath the thick pieces of copper was a slick silver base. A large door dropped to the sand.

"Enjoy your lunch you two," he said waving his hand to the door. "Keeg, we need to catch up soon it's been too long." He kissed both of her cheeks.

We walked inside the empty ship. Stairs covered the walls to the top of the ship, and giant bulbs of light stretched out above us.

"Your friend was - different," I said.

"His father invented pretty much everything here, but he's nothing compared to some characters you'll meet in Undertown Anador," she laughed.

We sank underwater, but I couldn't see outside. Before long we hit the bottom. The ship jolted as we lifted off of the sand and leapt a few feet forward. The door pushed itself back to the ground, but water didn't come pouring in. A dome of air surrounded us. It surrounded a whole city. Crooked lines of light rippled onto every building, moving with the small waves of water above us. I heard loud screeching coming from the door closing once again as the submarine's claw-like legs walked back into the water.

"Isn't it incredible?" she asked.

Water surrounded us on all sides. An entire utopia existed underneath the teal sea. "How is this even possible?"

A stingray soared through the water just above me as if it were a bird in the sky, casting a cool blue shadow over us as light reflected off of its large wings. I stretched my hand to touch it. As my hand hit the cold water, it dripped down my arm without losing its perfect shape.

"It was a haven for people who didn't agree with the claiming process; the keepers forcing someone to be dark or light. People wanted to be in charge of their own destiny, but that would have destroyed the entire system," she said.

We continued to walk through the small cottage-like houses that sat in the sand. Their roofs were any color pastel imaginable.

"This city started the genocide," she whispered.

"I haven't seen Vestrin markings yet. What do they look like?" I asked.

"Alturus markings are branch-like patterns and Vestrin's have constellations."

We walked past a group of women, and Keegan pointed to the one on the left end. Her bicep had a dark constellation engraved on it. My mother had a similar marking on her right forearm, but she never told me what it was. Even on that last day before she died.

There's a lot she never told me.

"I agree with them. I think we should be able to choose-" Keegan slapped her hand on my lips.

"You can't say that," she said close to my face. "We don't have opinions about that. We're already being watched."

Watched by who? I looked around us and noticed people wearing dark navy suits scattered around the rocks. They stared at us as we walked deeper into the city. I kept my mouth shut and tried to keep my thoughts away from that topic.

The pastel buildings around us shimmered in the light of the water. The tops of the buildings spiraled upwards like seashells. It was an easy city to keep you distracted. The people down here dressed just like Brav and talked like him too.

"Hey Keegan, you look stunning today," a girl with hair swirling two feet above her head said.

"Thank you beautiful," she said kissing the strange woman's cheek. "I have no idea who that was," she whispered.

To the right of us was the building I saw before I came down. It was a large palace with blues, pinks, and greens twisting around the different pillars. There were seven pillars plastered with different shells and curled at the top. A sign on the watercolor base of the building said *Brav's* with bright neon lights.

"This is Brav's store?" I asked.

"Yeah, he is practically the creator of fashion over here," she said. "I have to take you there one day."

"I think I'll pass."

A painting of Keegan wearing a dress that looked like a ton of bubbles stacked on top of each other covered the wall. "What is this?" I laughed.

"He likes to test clothes on me," she said. She covered her eyes and pulled my arm. "This is embarrassing. Come on."

"You look incredible," I said.

Her cheeks turned a rosy pink color while she shrugged a small thanks. She knew she did, but I could tell that she appreciated the comment.

"So you're like a model," I said.

"No, I swear it's just for fun," she said. She grabbed my arm and pulled me away from the store.

We reached the edge of the air dome around us. A covered path led into a circular shaped building in the water. We walked silently through the path with an ocean only being separated by a transparent roof. The door greeted us with two starfish-shaped handles and green turtles engraved in the stone. The girl at the front wore a strange, light blue dress with slits all around her waistline and stomach.

"Keegan, it's a pleasure to see you," she said kissing her right and left cheek. "You've been such a stranger."

"Evelina, it's good to see you," she said. "I've been booked with school and gimbat, so I don't have time to come down here as much."

"Well it's great to see you," she smiled. Glitter from her lips hung to her teeth. "Your groups in their usual spot, follow me."

We walked through the clear circular building. The ocean was all around us. A small cut in the top of the building allowed a thin waterfall to pour into a pond. We crossed a red bridge over the pond and Foster, Miller, and Jin sat around a table shaped like the wheel of a boat with glass on top.

"Finn," Miller shouted. "What's up? Here, sit next to me." He slid over, and I sat on the large red couch next to him.

Keegan sat across from me and next to Foster. I only saw Foster at night because he never hung out with the Craved. He wasn't as unpleasant as I remembered him to be. He stared at me as if I already wasn't uncomfortable enough. He continued to stare at me with a stupid grin on his face.

Foster whispered into Keegan's ear and started laughing.

"Is there a problem?" I asked.

He raised his eyebrows while he stared at my shirt and laughed.

"What?" I pulled at my shirt.

"Are you dumb?" he asked. "Wearing that shirt is the equivalent to putting a target on it." I looked down at the DU that covered the front and shrugged my shoulders. "The circle that's half light and half dark tells people you're a Craved." He shook his head. "You know what Craved is, right?" he asked in an even more condescending voice.

"Foster, stop," Keegan laughed as she hit him in the stomach.

He didn't stop. "I mean seriously, this kid hasn't even tried to learn about Centure."

He was about to say something else, but a seal swam up right behind him. I nodded towards the sea and right when Foster turned around, its open mouth crashed into the window.

He jumped back. "Jin, not cool."

"I wish I was sorry," Jin said.

We all cracked up. She waved her hand forward, and the creature swam away. It followed every request that Jin desired from it.

"You manipulate animals?" I asked.

"Yep." Jin said with a smile.

"That's amazing."

"It has its perks," she said. "All animals are in love with me."

"Like Keegan with boys," Foster laughed.

"Hilarious," Keegan pulled the water from his cup onto his pants.

Foster tried to move out of the way, but water covered him from the waist down.

"Finn, mind drying me off?" he said.

I squinted one eye and shook my head.

"Fine, I'll do it myself." He swirled a small gust of wind in his lap when Evelina walked to our table.

"You guys always make the biggest mess," she said shaking her head. "You ready to order?"

I hadn't looked at the menu yet, but everyone seemed to know what to get. Evelina looked at me knowing I'd never been here.

"Have you had our squalis?" she asked. "It's a moist chocolate bread topped with angelfish scales, sweet snail slime, and a sour shell on top. It's our most popular dish."

That didn't sound like something I'd eat, but I ordered it anyway. Everyone looked at me as if I killed a man.

"I've never been with someone who ordered that," Keegan said. "And I come here a lot."

"I figured that was normal food for you guys," I said.

"The people down in Anador eat it," Jin said. "The people down here are weird."

Teenagers proved to still be teenagers even when they possess incredible power. Conversations consisted of twisting different memories of the same story and trying to be the one who tells it the best. The waitress walked back to the table with the plates levitating above her hands. The seashell shaped plate floated onto the table just in front of me. My food looked like a piece of art glimmering in the light above us.

"If you need anything else let me know," she said as she walked away.

"Well, are you going to eat it or just look at it?" Miller said while I stared at my plate.

My fork glided through the bread and scales, and I brought it to my mouth. It felt like pudding until I crunched on the rock candy-like scales. It was an odd taste, but it was delicious. I dug in.

"You have to be kidding," Foster said. Everyone was staring at me.

"You guys should try it," I said with my mouth full. I swallowed. "It's incredible." I passed the plate over to Keegan.

"I think I'll pass, thank you though," she said pushing her hand out. She looked up at the clock with panic. It read twelve. "We need to go." She grabbed my arm. "Fost, can you cover us, since I've paid like the last eight times?"

"Sure, go have fun on your date." He laughed.

"This is not a date," she yelled back at him while we ran out of the restaurant.

I still had half of my food on my plate. The waitress tried to say bye, but we walked right past her.

"Why do we have to go?" I asked while swallowing whatever remained in my mouth.

"Class starts at one, and I wanted to show you one more place before we leave," she said.

We stayed close to the edge of the air dome around us, walking silently until we got to a large rock covered with dried coral. It climbed up sideways to the edge of the water and dropped off. There was nothing past it except a wide-open sea. I climbed the rock and reached my hand down to pull her up.

"I got it," she said pulling herself up. "This is one of my favorite places I've seen here."

I could see why. There was something unreal about the way the dimmed light reflected with a bluish hue. We were at the end of the world staring at the next universe over.

We stopped talking for a while. She pulled small dots out of the water and placed them on the rock, creating a sphere of water that never broke its shape. Waves of light scattered white trails across her face. She looked over at me, and I was already looking at her. I couldn't take my eyes off of her. She looked down and tucked her lips in her mouth. A patch of pink changed the tint of the water just above us.

"Look." I nudged her shoulder and pointed overhead.

A group of jellyfish pulsated through the water just above us. Their stingers stretched about ten feet. They were a light pink with thick ribbons of white coursing behind. They looked like birds flying above our heads, peaceful and mindless travelers, and then they were gone. While I was watching the jellyfish fade, I noticed a seiron floating in the water to the left of Keegan. Browns and blues covered the mask, and the odd wings behind it were a scorched red.

"Keegan," I uttered, "we need to le-"

A shadow reached out from the dome and grabbed me, pulling me into the ocean.

I could barely hear her yell my name as she jumped into the sea. She moved fast in the water, but the seiron moved faster. The creature dragged me to the surface and soared through the air. The shadows that wrapped around me were cold and paralyzing.

Keegan was right behind us. She ducked her head back under water, and then quickly propelled herself on a pillar of swirling water towering up to us. She tried to drench the seiron, but the water went right through it. My foot became tangled with icy water while a similar shadow pulled on my arm. The seiron released me, and I plummeted to the waters below. The pillar of water curved towards me, and Keegan latched onto my arm.

We slowly moved back down to the water as the seiron soared away from us until it was out of sight. "What happened? Why did it just attack me?" I said coughing up water. "I wasn't thinking anything even close to dark thoughts."

"Seirons will attack anything they feel threatened by," she said. "Maybe the jellyfish scared it."

I wanted to tell her about what I saw on the bridge. I wanted to ask if they can see right through me, but I never did.

Keegan brought us back down to the freezing water and propelled us to the island. We were on the backside of colorful buildings furthest away from the volcano. The ocean water passed through the little town underneath a system of bridges. Out in the distance, an enormous statue of a sea serpent coiled up and down through the water. Dark skies covered the air just beyond that.

"What is that?" I asked.

"That's the border. Nothing goes past that serpent," she said. "Are you going to thank me?"

"Thank you," I said. "Why are the clouds so dark over there?"

"So people can't come in or go out. There's a constant storm between us. Only the council can bring people in and out," she said.

"So, Sylvic's a part of the council?"

"Nothing gets past you. There's one member per city," she said. "We need to walk to class."

She was not the same girl who'd been sitting on the rock. She didn't want to talk or laugh. She didn't jump up on the arm of the bridge, she didn't dance with the falling leafs, she just walked.

Although we'd been taking classes for the last couple of weeks, we had to take a few Tangible Manipulation classes before we did Altercations because of how advanced the class is. So today was the first class with our other mentor.

Large, tan columns held a long hallway leading to a couple buildings. The rest of the Craved, except for Jin, stood in the hallways or sat on the pillars. Miller waved at us and then walked over.

"How was your guys' date?" he asked.

"That was not a date, grow up." Keegan punched Miller's arm.

A short but wide built man walked outside the building. He had golden hair that spread in every direction and only looked ten years older than us.

"Looks like everyone's here," he said. "Let's get started."

He stopped me as the others walked a tall, dark brick building that had *Altercations* engraved in big letters at the top. "I'm Nax," he said. "I'm the other mentor for the Craved."

"Finn. Kira told me you branch in fire. I'm really excited to learn from you." It sounded a lot sincerer in my head.

He was a handsome guy, especially when he smiled. He nodded his head, and I followed him inside. Human shaped dummies, steel cylinders surrounded by some foam, targets, and weights scattered the building.

"This week, we will be working with weapons, and Finn, I know this is your first time in this class so just let me know if you need help. You have the basics of the weapons, but you must use your specialization to finish it."

I looked to the wall behind us and saw sword hilts with no blades, empty chains, and other half-finished weapons. I grabbed the bow that lacked any arrows.

"I gotta go over the rules for Finn," he said.

Everyone groaned.

"Stop complaining, I'll be quick. You can't use these weapons on anyone, you can't take these weapons outside this room, and I'm sure Sylvic told you this already, but there is no manipulation outside class or the field."

I nodded, showing I was listening to some extent or another.

"Great. Does anyone want to go first?" Nax asked.

Keegan boasted in front of a board with a target in the center. Everyone surrounded her. She pulled water from a bowl on a steel podium and shaped it into a small star with four sharp blades. She stared at the white sheet that had three different colored circles on it and threw it at the board. The middle circle split in two and water dripped off of the brick walls.

"Looked good, Keegan," Nax said.

She held her chin up high.

Nax walked over to the wooden board and wiped the water off of it. "Next time try to keep the water intact with contact."

She nodded her head and walked behind us.

"I'll go next," Miller said grabbing a stick.

I walked towards Keegan. She poured a cup of water for me and herself in the back of the room. "Where'd you learn to do that?" I asked.

"I practiced. It sucked being the weakest one, so I decided not to be anymore. You should do the same," she said bumping into me. "You're going for the bow?"

"Yeah, I've always thought they were cool, so might as well use it," I said.

"Good luck, that's the hardest weapon to control." She was back to her old self, just like that. Confident and well collected.

We walked back to the crowd as Miller smirked at Keegan. The dummy that was shredded into pieces pulled itself back together as if it were one magnet.

"Show off," Foster said as he twirled the base of the sword in his fingers.

He walked in front of everyone and held the handle just in front of his mouth. He breathed out of his nose and a thin blade of air attached to the handle. He walked up to a dark dummy and pulled back to swing at it. When he brought it past the dummy, nothing happened. The blade of air didn't stay together. I let out a laugh.

"Try doing something better, Finn," Foster yelled.

"You could've done something back there if you focused on yourself," Nax said. "You're worrying too much about everything around you. Worry about the air. Okay Finn, you're up."

"This should be good," Foster said.

I walked up to the line Keegan was at earlier, held the edge of the bow with my left hand, and made a small flame on my fingertip. I pulled back on the string and tried to pull the flame with it, but it wouldn't budge. "Can I grab a new weapon?" I asked.

"You chose the bow for a reason, so try to stick with it," Nax said.

"It's just a little fire, hothead. It won't hurt," Foster blurted out.

I had about a hundred things I could've said about him.

"Have you ever shot a bow?" Nax asked.

"A couple times at a summer camp, but with arrows, not fire."

"I manipulate fire too, Finn. As much as it feels like a liquid, you have the capability of holding its shape." Nax held a beating fire in his hand, but as he focused on it, an invisible wall seemed to keep all the flares and breaths of the flame intact. "Try shooting one."

I walked up to a red box painted in the wood and pulled on the string. As my fingers traces back, I set a small flame in between my hands. When I released the string, it diverged into sparks hitting the steel walls. Foster lost it and began clapping.

"You need to use your breath." Nax grabbed my shoulder. "Pull back on the string again. Now, when you have a fire, what keeps it alive?"

"Oxygen," Hadlee said standing behind everyone.

"That's right. I need you to think about your oxygen. Think about the thing or person who makes you breathless," Nax said, "and then breathe it out."

The first thing I thought of was Keegan, not Kate or my mother, but a beautiful stranger. I thought of her face rippling with the water and smiling at me with those big, blue eyes. I looked back at her, and she was looking right back at me. I felt guilty thinking about her when I didn't even know her, but I couldn't help picturing her face. She nodded her head with a smile.

I breathed out of my nose and pulled back on the string. A thin, long flame rested between my fingertips. I focused on the center of the two half circles and released the bow. Heat travelled out of me as the arrow struck the thin sheet to the right of the center. The flame faded into air, and smoke rose upward. Everyone in the room was just as breathless as I was. Nax clapped slowly, praising my flame. Keegan was my flame. *She was my oxygen.*

CHAPTER FIVE
CONTROL

The past few weeks were almost a repetition. I had three tests in the last two days, and I've been preparing this presentation for Kira's class since she told us about it. Keegan and I took a quick study break in Undertown Anador yesterday, but I rarely saw her on the days we don't have classes.

No one knew where she went these days, and she liked being ambiguous. Miller had been planning something in Anador all week, but Keegan kept affirming she couldn't go. It's something different every time, but I think she goes to Brav's and models.

On mornings when we don't have class, I try to spend an hour or two alone. It gets draining being with people every second of the day. I love the marble courtyard, and the Atlas Atrium is always relaxing, but today I went to a plain hill sitting on the backside of campus.

There weren't any elegant buildings or gorgeous lakes, just a field. Something about it brought me back home. The pine trees scattered around the mountains and the cool sea breeze brought me back to California.

I don't miss it as much as I thought I would. I thought without Jeremy, Kate, and Jim, life would be stale, but everything has been so exciting. Miller, Jin, Hadlee and I can all talk for days without getting bored, and Keegan — Keegan was so different and free and refreshing. Everything would be perfect if my mom was here with me.

I often wondered where I would be if we stayed. My dad was a high-ranking officer, so I guess he would've had to be a Vestrin. We could've lived in Emor, but I guess when they had a child who was a Craved they'd have to leave. Caltus looked cool on the Atlas; a large city right by the beach.

When I got back to my room, two women stood in front of the door facing different directions. They did not stop me or say anything as I walked to the door. They wore the same navy-blue suits with a disfigured oval hat. I slid the door open, and only Miller and Hadlee sat on the floor reading *Outworldly Tales of the Awestruck Man* again.

"Hey Finn." Miller looked around me to make sure the door closed.

"Hey Miller, hey Hadlee." I sat on the floor. "What have you guys been up to?"

"Reading," Hadlee said with her dark brown hair covering her face. "Finn, did you ever hear about the Mallux?"

"You mentioned it, but I don't know what it's about."

"It's not even allowed to be printed or read anymore. It was a children's story about an object that let people choose if they want to be claimed for light or dark," Hadlee said.

"Hadlee, there's two Vestrin guards right outside," Miller whispered.

"I've been doing research, and I think it's real. There's missing pages in my story, but all of the objects used to make it are real. We could-"

"Hadlee, stop. Do you want us to get kicked out?" Miller closed the book.

"Sorry, I just got excited."

"What's up with the ladies outside our door?" I asked.

"They're here from the City of Light," Hadlee whispered. "They're watching us. Something about the Keeper coming to Domister."

"If we misbehave they're gonna get rid of us," Miller said.

"Shut up," I laughed. "Are we still going to Anador?

"Yeah, we gotta get going. You ready?" Miller asked.

I threw the maroon jacket back on and nodded. "Hadlee you coming?"

"Yeah," she said. "I'm meeting Jin at Herba's. Could she tag along?"

"Yeah that's fine." Miller reached his hand towards Hadlee. "Let's head out." She grabbed his hand and pulled herself up.

We walked out of the door, and one of the two guards followed behind us. We stayed silent through the woods and long after that. Hadlee made sure we kept quiet by standing between me and Miller. The guard only left after we got to the beach and walked towards the city.

"Seriously, why are they here?" I asked. "I mean why are they watching us."

"We are the oldest Craved that have yet to be claimed," Hadlee said. "We're supposed to get claimed around eighteen and some are close to that."

"Why does that matter?"

"I don't know," Miller whispered. "Vatius hasn't cared about us in years, something must be happening."

"*Shh.*" Hadlee nudged Miller. "We're almost in the city, people will be listening."

We hopped off of the black sand bridge and onto a cobblestone path. We walked past the lagoon and towards the towering mountain standing at the back of the town.

The inner city of Anador was quiet and peaceful, almost the exact opposite of the city underwater. The buildings stood two stories tall but had different shapes. Some of them had pushed out corners and circular windows while others had cylindrical towers and large domed roofs, but every building had vibrant colored plants growing off the side. A small river trailed in between the buildings and cobblestone paths on each side. The large volcano dripping a cool blue lava stood behind the town, but as magma trailed down the mountain, it became a vibrant red.

We reached a pearl-white bridge connecting the paths with a circle carved under it proportional to the arc of the bridge. We walked across it and into an open alleyway. A garden with a strange assortment of dull flowers enclosed by a white fence hugged the front walls of a brick building. *Herba's* was written in big black letters on the tan building surrounded by twisted vines and bright white daisies.

Inside Herba's were tall, white brick walls devoured by green vines. Plants hung from the ceiling by a rope in small clear domes. The walls had different words spelt with the vines on them; *the shadows only show when the light shines* hung in cursive on the far-right wall.

"Guys," Jin said from a white table with her hand raised.

"Hey Jin," I said.

Miller walked with Hadlee to the counter to order drinks, but I didn't have money to spend on an overpriced coffee. I sat just across from Jin who sipped a steaming blue drink from a marble mug. I looked up at her, and she was staring at me. Long brown ropes and braided vines held different succulents in clear bowls above us.

"Do you wanna try some?" Jin pushed her mug towards me.

"What is it?" I asked sniffing the drink. It smelled sweet.

"Kavazul," she said with a strange accent. "It's named after the volcano."

I grabbed the cup and took a sip of the hot beverage. It tasted like white hot chocolate with the slightest hint of mint. Jin laughed at me and pointed to her upper lip. I grabbed a napkin and wiped the blue off of my lips.

"How's your new class schedule?" I asked. She hasn't been to Tangible Manipulation in weeks.

"It's fun, but I miss you guys. Everyone in there thinks they own the school because we're in Spectral Forces."

"What's the difference again?" I asked while she took another sip of her drink.

"Tangible branches are physical ones with visible reactions. Spectral branches deal more with the brain and internal changes."

"What do the others in your classes branch in?"

"Well there's like nine of us total, so it's a small group. We have two who manipulate minds, one kid can control speed, another can change terrain, and this girl can change her appearance. It's incredible seeing what some of these kids can do."

Hadlee and Miller walked to the wooden table. Miller sat down next to me.

"We just had the weirdest conversation," Hadlee whispered. She looked behind her to make sure no one was close.

"What happened?" Jin laughed.

"So, I ordered the special today, and it was called The Driftless."

"That's a weird name," Jin interrupted her.

"That's what I thought," Hadlee continued. "I asked the guy why he called it that, and he asked if we were Vestrin. Usually I go with it, but I saw his Alturus markings and told him we weren't. Then he asked to see my markings."

"No he didn't," Jin gasped.

"It was so creepy," Miller said.

A man with a collared white shirt covered with dried paint walked close to the table with another steaming drink. He put the marble mug on the table just in front of Hadlee, but she refused to make eye contact with him.

"A Driftless for you," he said.

Hadlee uttered a thank you.

He leaned in close to the table. He had long black hair pushed to the side of his head and crooked teeth. "The darkness only shows when the light shines," he whispered and crept back to the counter to help more students that walked inside.

It was a weird interaction, even for Anador. Hadlee waited until he was talking to the others before she finished the story. "I was stammered by the question, and then I told him I was a Craved."

"He seemed so excited about this instead of pissed like most people," Miller said.

"He grabbed my hand, said it was such a pleasure to meet one of us, and then gave me the drink on the house." Hadlee took a sip from the mug. "This is one good drink though."

"Why did he care so much?" I asked.

I looked over at Hadlee's drink. A white foam sat on the top of the cup with a small star shape made in the middle. Hadlee stirred the drink, and a dark liquid corrupted the white foam. My mind traveled back to the bridge again, to the darkness I've dreamt of. It swirled around me, covered me, *consumed me.*

"Finn." Miller nudged my shoulder.

"Do you want to try some?" Hadlee asked.

She pushed the mug down towards me, and a cream-colored foam with a few dark streaks sat at the top of the drink. It was not as sweet as Jin's; it was a little salty and caramel flavored.

"Thanks," I said.

I looked back down at the drink, but it was still light. I passed it back to Hadlee, and she asked if I liked it.

"It was great," I said.

"I will try to finish it quick," Hadlee laughed. "I don't want that guy to draw more attention to us."

Hadlee drank half of her cup, but once she saw Jin finished, she hurried us out of the store.

A young woman wearing a small white dress with paint covering the lower half took the empty cups away. Jin left a few coins on the table; some were half circles, others square. We walked out of the door and towards the huge mountain.

"I know you're on a time crunch Miller, but I have to get ink for this ethics project. I'm gonna try to get free stuff from the girls at the tattoo parlor," Hadlee said.

"You don't have any tattoos," Miller said.

Hadlee grinned at him.

"You have tattoos? How many?"

Hadlee didn't respond. She shrugged her shoulders and stood up.

"Okay, we can do whatever but we have to be at the top of Mount Kava by five," Miller said with a huge smile.

Most of the buildings had similar features: bright colors, unique shapes, and stood no taller than two stories. The first building that didn't meet the criteria sat at the corner of the street, closest to the volcano.

All the letters in *INKED* rested at different angles above the door. The walls were a pure black color, but a thick white liquid dripped from the roof into holes on the ground. A girl with a half-shaved head welcomed us as we walked inside.

"Hadlee," she said leaning up against the desk, "it's been a while. How have you been?"

"Hey, Creda. I've been doing well." Hadlee walked over to her.

"How are your inks?" she asked.

Markings covered the artist's arms hiding her skin. She had the branch markings of the Alturus, but she didn't cover them up at all. Being this close to it, I saw it pressing up out of her skin like roots twisting from the ground. Light pastel flowers scattered around the markings like a garden of roses and thorns.

"They are still looking good," she said. She looked back at Miller and raised her eyebrows.

"Glad to hear that." she said. "Do you or your friends want one?"

"Not today. We needed to buy ink." Hadlee pulled out a bag of metal coins.

"We're just going to throw out this black ink." She grabbed a bottle off of the shelf. "No one wants to risk looking like an Alturus."

"Are you sure we can just take it?" Hadlee said.

"Yeah." Creda handed over the bottle. "Things are bad for us outside Anador. Alturus are getting beaten in Obrum's and losing jobs. No one will be getting black ink tattoos anytime soon." Creda grabbed her arm with her left hand to cover the pulsing marking on her bicep.

"I'm so sorry." Hadlee grabbed her hand. "We will try to fix all of this."

"Well, they'd appreciate it," Creda laughed while trying to keep tears from falling down her cheeks.

"Thank you so much again," Hadlee said grabbing the ink. "I promise, I'll be back soon."

"You better," she said as we walked out the door.

We walked to a clock tower at the base of the mountain to the left of us. The beige bell tower below Mount Kava stated it was already five. A gondola train that climbed the mountain like a beast digging its claws into the rocky side stopped at a platform just a few feet up. We stepped onto the train, and it ascended the mountain.

The steel beast took long strides, jerking us with every step. The walls were glass, and the inside was cold copper that kept the heat outside.

"What's an Obrum?" I asked.

"It's where most of the Alturus live," Jin said leaning up against the cold steel. "That's where I'm from. I can hardly call it a town."

"What's it like there?"

"Not too nice. We can make better houses from scrapped steel, but everything is designed for us."

A piece of the mountain clipped off from the claws of the machine, and we jolted to the side. I fell into the wall, and Jin fell into me. The gondola got ahold of its footing, and we climbed the mountain again.

"I'm sorry," I coughed taking a half step away from Jin.

"It's okay," she smiled. "Coming from a place like that to here was the best thing that happened. You never know what will happen next in Anador, or who you might meet. This experience wouldn't have been so vivid if I was from Emor or Pravon."

The train stopped and lowered itself into the mountainside. We walked out onto a ledge just below the peak of the mountain and towards two guys holding huge gliders.

"Miller," a slender guy with copper hair said.

"Hey bro," he said giving him a hug. "It's been a while."

I walked towards them with shaking legs. I've always hated heights.

"This is my friend, Finn."

"Nice to meet you," he said. "I'm Miller's cousin, Jericho." He looked just like Miller, except with darker skin and more controlled hair. "Are you gliding with us?"

Two oversized kites sat on the ground near the edge of the cliff. One was a dark blue, and the other a tattered green with a rusted metal bar hanging below it. The cliff dropped straight off the side of the mountain.

"Uhm," I looked down at the waters below me, "I'm not the biggest fan of heights."

"It's not that bad," Jericho said. "It's peaceful. And you'll be under my control the entire time." His leg was covered with the same dark markings that Creda had.

"I'll do it first if it makes you feel better," Hadlee said.

"Don't count me out." Jin walked towards the gliders.

Jericho attached them to the glider and in a few minutes, they glided. It looked like the entire thing was orchestrated by Jericho manipulating the winds. They were twisting around one another, touching the water way below us and the clouds up above.

"Have you done this before?" I asked Miller.

"Nope," he said, "and I'm not too sure I want to anymore."

I heard Jin laughing from above us. She looked right at me as she curved around us. Pieces of her hair blew in front of her face. She let go of the bar and let the straps across her shoulders keep her attached to the glider.

Jin swung upwards and rose to the clouds. The blue and green twisted around each other, heading straight towards the bright sun. The reflections from the gliders rippled off the mountainside. Jin and Hadlee flipped in opposite directions, and Jericho directed them back to the cliff.

The gliders landed back on the ledge right in front of us. The girls were laughing hysterically. Jin took a deep breath, and then she yelled with joy and relief.

"That was incredible," Hadlee said trying to catch her breath as the harness was being taken off.

"All right Finn, Miller, you're up," Jericho's blonde friend said.

I walked as close to the mountain as possible and he hooked me up to the glider. Miller stood next to me. His glider was a dark blue color and looked like it was about to tear into two. We crept to the edge.

"You sure about this," I yelled.

"Yeah, we should be fine," he said.

"I'm not too sure," I screamed over the wind.

"You jump, I jump, okay."

"Okay. On the count of three. One. Two. Three."

We jumped off of the ledge, and I plummeted towards the ground. The side of the mountain approached me fast. If I reached my hand forward, I would graze the rocks. A strong breeze lifted from behind me, and I flew back up into the air. A relieved laughter broke out of me as I soared right next to Miller.

"This is amazing," he screamed.

I couldn't speak. I could hardly breath. I let out a loud cheer because that was all I could comprehend. My palms were sweating as I gripped to the rubber bar. I was pulled towards Miller, and then I flipped just under him. Jericho swayed his arms, keeping me up. I was in his control. I let go of the bar and trusted the winds.

My glider shook as a vacuum of air forced me to nosedive towards the water. Right before I dove straight down, the winds shifted me until I soared just above the waves. My fingers grazed the surface, marking my path as I traveled these remote areas between the sky and sea. A flame torched from my hand, and the glider twisted upward. I swirled towards the sky as I continued to let flames come out of my body. Fire spiraled behind me and dissolved into air.

More heat brewed inside of me waiting to erupt. I bent my knees forward and when I kicked them out, fire came from my feet. Flames propelled me forward. Jericho screamed at me, but I couldn't make his words out. I twisted around Mount Kava and felt a loss of control.

I hurtled into the little town, so I grabbed onto the bar and leaned, trying to get back in Jericho's reach, but I couldn't turn. Buildings became stepping stones barely under my body. I leaned my body far back, but I couldn't get enough lift. I projected fire out of my feet and closed my eyes.

The sound of rushing waves gave me enough confidence to open my eyes again. There was only the clear ocean around me, and the crisp wind pushing at every inch of my body. Loud claps and cheering came from high above me, and I couldn't help but cheer myself as I turned back towards the cliffs. Jericho held his hands high in the air to show he wasn't controlling me at all. *I had control.* I reveled in my moment of true freedom.

The sky was already a pinkish-orange color. The clouds were a light purple. The heat never stopped rising in my chest, no matter how much fire I used to keep me in the air. I pushed fire from my feet, but needed to use my hands to turn. The only problem was I'd never manipulated from my feet, much less my feet and hands.

I took a few deep breaths and focused on what I felt. It was freedom. It was power. *It was magnificence.* My throat was warm, unlike anything else I'd felt before, but it was dense. I stuck out my right hand and let the heat from the depths of my body come out. Both of my feet exuded flames, and now my hand did too.

I turned towards the cliff, but I didn't want to land yet. This was perfect. My flames kept me from falling. Not his wind, not the glider - just me. It seemed to be one of the first times I ever had total control of myself, and I never wanted to let it go.

CHAPTER SIX
WHAT WE BECOME

The morning was colder than any I had experienced here. The warm colored leaves didn't fit in with the crisp breeze that surrounded us. Keegan loved it. She danced with the leaves and seemed tranquil in the wind almost like she was a part of it; a constant breeze altering everything it touches.

Keegan and I had a group History project due today that we've known about for weeks, but we started it the day before it was due. She assured me it wouldn't be hard once we got an idea down.

We had to depict an event and make an artistic piece based off of it. We wanted to show the creation of Undertown Anador during the war, but our professor said we would get kicked out of his class if we do anything to disrespect the Vestrins. So, now we are making a piece about Our Sovereign Lady and her beast. We went to the courtyard with her marble statue for some inspiration, but Vestrin guards surrounded it. We walked to the field off the campus' beaten path.

I drew on a large piece of firm paper, but Keegan reached under my hand and pushed it off the page.

"We don't need to do that," she laughed.

Hadlee gave us her leftover ink she used for her project a couple weeks ago. Keegan reached right over my lap, grabbed the glass bottle, and twisted it open.

"I told you we could do this super quick."

She smiled as she pulled ink from the bottle. The liquid hung suspended over the clean page, taking whatever shape Keegan wanted it to be.

"So dragon in the back and Vatius standing boldly in front of it?" she asked.

"Sounds good," I laughed.

The ink splattered on the page with a long, dark serpent wrapping behind a dark silhouetted woman. Her finger cut through the beast to give it some texture, and then she pulled two long wings from its back. Rings of gradient ink became eyes, and she made a sharp jaw using shading methods based on how much ink she settled into the paper.

For Vatius, the first thing she focused on was her hair. Keegan pulled her bottom lip inside of her mouth, just like Kate did when she focused. The hair separated into a ton of small braids stretching down past her ribs. She wore a long dress with a gray crown resting at the top of her head. This would've taken me a couple hours to do, but she finished in a few minutes.

"I can't thank you enough Kate, you're incre-" I stopped talking, but my mouth froze open.

"Kate?" she asked. "Is that someone from home?"

"Yeah," I said. "Sorry you guys just have the same hair color."

That was the first time I had thought of Kate since I'd been here. I had hardly thought of my family since I left. I wasn't sad that I hadn't seen them, I was sad because I might never see them again. After I came here, after I knew everything I could do, I belonged here. Fire shouldn't be around people who can't extinguish it. I couldn't stop myself at the church. *The Church.* I didn't even know what happened after the church burned down.

"Are you okay, Finn?" she asked. She stretched her hand out towards my knee.

"I'm great," I said.

She moved her body closer to mine. "Seriously, you can tell me what's wrong."

"Do you remember telling me about that girl? The one you-"

"*Killed?*" she paused. "I always do. I can't forget it."

"When I found out the extent of my fire, I was at a concert. I saw something. A seiron attacked us and I tried to protect my friends, but before I knew it the entire place caught on fire. I ran. I didn't see if everyone made it out. I probably killed someone. The flames kept getting interrupted by the crowd running through them." My eyes glossed with tears I wouldn't let fall out.

My chest started heating, like it did when I destroyed the church. "That isn't me."

I punched my hand downwards, and flames scorched the floor inches from Keegan's legs. Even then, I could not control myself. I was about to apologize, but she saw the regret in my eyes.

"Finn, I'm so sorry." She put her hand on my leg. She didn't back away from the fire as it came toward her. She understood it. "We're all magnificent people with a destructive inheritance. That's why we are here, though, to be something more. We could be anything." She looked down for a second then directed her eyes back to me.

"What if we can't though? What if we're claimed for dark?"

"I know you won't let a few world leaders tell you what you can and can't be," she laughed.

"I keep having this dream. Darkness surrounds me, and-" The bells vibrated through the lawn, telling us we had to rush to class.

"Shoot, we're going to be late for class," she said standing up. She settled all the ink onto the paper and pulled whatever remained back into the bottle. "We should be careful about what we talk about when we walk back to class, but I would love to talk about this with you soon."

I agreed, and we walked to Altercations. The chances of us talking about that again were slim. I didn't want to. I hated allowing people to see me like that. I rarely let my emotions get the best of me, but cage something up for that long, and it will come out screaming.

We were a couple minutes late, which happened a little too often. Nax sighed as we walked in the door.

"Is there at least an excuse this time?" he asked.

"We were working on a project for our other class, I swear," Keegan responded.

"You're in the clear today, Kira is running a few minutes late," he said.

Kira hadn't taught with Nax yet, but Hadlee said she always sees the two of them hanging out with each other outside class. Kira came inside just a few minutes after me and Keegan. Nax didn't know how to greet her as he put his hand on her shoulder and introduced her to the rest of us.

"I teach these kids too," she laughed.

"Yeah, of course," he stuttered. "I'm sorry I'm trying to stay professional."

"Don't," she laughed. "This entire lesson is based on relationships. We shouldn't act like we don't know each other."

He smiled and looked up at her. He was a couple inches shorter than her, but they both had a strong build. Hadlee looked back at me and mouthed that she told me so.

Kira grabbed Nax's hand and walked to the pool of water. It wasn't as big as the one in the Confines, but I liked class in this building more. A clear roof let the light and warmth of the sun surround the room, and it helped me manipulate.

"We will be trying to show you guys how powerful two different branches of manipulation can be when used correctly together," Nax said. "This will be great practice for when you will all be able to manipulate another substance after being claimed."

I had thought little about what I would control after claiming. Anything Spectral would be so different from what I know and seeing into someone's mind could get exhausting. Being able to move something solid like the ground would be ideal. Miller doesn't have to worry about what repercussions might come from manipulating rocks because they won't move without him. Fire is alive; it doesn't need someone to make it move.

"We will pair you up with what you might think would be the most unlikely pair to work together, and both of you will find a way to better your own strengths," Kira said.

"We'll show you what we mean." Nax walked up to Kira. "You guys might wanna back up."

We inched back to the wall and watched them with anticipation.

Water froze as Kira pulled ribbons of ice in between her and Nax. Nax took a step back and stretched his hand far out. A flame sat five feet away from him, resting in the middle of the air. Fire exited just past my palm, or the tips of my fingers, or the bottom of my feet because that's where heat rushed to. Something about his fire was calm, restrained, and under his control.

Kira wrapped a tight ball of ice around the flame. The ice was a bright orange color, but she kept forming a larger sphere until you couldn't see the light from the flame. Kira backed up towards us and held her hand out in front of her. She nodded towards Nax, and he stretched his hands apart. The large ball glowed again, and then Nax pulled his hands open as fast as he could.

Sharp shards of ice scattered across the room with a loud explosion and intense heat. Hundreds of ice particles sat inches from my face as Kira kept the shards away from us. Nax made sure the overwhelming fire never came too close. I've never felt such an intense heat, but it eradicated to nothingness almost immediately.

Hadlee clapped, and soon enough the rest of us were too. Kira let the small shards of ice fall to the ground as she walked to the front of the room. Nax grabbed her by the waist and exclaimed how awesome she did.

She pulled his hands off of her and turned back towards us.

"What do you guys think would've happened if we weren't trying to protect you?"

"Well, the ice would've gone into our skin and the explosion would've burned us, so that wouldn't have ended too well," Foster said.

"If we stopped one thing, the other would've likely disposed some serious problems," Hadlee said.

"Exactly," Nax said. "It is a lot harder to predict what two different branches might do when they combine. Everyone come close. We will split you up."

We walked into the center of the room. Keegan was busy talking to Foster, so she didn't notice me looking at her. I thought Keegan and I would pair together. It would've made sense because of how opposite fire and water were.

"Miller and Keegan," Nax said.

I guess we weren't.

"Finn and Hadlee, and then Foster and Kira," he continued.

Hadlee looked at me with excitement, but I was a little irritated. Hadlee was a lot better at manipulation than me, no matter how much she wanted to deny it. She might be better than any of us, but she doesn't seem to enjoy it as much as Keegan or Foster do.

"Foster, you and Kira will go first because you saw ice in action." Nax walked towards a metal staircase and gestured his hand so we would follow him.

The rest of us stepped up to the little balcony to stay out of their range.

"It's a quick-thinking exercise so Foster take initiative," Nax yelled.

Foster whispered something to Kira, and she smiled and nodded. Foster spun the air feet in front of him. Leafs and dust got picked up by the whirlwind. Foster pulled the swirling air over the pond and water lifted into it, sloshing around until Kira froze it.

Wisping sheets of ice stacked on top of one another making a tornado of ice. It was beautiful and massive. Every inch splintered in a different direction, becoming something different from what came before it. I wanted to walk down and look at it, but Kira flipped her feet over her head to get the momentum needed to catapult the structure at the metal wall.

When the ice made an impact with the wall, a loud thud vibrated the room as the once massive object shattered into complete nothingness. Kira looked up towards Nax and gave an almost condescending smile.

"That was awesome," Nax applauded. "But now we are all out of water, so Miller and Keegan get to wait until next class."

Kira's smile faded to embarrassment as she looked at the empty pool. She and Foster walked up the stairs.

"Sorry about the water," Kira said.

"Don't be," Keegan replied, "that would've been hard to top."

"All right. Hadlee and Finn, I guess you're up," Nax said.

We walked down to the center of the room, and Miller gave me a thumbs up. An assortment of plants covered the wall behind the dummies. Hadlee closed her eyes and reached her hand out towards them.

"Okay, a few of these vines are very strong." She put her hand down. "I will grab a few of them, and you can ignite the ends. Just make sure you don't let the fire get too close."

"Sounds good," I said.

It didn't. It was difficult to stop something after it caught flame. All fire wants to do is overwhelm whatever holds it. That's what happened at the church.

Hadlee ripped the vines from the wall and stepped on the ends of them. She looked over at me, and I ignited the six long vines. They weren't burning until Hadlee whipped the vines towards the dummies. Her hands flowed with ferocity as she moved the half dozen vines with different speed and direction.

The fire engulfed more of the plant. A rotten smell surrounded the room as three-fourths of the vine caught a wild flame. With each whip, fire would go astray and speed into the walls. She looked back at me as the fire came close to her foot. I closed my eyes and felt heat coming from everywhere.

Three deep breaths.

I focused on where the heat was the strongest, right where they were coming close to becoming one. The magnitude of the fire became tangible in the air. I stuck my hands out and made sure the flames didn't move closer.

The vines still burned, but they no longer move closer to Hadlee.

She smiled at me as she prepared her final blow. Her hands stood at a momentary standstill, and then she pushed them together. The vines and flames all became one massive line of fire, but I kept it from growing past the point I had assigned. She stretched her arm back and grunted as she whipped the flame through the dummy.

She let her foot off of the vines and took a step towards me. The long, burning vine crackled as the flame finished devouring it. Nax brought the rest of the class down the stairs and to the center of the room once again.

"That was great you guys. Definitely something that would be hard to stop," Nax said.

Hadlee looked over at me and smiled. I controlled it this time. I stopped the flames from doing what they were created to do – destroy.

"I'm going to let you guys out early today, but don't get mad at me when we stay late next class," Nax said. "There is a mandatory lunch in the Alure, so you guys should head over there. Sylvic is talking about the end of the semester dance and some other events coming up."

We all moaned. No one liked the Alure, and we ate there almost every day. It was the only place in Domister to get food, and the wait was always half an hour long. The building itself was beautiful, but there was no privacy.

"As in walk there now," Kira laughed, pushing us out the doors.

The Alure was in the center of student life. Six of the dorms sat around it and tall pink trees occupied the space between them. A cobblestone path twisted around beds of pastel colored flowers and led to the grand doors of the hall.

The massive wooden doors swung open. The line to get lunch almost reached the doors. Jin stood by herself about halfway up the line. I wouldn't cut up with her most days, but I was hungry and didn't have the patience to wait.

As Miller and I walked up towards her, everyone glared at us and murmured insults under their breath. This place was a battlefield. Someone always watched me and made a quick judgement based on where I sat, what I ate, or what I wore.

Vestrins exposed their markings for the rest of the school to see. Domister prides itself on being inclusive of both groups, but there was a clear division almost everywhere. Only a few tables had both Vestrins and Alturus sitting together, and then there were the Craved.

A few groups on campus would like us because we were Craved, but we didn't want people to know about us. Nothing too terrible had ever happened to me, but Hadlee told me about some things that happened to her. A lot of name calling and looks, but one time a group of guys pushed her up against a wall and drew markings on her with handfuls of mud. She said they got kicked out of school for a couple days and since then, nothing else had happened.

"How was class?" I asked Jin.

"Our professor cancelled it because of this lunch, so I guess one good thing came from it. How about yours?" she asked.

"It was fun, Kira taught and I think Hadlee was right about them dating."

"You should've seen Finn," Miller shouted. "He and Hadlee were paired to manipulate together, and she pulled a bunch of vines and then they ignited them and she whirled them all over the place."

"You guys all got to manipulate together?"

I nodded.

"I hate not being in class with you guys," she pouted. "It looks like we're having pasta again."

Long tables sat at the back of the room piled high with trays and trays of food. A couple elderly woman marked everyone once they passed to make sure we only had one plate of food. Today was all food from Emor, which were the most eloquent dishes I'd seen served at lunch. White pasta with light blue flowers twisted high in a ceramic bowl. A light meat tossed with a pink seasoning and breadcrumbs then smothered with a multicolored sauce sat over the pasta.

I filled up the plate with pasta and shoved the large piece of meat on top of the noodles. There weren't any desserts today, which was for the best. Miller and I had been going to the weight room every other day of the week. Well, it was more like two or three times a week, but at least we were trying.

A couple dozen long tables spread throughout the Alure, so even if we wanted to sit with just our group, another ten people could fit right next to us. We claimed a table right underneath one of the large, twisting columns. It was far away from where everyone walked, and there weren't too many tables around us.

Jin sat right next to me, and Miller sat on the opposite side. I should've waited for the rest of us to sit before I ate, but I was so hungry and this looked too good. It tasted better than it looked too. The blue flowers in the pasta were salty and balanced the white cheese sauce, and the chicken was cooked to perfection.

"Are you gonna breathe?" Jin laughed.

"It's so good," I tried to say over the food in my mouth.

"This meeting has to be bad. They never feed us this well," Miller said.

Keegan walked next to Foster, and Hadlee followed behind. I lifted my hand even though they already walked towards us.

"This looks so amazing," Keegan said.

She sat down next to Miller, and Foster sat next to her.

"Finn must've hated it," Foster laughed at my almost empty plate.

Steel shutters screeched throughout the room as windows closed and opened to grab our attention. It worked. Sylvic stood at a podium a couple feet off the ground near the front of the room.

"Good afternoon," he yelled. "I will keep this as short as possible for you. As you all may have noticed, we have welcomed Vestrin guards to our campus for the last couple of weeks. They have been inspecting every corner to prepare us for a great visitor. The semi-annual ball is held at the end of each semester, and in four weeks, we will have ours."

I didn't realize that we were already so close to being done with an entire semester.

"I know, it's hard to believe we've already gone through a

hundred school days," Sylvic said with a sarcastic voice. "After much evaluation, we have received word that our Sovereign Lady, the Keeper of Light herself, is coming to the ball."

The room erupted with quiet conversations becoming one indisputable loud one.

"There's no way," Jin whispered.

"They wouldn't just say that." Hadlee was gleaming, even Miller seemed shocked by the information.

Sylvic tried to get everyone's attention once again, but no one listened. One of the elderly woman walked up to the podium and pushed Sylvic to the side.

"QUIET!" The walls vibrated as she screamed.

My drink shook and spilt over my lap. Everyone covered their ears and stopped talking.

Sound manipulators are the worst.

"Thank you," Sylvic said as the woman walked off the stage. "With all of that being said, you cannot talk to her while she is here. She will talk at the end of the night. We also expect you to keep this all under wraps, if word gets around to Anador or neighboring cities, she will no longer come and risk her safety. Word travels fast in Centure and the last thing we want is-"

Darkness swarmed around the walls. The windows were still wide open, but there was no longer any light coming through. Sylvic stepped off the podium and walked to the middle of the room, scanning every table until his eyes stopped on us. Another professor stepped next to Sylvic and raised his hand with a fist of bright light. It was the first time I'd ever seen a light manipulator, but the white glow he created around the walls did not last.

It seemed like any amount of light that was once present was no longer capable of showing itself. A glowing black light sailed through the ground from different directions until it stopped in an octagon around us. The octagon rose into a pyramid around Foster's chest, pulling him up and keeping him still in the air. An agonizing scream came muffling out of his body.

Shadows traveled through his skin, trailing its way from his chest and out his hand. Just as it began, it ended. The light returned, and the darkness expelled. Foster looked down at his arm covered with throbbing branch-like markings.

There wasn't a single person who wasn't staring at him. Sylvic tried to tell everyone to stay calm, but no one listened. Foster shook as he looked down, and then he sprinted towards the door.

"Foster," Keegan yelled.

He didn't look back.

The room fell quiet until one kid screamed half-breed. Chaos erupted, and we were at the center. Keegan's entire body tensed because she knew reacting would only make matters worse. She stood up and walked out of her seat, tightening the grip on her fist. Heat rushed through her, like I often felt in me. It was in her head while mine resided in my stomach. Miller, Jin and Hadlee followed her out, and I ran to catch up with them.

Sylvic and other professors made sure that no one followed us. Kira sprinted after us, telling us to wait, but no one stopped running.

When we got to our shack, the two guards were not standing outside. Our massive steel door was crumpled like a piece of paper lying on the ground.

"Foster," Keegan screamed, "are you in here?"

"Guys, be careful." Kira caught her breath. "We need to give him some space.

We walked inside our dorm. Strips of metal covered the floor, and the steel walls looked like a wild animal clawed them. Sitting in the corner of the room was Foster. He whittled with the steel from the walls and molded it into flower petals. His slicked back hair was falling down on his face.

"Foster," Keegan put her hand on his shoulder.

"Look at this," he said as he stood up.

He handed her the strips of steel folded over each other. It looked like a daffodil. A cold, heartless flower. Dark markings covered his right arm; the same ones the girl at the tattoo parlor had. They looked like dead tree branches stretching to his shoulder.

"I thought it would feel different. I thought it would hurt, but now I feel whole. I feel good."

"Did you want to be claimed for the dark?" I asked.

"Yeah," he said looking at me, "I *wanted* to be treated worse than half the population. No. I'm just glad it happened. I'm glad I finally know."

He was the first person claimed out of the six of us. The first to know what he is. A big part inside of me wished I knew the same.

"So," Jin hesitated, "how do you feel?"

"It's like someone has been holding something two feet from me my entire life, and I get to see what it is," he stood up.

"Foster, this isn't who you are. I want you to know that," Kira said. "I want you all to know that."

"What if it is?" Foster said. "What if it's who I've always been? Is there something wrong with that?"

"You can be whatever you decide. There's nothing wrong with that. The only problem comes when you let what others perceive about you become you," she said.

A quiet inquisition crept throughout all of us. Nax told us we would manipulate two substances soon, but no one guessed how close soon was. Maybe Kira was right about how being light or dark didn't change who we are, but being claimed does.

When we're claimed, we become twice as powerful and even more feared than we were before. There was a dynamic shift within all of us; our claiming was coming, and there's nothing we can do to stop it.

CHAPTER SEVEN
DRAGON'S DANCE

Foster still lived in the shack even though he was already claimed. I didn't know if he was still considered a Craved, but he was definitely more powerful. He understood metal manipulation within just a few weeks. Kira and Miller had been helping him out a lot because they both control stable solids.

It was interesting watching him understand how different it was to control two very different branches. Every aspect of air was gentle and easy to diverge, but metal was stubborn. He controlled steel differently than most would because he was used to manipulating the winds. Instead of planting his feet and using brute strength, he danced with small strips of steel until he released the energy he stored up.

Nax told us about essences after Foster's claiming. They carry the gift of manipulation, but they come with the cost of being marked. Once one person dies, the essence leaves their body and searches for an empty one. Kira said if we looked in the right place when it is dark out, we could watch glowing essences travel through the night.

All of us have a light and a dark essence inside of us. We get the ability to manipulate from one immediately, but claiming only happens when one becomes stronger than the other. The odds of us being Craved was slim, but the probability that two essences came from Centure to California to claim Keegan seemed impossible. It was likely that manipulators created a life in California just like my mother did.

We were all around the age when Craved get claimed. Who knows what will happen to us when next semester comes around. All of us planned on staying here for the two weeks between semesters, but I wish I could go home, if only for a day. I wondered what Sylvic told Jim. Maybe it was boarding school, or I joined the army, or left a fake runaway note.

I wonder if they miss me.

Christmas wasn't celebrated anywhere here. There weren't many holidays at all, not even birthdays. I turned eighteen a couple weeks after I came to Domister, but because we don't have dates, we don't have birthdays. Vestrins celebrate the first day of every season in the major cities and that's about it.

I wish I smelled the pine tree and the firewood that filled my living room and tasted the warm hot chocolate and watch a movie. Last year, we all went out to see some new movie called *A Christmas Story*, and then we drove around and looked at lights for hours on end. What were they doing this year without me. It's not even winter yet here, but it should come any day now.

My last test was this morning, so there wasn't too much I could be upset about. Tonight was the ball. Jin and I were going together. When Sylvic said we would have everything we needed, he meant it. All the guys had the same button-up shirt, black coat, black tie, and dress pants. The guys were ready, but the girls took a while to get dressed.

Dates worked out for all of us. Miller and Hadlee were the closest, so they're going together. Even though I wanted to go with Keegan, Jin and I can talk for hours. Foster and Keegan were better friends than I would've imagined, but they both came to Domister around the same time so it made sense.

The girls walked out of the bathroom wearing the same black dress engraved with flowers and cut open in the back, but Keegan was putting on a light blue dress. She asked me to button the top as she pulled her blonde hair in front of her shoulders. Her blue eyes were cloudless compared to the sparkling blue dress she wore.

Jin looked beautiful tonight too. Usually, her hair went everywhere, and she wore loose clothes. Not tonight. Dark makeup created a sharp point just outside each eye. Braided strands held her bun all together.

"Wow," I said. "If I'm going as your date I need to clean up." I walked to the bathroom.

I stared into my eyes for a while. They were the opposite of Keegan's. I had a dark blue hue, like the bottom of the ocean. Hers were light, like the galaxy. My hair frizzed to the right side of my head. I put it under the sink and it became a near black color under the water. It almost stretched down to my mouth now. I pushed all of my hair back.

"How do I look?" I asked as the door swung open.

"Amazing as always." Jin smiled. "Everyone kind of ran off while you were doing your hair," she laughed.

"I didn't realize I took so long." I reached my arm out, and she linked onto it. "Shall we?"

We walked in synch despite her legs being shorter than mine. The moon was bright again tonight, making the stars hardly visible. Her arm wove around mine. She stood taller than I had ever realized, only a couple inches shorter than me.

"Finn," she whispered, "why did it take so long for you to come here?"

"I've been waiting to come to this world," I said. "My mother told me about it before she died, but after years I thought Centure was just a make-believe world."

"You're from the Common?"

"What?"

"The Common World. The other side of this world where they can't do what we can." She pushed her bangs to the side of her face. "I guess some *can* do what we can."

"Yeah, I guess I am," I said.

"How did you not tell me that already?"

"You never asked," I laughed. "What happened to you when you found out you were a Craved?"

"My parents were both Alturus, so when they found out they couldn't have been happier. They told me I had to be light to bring honor to our family." She looked up at the night sky. "I don't want that kind of pressure."

We walked past a garden of flowers, and I picked up a big, white tulip. It was almost dead. Half of the petals fell off, but the part that was white was a vibrant color. I put it in one of the braids wrapping her bun.

"You will make them proud," I said pushing a stray piece of hair out of her face, "no matter what you're claimed as."

The dance was on the marble courtyard I had grown so fond of. They filled the fountain in the middle with red rose petals, and strings of light hung above. The music was soft and slow like at an elegant ball. Hundreds, maybe a thousand-people crowded here, but most of them were unknown faces.

We walked over to the center of the courtyard in between the two staircases. A bright orange punch tasted like a poor mix of every fruit they could find. It was tangy and filled with pulp.

Keegan pulled Foster over to the table. He grabbed one of the flower shaped cookies and stuffed it in his mouth.

"You hungry?" I asked.

"We had like two eggs for breakfast, how are you not?" he mumbled. "These are fantastic."

I grabbed a cookie and ended up grabbing four more. It smelled like lemon with a spicy kick. No one in the crowd danced yet because the surrounding professors could still see is in the last minutes of light. This music was boring despite how pretty it sounded.

A man walked up on stage carrying a red trumped bigger than his entire body. With one loud, long blow, the crowd went wild and swarmed up close to the stage.

"Is that Lemair Hones?" Jin stretched up on her toes to look over the students.

"No way," Foster said. He smiled bigger than I had ever seen him. "We have to get up there."

He grabbed Keegan's hand and made her drink spill as he pulled her into the crowd. Jin grabbed my hand and followed Foster. I finished eating while we pushed through the sea of people.

The music picked up after Lemair took the lead. It sounded like the jazz that my mom and step-dad would listen to when they danced around the living room. She could swing better than anyone else I'd ever seen. She taught me and Kate when we were kids.

We found space to the left of the stage. To none of our surprise, Miller and Hadlee danced at the front of the stage. He looked over and walked towards us.

"This is crazy," he yelled over the music. "I heard they hired him because Vatius isn't coming anymore, so they had a lot of money left over."

"This is way better than hearing Vatius speak, no offense," Jin said.

After a song or two, the crowd of people became less dense. We had our own little area to dance around. I grabbed Jin's hands, and we spun around each other. She and most of the other students knew what they were doing.

She taught me a new move where I pull her behind me and we both spin in opposite directions twice, and then we're back in the position we started in. The different twists we had to make with our hands made this super difficult, but every time we messed up we laughed it off and tried again.

We figured out some moves, but Foster struggled next to us. Jin asked Foster if he needed any help, and he took her up on the offer. She grabbed his hands and left me alone in the crowd. Keegan stepped over once Foster and Jin started dancing.

I didn't grab her hands. She stared at the band with the fleeting orange light painting the sky behind her. She moved in a way drastically different from anyone else, letting herself live in the exact moment that surrounded her. Her hands rolled above her head as she reached towards the sky. It was hard to speak when she looked over at me.

"Are you having fun?" she asked.

"Yeah," I said.

"Where'd you learn to dance like that?"

"My mom, but my ex liked to dance a lot."

"Kate?" she said.

I nodded.

"Are you going to ask me to dance or are we gonna sit here?"

I laughed and reached my left hand out towards her. Her body twisted around my arm and pulled away from me. She grabbed my other hand, crossed over my head, and slid her fingers down my forearm. She twisted around me again, and then she stood right in front of me. We swayed for a second until the song ended, and Foster walked back over to us.

"We're going to take a short break," Lemair said.

Everyone cheered as the music ended with a loud beat of a drum.

The crowd diluted as students walked away from the stage.

"Let's get something to drink," Jin said grabbing my hand.

The light from the day faded, and stringed bulbs overhead lit up the floor. The fountain glowed with a pink colored light, and a magnificent purple lit the statue of Vatius.

"Why isn't she coming anymore?" I asked.

"Vatius? Too many people found out, and she didn't feel safe coming anymore. Which makes sense. Kendrax would be here the second she found out Vatius was out of Emor." Jin handed me a drink.

"Kendrax is. . ."

"The Keeper of Darkness," she laughed.

"I knew that."

"I bet you did." She tapped her hand against my shoulder.

A woman wearing a long white dress walked up to the stage and sat at the maroon piano. As she hit the first few keys, everyone became silent once again.

"This is my favorite song," she whispered. She grabbed my hand and pulled me away from the statue. I spilled my drink all over the floor. "Mind if we dance?" She wrapped her hands around my neck.

"Of course."

I put my hands around her waist. This song was slow, and the tempo held steady like a heartbeat. Her head rested on my chest. Miller looked at me from the top of the staircase with Hadlee. He formed his hands into a heart while Hadlee blew kisses at us. I shook my head, and Jin looked up at me.

"This is the song I would dance to with my father."

"Is that why it's your favorite?"

"Yeah, it reminds me of my family."

She placed her hands around my neck as we continued to dance. She was the perfect height, standing right beneath my chin.

"Did I tell you I have four older sisters? I haven't seen them in years."

"Four sisters? I can't even imagine having one."

"My parents kept hoping one of us would be claimed for light, but none of us were. If I were a Vestrin, I could give my family a better house, and medicine, and substantial food."

"You could still be."

"I couldn't imagine that. I could help them" She looked up at the lights hanging above us. "Everything would finally work out." She looked back at me and leaned towards me. Her lips grazed mine. I backed up.

"Sorry Jin, I-"

"No, I'm sorry." She let go of my head and turned around. "I should've known."

The song ended, and it seemed as if the entire world became mute. She ran off to the top of the staircase. I followed her up. Her hands cradled her chin, resting on the balcony overlooking the forest below. She pulled out the braid in her hair and locks fell just below her shoulders in small waves.

"Jin," I said as I sat on the balcony. "You're amazing and beautiful-"

"Not as beautiful as her, not as beautiful as Keegan," she said still looking over the dark trees. "I see the way you look at her. I saw the way you did tonight. You love her."

"I barely know her," I said. "I don't love her." My face became red hot.

"You look at her the way every girl wants to be looked at."

"You will find someone who looks at you like that," I said trying to get off the topic of Keegan.

"Maybe one day, but it isn't you, and it isn't anyone I've met yet." She walked away again.

"Jin, wait," I said as I grabbed her hand.

"I'm not in the dancing mood Finn," she said pulling her hand from mine. "I'll see you tomorrow. Thanks for taking me."

My eyes followed her walking down every step. She did not lift her head once. As she walked through the crowds of people, she held her chin high with a smile.

As I stared at the hundreds of unrecognizable faces, I thought about what tonight would have been. We'd be at Winter Formal, in my sweaty gym listening to music I knew. My feet would move way off the rhythm of Fleetwood Mac or some new Michael Jackson in a circle with everyone who knows me, with people I love. During the slow song, I would hold Kate like Foster held Keegan. If I were home, I would not feel like this. I would not be standing here by myself.

A loud thudding came from the forest below the balcony. No one else seemed to notice it because the loud jazz music echoed through the courtyard. It kept getting louder and louder, and the balcony I stood on trembled with every step.

The stomping stopped. Nothing stood anywhere around me, but I felt something. The heat inside the creature had the capacity to warm my entire body. It was bigger and warmer than anything I'd ever felt.

I crept to the balcony, dragging my feet until they hit the edge. I tilted my head over the railing, and through the trees a warm light illuminated the forest. A barrage of flames was directed upwards towards me. I closed my eyes and redirected the flames away from my body, but when I looked up, nothing was there.

Everything was ablaze. I ran down to the crowd of strangers, helpless, looking for an escape. *I'm not running this time.* A large tail knocked over the balcony I was standing on and a gray colored beast with six legs landed on the remaining pieces of the balcony.

Loud screams came from the hundreds of students as they pushed into each other and knocking each other on the floor. The beast had four wings covered with long thorns. Its face was round and its jaw covered half of it. Its legs ignited with flames. The towering wings knocked the stone statue down. The serpent that enveloped the lady on the statue resembled this creature we stared at.

The beast spoke, but did not need to open its mouth. "I am here for the one that wanders."

Its voice was low but belonged to a woman. A bolt of lightning struck the creature just below the eye, and it let out a painful shriek. Her four eyes were a white color. As her mouth opened, a ball of fire brewed inside. She shot the flaming sphere at Nax as he rushed onto the staircase. He controlled it and fired it back at the beast.

"You have wandered," she said, "but you are not the one I am looking for."

"She wants you guys, she wants the Craved," Kira screamed. "Get them now. You need to leave."

"You need to leave too, it's not safe here," I said as I pulled her away from the stairs.

"Trust me, I can handle myself." She walked up the stairs, freezing the moisture over the railings as she passed.

"Little girl, you are not what I am looking for," the beast said with almost a whisper.

"Well you won't find anything," Kira screamed.

The water from the pond froze, and then Kira hurled large sheets of ice towards the large beast. They shattered like glass as they came into contact with the beast's harsh skin. I searched through the dense crowd until I saw Miller and Hadlee being pushed into each other by the students who were using all means to escape.

"Guys we need to go," I said pulling them out of the crowd. "We need to find the rest of the Craved."

"I'm not going anywhere, these people need to get out," Hadlee said.

She pushed the students and walking up the stairs towards Kira. The beast flapped its wings to create a whirlwind I struggled to walk against.

"I can feel this one," the beast said while shooting her tongue out of her mouth. "You're so close to being chosen. You could be either one at any second."

"You can't control what I am," Hadlee said, "but I can control you."

Hundreds of roots came flying from below the balcony and wrapped around the beast, closing the enormous jaws shut. Kira pulled moisture from the sky, and ice crystallized around the large snout.

"Everyone needs to leave," I yelled.

I pushed the wall of fire blocking the exit forward. People ran from every direction; ramming into my shoulders and tripping over one another until the only people left were Hadlee and Kira. I ran to the stairs and the beast struggled to get out of Hadlee's vines.

"Hadlee, we need to go," I screamed.

"I can't leave, or it'll get out," she said as she clenched her fists.

"Figure something out," I said.

Hadlee closed her eyes and took a deep breath in. She yanked her hands towards her body, and the roots pulled down on the beast. Vines dragged it off the broken balcony and slammed it into the ground below. We ran out of the courtyard, hearing the loud cries of the beast echo throughout.

"Go back to the dorm," Kira said. "I will come find you guys in the morning, I need to make sure everything gets locked down."

We sprinted back to our dorm, but there was nothing there. Hills covered the pocket of land we lived in.

"There's something below us." Hadlee held her hands over the grass. "It's underground."

The cold wind picked up. We looked at each other with a confused frustration because neither of us knew what to do. As she looked at me, a hole was pulled into the ground in front of us with a stone staircase leading into darkness. Miller walked up the staircase and told us to come down. We followed him in. The ground above us closed, leaving us in complete darkness. We walked down maybe thirty feet until a light shined on the surrounding tunnels. It appeared as if our dorm was dragged down here because nothing inside of it changed.

Nax sat in the room with everyone in a large circle on the floor. "I'm so glad you guys all made it here," he said. His blonde hair curled over his eyes. "She was after you guys, the Keeper of Dark, but you guys are safe for now."

This group had never been so quiet since I've known them; it might have been the first time any of them experienced real fear.

"You guys should get some rest, it's almost midnight." Nax walked out of our room. His steps echoed throughout the hall.

I knew I wouldn't sleep tonight, I doubt any of us would. After being told all semester we were in danger, that danger came. We were told that we needed protection, but none of us quite knew the capacity of what was after us.

Part Two

CHAPTER EIGHT
THEY CAME FROM BELOW

I dreamt of her again. It was a new story mixed with a faint memory of her. We loved to drive together. It seemed like that was all we did. I would lean on the door, and she would put her hand on my knee. When she stretched her arm, I saw the markings of a constellation. She always hid them under a long-sleeved shirt, so I'd never seen where it started. I imagined it stretched all the way to her shoulder. She smiled at me. We were in between the forest and the ocean.

"There's so much more out there, Finn." She spoke softly.

The windows were rolled down. The warm, salty breeze flowed throughout the car. She grabbed my hand with hers. "I can't wait to see it all with you." She put her hand back on the steering wheel, and we continued to drive.

I woke up in a panic. I didn't realize I fell asleep, but it looked like everyone else still slept. My neck was tense from sleeping how I did, sitting upright and holding onto my backpack. I rolled my head around and stood up.

Three voices whispered just around the corner. It sounded like Hadlee, Nax and Sylvic.

"Are you sure about this?" Nax said.

"Yes, we have to do this," Sylvic said. "Not just for them but for everyone."

"Sylvic, it might not even be a real thing. It could just be another myth in the book," Hadlee said.

Is she talking about the Mallux?

"It is. I've talked to Vatius about this. I saw Finn holding it when I crossed the bridge," he said.

The thumping of steel crept towards me. I threw my backpack on the bed and crawled under my blankets. The bright lights turned on, and everyone awoke with a moan. Kira stood behind Nax.

"Wake up and pack," Nax said. "After last night's events, we realized that you aren't safe here."

"Where are we going?" Jin yawned.

"Have you guys heard of the Mallux?" Sylvic asked. No one responded. He nodded over toward Hadlee.

"The Mallux is a relic we've been researching. If it is real, we and everyone else will choose whether they want to be Light or Dark," Hadlee said.

"If it's real," Foster laughed, "half of the stuff in your stupid book isn't real." It looked like he slept about as well as I did last night.

"Hey," Kira said as she walked towards Foster. "Do you not understand that the most dangerous person on this planet knows where you are and wants you dead. If you want to make it past the twentieth year, I would consider dropping your attitude and getting packed up."

"This is the chance for you guys to see the world and not exist in this shack," Nax said. "Foster, you're claimed now, so if you don't want to come you can finish your year here."

"I'm in." Keegan jumped off of her bed. She threw on a gray sweater and zipped up her backpack. "You all ready?"

She somehow looked beautiful already. Her hair sailed all over her head, and she had dark circles around her eyes that only made her look more mature.

"No way I'm staying here without you guys," Foster said. "I have no one else that cares about me."

"Count me in," Miller said.

Soon, all the Craved agreed to get out of this place. I didn't know where we're going, but that didn't matter. I waited for everyone else to throw on all their clothes before I took the blanket off of me. Everyone followed Nax and Kira through the halls and up the stairs. Keegan floated to the back of the group where I stood.

"You were already awake when he came," she whispered.

"Yeah," I said, "I couldn't sleep after everything that happened."

"Like you've never seen a dragon before," she laughed.

"I didn't think we were ever in real danger. I thought this stupid shack was just to keep us away from students."

She said nothing, but she grabbed my dangling hand and squeezed it for a second. It was insignificant, but in that moment, it meant the world. Light transpired around the stone walls as we walked up to the hills we hid under.

The sun rose, and everyone walked as if they rose from the dead.

We walked through the forest I'd grown almost familiar to. Morning dew covered the broken cobblestone, and the sun reflected from over the horizon of the waters. Just past the bridge to Anador was a large ship made of dark brown wood and covered with tattered black sails. It rested on the sand, but I had no idea how it got there. It was not in a close to good enough condition to sail anywhere. The wood was about to snap in half, the base was filled with holes, and the two sails were torn at all edges.

"Welcome aboard," Nax said. "Find a spot and get comfortable. We may be on this thing for a while."

"I'm not sure how you expect this thing to move even two feet," Foster said.

"We're not sailing this ship on the water," Nax said.

We weren't going to make it far on that thing by land either.

"Let's move now. We have to travel while everyone's still sleeping," Kira said.

Miller lifted the ground from beneath him to create a staircase leading up to the boat. It perplexed me how Miller couldn't move the sand. I assumed that they are the same. They were both minerals, one was just crushed.

I walked up the stairs and jumped into the wooden hull. The black sails frayed, and pieces of fabric hung just above the splintered base. A room with golden windows poised at the back of the boat. The inside looked brand new; two maroon curtains hung from the back wall beside a long couch. A large compass was in the middle. The compass was three dimensional, like a globe with a swaying red arrow.

"A tour of this beauty will have to wait, we need to get a move on," Nax said. "Keegan can you get us going?"

"Sure thing, Captain," she said bringing her left hand to her forehead.

Keegan stuck her hands behind her and moved them forward until the water carried us. The boat sunk down a couple of feet, and the top deck was hardly over the water. I walked up to the top of the boat, just over the furnished room. They placed all the weapons from altercations on a large black rack. My fingers grazed over the different objects and stopped at the bow for a few seconds.

"Nax had this all figured out pretty well," Kira said. She sat on top of a railing, sharpening a dagger covered in ice. "You've had quite the semester, huh?"

"Yeah, it's been a crazy couple of months."

"Last night was one of the most – unexpected nights we've had."

It was weird going on a trip with my professors. Kira and Nax were almost like our friends, but Sylvic was the odd one out. I didn't know what to talk about besides manipulation because that was the only area she existed in my life.

"So, were you a Craved?" I asked.

"No. I was lucky, claimed for light at birth."

The boat turned and drifted through the water. Nax stood at the front of the boat with his hands on the steering wheel. Everyone else was with him. Smiling. Laughing. Ready to explore their world.

"So why are you here?" I asked.

The sun rose over the waters, illuminating Kira's red hair in a golden glow. Freckles covered her face. Her orange hair and dark freckles only made her brown eyes a lighter, almost a yellow color.

"I've seen what claiming can do to people, it tears families apart. If this Mallux thing is real, it can change our entire world."

We headed into a small cave at the edge of Mount Kava. Waves crashed against the sharp opening of the mountain. The smoldering blue lava collapsed into the sea, making the island grow as the lava cooled.

"Keegan, is there any way you can stop those waves?" Nax yelled.

"We should go up there, looks like they could use help," Kira laughed. We walked up to the front of the ship, and we were on a crash course with the blue flames.

"Keegan, I need you to push us away from the wall. Finn, do you think you can diminish that lava?"

Keegan nodded, and we ran to the right side of the boat. The water rose at an angle until the ship was horizontal. The boat changed direction, but it was not enough to avoid the falling lava. I'd never tried to disassemble lava, only create flames. I was destructive not subversive. I tried bringing the flames to utter nothingness as heat fell repeatedly, but it wasn't a normal fire.

"Finn, you need to do this now," Keegan screamed.

"I can't. It's not just a flame."

"Finn. You have to do this," Nax yelled.

I kept trying, but I couldn't stop it. I felt the warmth. I felt the flames, but I didn't have the power to stop them. Miller ran and pushed the entire opening of the mountain over, causing cliffs to tumble down over us. A clear path flowed to our left, but it was too late to turn the ship. I shot as much fire as I could off the side of the ship and we moved out of the way of the falling flames.

"Finn, what happened back there?" Foster said. "You could've had us all killed."

"I don't know. It didn't feel the same as fire." I looked back to the rear of the boat. Rocks fell into the water until the opening disappeared and the cave became complete darkness.

"Looks like we aren't going back out that way," Jin said.

"We weren't planning on it," Nax said. "Finn can you give us some light?"

I lifted my hand out and centered my energy to the pocket of space between my wrist and fingertips. A large orb of fire illuminated the rocks and water. Nax also made his hand into a large candle. I walked to the back of the boat, and the warm light reflected along the water as I went. Kira walked up behind me and put her hand on my shoulder. She had a strong presence around her. I could tell who it was without looking.

"Don't worry about that Finn, it happens." She held both of her arms on my shoulders.

"Why couldn't I do anything?"

"Same reason I can't control water, or why Miller can't move sand," she responded. "The molecules in each are different. Ice and earth are stable and organized. Water and sand are loose and scattered. There was nothing you could do about it Finn."

"So it wasn't me?"

"No. Just trust a little more in yourself, you are a bright kid." Her mouth stretched out wide when she smiled. "You're an artist, right?"

"Not really. I mean I can draw, but I'm not great."

"Well then, I have a special task for you before we get airborne."

"*Airborne?*"

"Shoot, wasn't supposed to say anything yet." She looked at the crystals around us. The walls now reflected my flame and ricocheted it back in a spectrum of colors. "It looks like we're here."

Light from around us splintered off in different directions with different vibrancies and colors. We were in the center of the volcano floating through an icy blue river surrounded by crystals. There was not an ounce of darkness in this place. Light reflected in every direction imaginable. I looked up and sharp, transparent stones hung overhead.

"These crystals have a very strong magnetic force," Nax said. "Once the push and pull affect our ship, we'll float."

"Miller, we need you to pull a good chunk of the rocks from each side and keep them close to the ship so we will stay airborne," Sylvic said. "Do you understand?"

Gravity loosened its grip on us, and the ship lifted out of the water. I ran to the post that held the tattered sail and clenched onto it.

"Miller now!" Sylvic yelled.

We were going straight towards the sharp crystals overhead, but then we repelled away from it like the wrong side of a magnet. Miller ran to the middle of the ship and pulled towards his body. A loud crack echoed throughout the cave.

"Come on Miller, you almost got it," Kira said.

With a loud grunt, he pulled two long crystals to the side of the ship. There was a small opening in the side of the mountain, but we accelerated upwards towards the sharp crystals.

"Miller, tilt us forward towards the mouth," Nax said as he ran towards the back of the ship.

We jolted forward as Miller tried to keep us away from the jagged ceiling. Nax hurled fire from the back of the ship to push us forward. The post scratched the top of the cave as we raced out of the volcano and into the sky.

"Next stop, the City of Light," Kira said raising her fist high in the air.

"Nice work, Miller," Sylvic said grabbing his shoulder. "We need to keep some distance between the crystals so we don't go way off into the sky. We also need to angle them so we will continue to go forward, but you don't have to…" his voice became too soft to hear as he walked with Miller towards the back of the boat.

It felt like a dream as we pierced the gray clouds above the rising sun. The torn ship flew high above the silent streets of Anador. No one seemed to be awake in the town yet, which was good because anyone could see us without trying.

We were over whatever remained of the island. Jagged rocks stood high above the water until a wave crashed and suffocated the cliffs. I imagined the powerful sound that the crash and the rushing waters made as they pulled away from the rocks.

"Finn," Kira said walking down the stairs. "As you can see, we're in need of a new sail." I looked up at the black sail torn into three different sheets. "Nax and I want you to draw our emblem. We thought of the Mallux."

She threw down a large, white sail and some black paint in a small jar. "I don't know what it looks like," I replied. I wasn't lying, but nothing in me wanted to be *artistic* right now.

"It's in *Outworldly Tales*." She pulled the book out of her large brown bag and handed it to me. "Nax and I will help you out in a bit, *the Captain* wants to show me the living quarters." She smirked and walked toward the staircase.

What was the page Hadlee showed me? Page 65 talked about the wondrous beasts of Centure. Page 71 talked about a group of Windwalkers.

Page 78. *Gentry searched for something that could change everything. The Mallux was brought together with the Apex of Darkness, the Halo of Light, and the Libra Piece. With this object, everyone gets a chance to —*

The next page was ripped out. Then the story ended. The next page was another random story about the Keepers. I needed someone who knew more about this. I needed Hadlee.

Miller and Hadlee stood at the front of the ship in front of large mountains forming a large half circle and encompassing something in the middle. Miles to the right of that, towering buildings with a copper color skyline fixated my eyes. I've been to Los Angeles a few times, but it didn't look like this. Every building was a different shape, a different style.

"Finn," Miller held my name as I walked to them.

"Hey, I need help with the Mallux," I said.

"Of course," Hadlee laughed. "Why do you need it?"

"I'm painting something on the sail. I need to know what the Mallux looks like."

The ship plummeted towards the ground, and Miller quickly pulled the crystals back onto the ship. He grunted as he tried to pierce the rocks through the sides of the ship.

"Do you got it?" I laughed.

"Yeah," he said catching his breath. "I have to focus on these stupid rocks every second. It's exhausting."

"Don't push yourself too hard," I said.

"I won't. Sylvic has a good middle point we will stay at tonight. You go get your thing done. I'll be fine."

"The Halo of Light and Apex of Darkness are both going to be with the subsequent Keepers. All the Keeper information is in the dead center of the book," Hadlee said. "If you need anything else, let me know."

"I will." I smiled. "It shouldn't take long."

I walked back to the sheet on the ground and flipped to the beginning of the book to find no table of contents, but a small glossary with rough sketches. On the first page there was a map of Centure. The next page listed every manipulatable substance which stated some that I hadn't seen, like gravity and terrain. The next page listed all the Pulurves that existed. Human-fish creatures, eagle-people and even alokrites, the fox-seiron. I flipped through a dozen of pages like this until I reached a page about the Keepers. The top two were the Keeper of Light and Dark. Under the description of the Light was a series of constellations and a reference to page 54.

The winds flipped the pages of the book around and clouds seemed to appear from thin air. I scanned the book for page 54. Whoever wrote this did not have much to say about either of them. It was just a bunch of facts about them. Vatius was the Keeper of Light who lived in Emor. The Halo of Light contained her power. A painting of a ring-shaped crown on the right side of the page covered the margin.

The page before talked about Kendrax, the Keeper of Dark. She lived in isolation in Umbrous and was greeted with a power she couldn't control by herself. She made different creatures out of the darkness that created her. These creatures were supposed to be human, but turned out to be grotesque beings of darkness contained in her crown of lost souls. It contained the knowledge of those she has destroyed and was shaped like a C with the ends meeting at a point in the middle.

I still couldn't find the Libra Piece in the book. I looked back towards Hadlee. She stood near the back of the boat with Miller. She noticed me and walked towards me. The wind became fierce and cold. I wrapped my arms around my chest and tucked my hands under my armpits.

"How's your research going?" Hadlee asked. "You've been examining that book for almost an hour now."

"It's going. I know what the Halo and Apex look like, but I still can't find a sentence about the Libra Piece."

"I couldn't either but I had an idea." We sat together on the floor, and she flipped to the page she looked for, as if she had memorized every page of this book. "Do you remember the story about the Keeper of Death?"

"That was the child in the corn field, right?"

"Exactly. I think the blade of the sickle could be the Libra Piece." There was a picture of the blade just under the story. It was a curved triangle and sharp like a fang.

"Well it's better than anything I could think of. Mind spreading out the sheet?"

She grabbed the opposite corner and pulled it, stretching it at least eight feet away from me. I dipped two of my fingers in the black paint and started by drawing the Apex of Darkness in the center. My entire arm had to arch in order for it to fill up most of the sheet. Then, I painted a thick outline of a circle on the left side of the huge C shape already implanted on the white fabric. I put the curved triangle on the inside of the crown, right in between the two sharp endpoints.

"That looks amazing. Finn." Hadlee stood above the flag.

Kira and Nax walked up from below the deck. Kira smiled at Nax. She was usually looking at him. She looked down for a couple of seconds at the new sail.

"Finn this looks incredible," Kira said. "We need to raise it up."

Her nose became wrinkled with excitement as she pulled a rope all the way through each of the sides, and we pulled it up. It stretched high above us and looked much better than the torn black sail.

"I'm sure you guys are hungry," Nax said.

He threw a huge chunk of frozen fish on the ground and snapped the wood in half with a loud *crack*. Frozen fish fell through the ship, but Kira kept them up. She swayed her hand over and the ton of ice repositioned itself on a steel tray covering another hole. The already damaged boat now had a gaping hole in the middle.

"We needed firewood anyway," he shrugged.

I got the fire started and soon we all sat around it, waiting for the fish to thaw. It was an awkward division: Keegan and Foster sat on an old crate while Jin, Miller, Hadlee, and I talked about which weapon was the most useful during some war.

No one noticed the quick blackening of the fish, so I governed the fire while Keegan pulled the fish off of the resting logs, throwing the burning hot fish to the side. Foster got the handle of a knife from the weapons Nax brought.

"It would be nice if there were actual blades on some of these," Foster laughed trying to skin the fish with a blade of air.

After about ten minutes of trial and error, we ate burnt fish around our small little fire. Everyone knew Keegan was from the common world, but they figured out I was too. They seemed intrigued with our past, so we shared. Keegan was from Los Angeles, which was close to me. She modelled throughout her childhood, and sometimes that seemed like all her childhood was. When Sylvic came, there was no one in her life keeping her there, so she packed up her things and left that day.

I didn't have much to say about my past; I couldn't talk about it without grieving over it. I'm here because I lost control of myself. I was an untamable flame, a wildfire. When they asked me about my past, I told them about my small house in the hills up against the beach, and about my school and football. I told them about Kate, who I guess was my ex-girlfriend now. I told them how I could not say goodbye to anyone I knew. I didn't tell them about the church. I didn't tell them how I found out about this demon inside of me, and they did not ask.

We went around the circle telling stories from our past. It started like a seldom conversation, but then it evolved into something light-hearted. We all talked for hours. Eating large pastries that puff to a golden brown in the fire. This reminded me of the bonfires I had with all of our neighbors years ago. Sylvic, Nax, and Kira came and sat with us. The sun transcended its way behind the rolling hills that served as a constant background. Our conversations never paused, and I never wanted it to.

As the sun hit the horizon, Sylvic told Miller that we can head down. He stood up and brought us back towards the ground while Nax changed our course towards a patch of tall grass. Once we landed, we grabbed our bags and walked into the field. Hadlee covered our ship with the green grass until it was hardly visible.

When the sun set, the patch of flowers glowed and radiated our bodies in a lavender light under the dark sky. The winds would sway them from side to side, and the light radiating from them would move too. No one had to suggest it; this was where we were sleeping for the night. The grass below the flowers was soft and the purple glow created a tranquil atmosphere.

It was easy to forget everything else.

Jin and Miller laid on the ground next to me. I pulled out my warm maroon coat and a pair of soft pants. I laid the jacket over me and rested my head on the jeans I folded multiple times. Jin laid on her left side staring at me, and the light expelling from the flowers made her eyes a purple color.

A strand of her short black hair fell in front of her face. She picked a flower from the grass, and it immediately lost its glow. She put one in my hair, which was a tangled mess. We laughed quietly so no one would wake up. I took it out of my hair, turned my body towards the sky, and then lifted the flower until the light of the moon reflected over it. It was a dark purple when it was not disclosing its own light. My eyes squinted at the picture of the flower falling onto my body.

The next thing I know, Jin shook my shoulder telling me to get up. In a dazed awakening, I listened.

"You need to see this." Her smile was larger than I had ever seen. The lilac light kept a constant attachment to her face until she pulled us both to our feet. She took my hand and dragged me towards the silhouettes of tall trees.

"Where are we going?" I yawned.

She put her finger over her mouth, "SHH. We can't wake everyone up."

The flowers seemed to be boundless, all glowing with the same vibrancy. I'd never seen something more astonishing than that. We walked through the forest. I realized her hand was still enveloped in mine, so I pulled away and pointed to the turquoise glow coming from deeper in the trees. It felt alive. The leaves were not as luminous as the flowers, but they made the dark roots noticeable in their light. My fingers gripped a leaf and plucked it off of the branch. The white-blue color faded as it fell to the ground.

"This is amazing," I whispered.

"You never been out during a full moon?" Jin said hopping up on a tree stump.

"I have, but it's nothing like this." I sat down next to her and she slid her body over.

She crossed her arms around her big gray jacket. "What's it like?"

"Boring. Dark. Everything over there seems normal compared to here."

"There has to be something over there that you miss."

My mind traveled back to my house. The dull kitchen with that old, splintered table, my step-father's dark coffee, the clicking of our old van. "I guess all the small constants in your life. So far, I don't have constants here."

Clouds moved over the moon, and the forest became dimmer as the plants lost their glow. "I've never had many constants. The war just ended when I was born."

"What war?"

"It wasn't really a war, it was more like a genocide. Uprising from

Alturus happened in almost every city, but they never stood a chance. They killed Alturus people until the Keeper of Light got her message across. Domister is one of the few places where both live together." The clouds unveiled the moon, and the trees glowed again. "It's funny. At Domister, everyone acts like we are all equal, but the second we get out of there the discrimination continues."

Wolves howled together in the distance until Jin shut her open hand to silence them. A silhouette that looked like a small dog casted on the tree. The face of the fascinated creature sniffed the dirt below us. It walked towards the stump we sat on.

As it looked up towards me, the white mask of a seiron became noticeable. A big, yellow dot sat just over the middle of the eyes and black lines swirled into cloud like shapes on the side of the mask. Its eyes were a bright green color and looked curious. It pressed against my face, and I didn't move a muscle. I closed my eyes and breathed slow although my heart raced. Jin's laughter turned the face of the beast away from mine. She stroked the fur resting over the mask.

"Aren't these things dangerous?" I whispered.

"Alokrites?" she giggled. "These little guys won't hurt you unless they feel threatened. People say they're good luck."

I stretched my hand out, and the creature pressed its head against my thigh. There wasn't a separation between the mask and the face of the mysterious creature resting on my leg. It looked like the mask attached to every muscle of the face.

"Looks like I made a new friend." Its fur was soft.

"Consider that a good thing," she said. "Light attracts them."

"I thought they were seirons?"

"They were, but when the seirons tried to possess the foxes, it gave them the opposite mission. The alokrites chase the light. It's obvious he sees light in you." She lifted her hand from the pale-orange creature. "I'd hoped it would see light in me."

"You seem like you want to be claimed more than anyone. Why?"

"There's a second chance for everyone. If anyone in your family is claimed for light, the direct family gets a better life in the Obrum. They get medicine, and food, and clothes." She smiled at the idea. "The opposite of that is true. Foster's family were Vestrins. Both his parents could manipulate light. When he was born unclaimed, they tried to kill him and act as if nothing happened, but they couldn't do it. When I was born, I was some huge miracle. I can still hear my father saying 'be good for me Jin. Be good for all of us.'"

"You don't need to be some restoring being for your family."

"No, I do. That's how things work here."

"What if it didn't have to be like that? Maybe we are all here to bring change."

She looked disgusted with the thought of change. Her rolling eyes wrote stories about this place. Her mouth opened to say something, but she held her tongue back. "We should head back. We have a long day tomorrow."

The walk back was a lot darker. Jin usually exuded a light, but tonight she was static. The small fox walked back to camp with us until Jin looked back and flicked her wrist. The beast let out a loud cry and limped back into the woods. She picked up a bundle of the bright purple flowers if only to make them stop glowing. We got back to the soft grass where everyone was still sound asleep. She laid down next to me, but turned her body the opposite direction. The lavender flowers above blended in with the night sky.

CHAPTER NINE
TO BE LIGHT

In the daylight, the flowers were a dark purple color with a red tint. I seemed to be the last one awake. Miller picked flower petals and let them fall on my face. I opened my mouth to talk, but a petal fell on my tongue and left a bitter taste. I shot up and spit it out.

"It's about time you got up," Miller laughed.

"Am I the last one?" I yawned.

"Yeah, Sylvic made breakfast already."

The scent of savory meats dissipated through the air. There was a small fire in the middle of all of us, and Jin stood over it with a small rabbit burning on a stick. She waved the burning meat at me with a smile.

"Good morning," she said.

She grabbed another small, skinless animal and handed it to me. I took a big bite from the white meat. It didn't taste like rabbit, but I was too dazed to ask questions.

"Thank you," I murmured. "How close are we to Emor?"

"We're gonna be flying for about an hour," Sylvic said. "Keegan, Hadlee, and Foster are already getting the ship ready, so we can walk over once you're up."

I stood up and threw my jacket back on. The sun wasn't too high, and the air was still crisp. Jin finished cooking her rabbit, and Nax settled the fire. We picked up our bags and continued eating while we walked to the ship.

"Ahoy!" Keegan screamed from the deck of the ship.

Hadlee threw down a long vine and lifted us up one at a time. The sail looked better than I remembered it. Keegan pulled on the ropes without moving the sail at all.

"You a little tired?" Keegan laughed.

"Jin and I stayed up way too late last night," I yawned again.

She raised her eyebrows up repeatedly. "Oh, you did?" she asked.

"Yes, we were just talking."

"Oh, I'm sure."

"I swear," I insisted.

She punched my shoulder. "I know, I'm just messing with you."

As Miller pulled the crystals back towards the ship, the quick jolt made me fall into Keegan. I grabbed onto the wooden mast with one hand and held Keegan up with the other. I pushed off of her and regained my balance.

She pulled some of her stray hairs back behind her ear. "Miller should warn us before he lifts us up like that," she laughed and looked away.

Foster, Nax, and I switched off pushing the ship forward faster because of how cold it was. I pushed flames from my hands for as long as I could, and then I walked down into the ship.

Keegan and Miller sat on a large gray couch staring outside a smudged glass window. I sat down next to them and wrapped my jacket around me.

"You cold?" Miller asked.

"Yes, it's freezing up there. How did you stay inside?"

"I interlocked some crystals, and Hadlee tied them to the ship this morning so I wouldn't have to hold them up anymore."

"Smart."

"It was all Hadlee's idea," he laughed.

"You guys, look," Keegan said staring out the window.

We flew over another city. It was a dull brown color as if someone formed it from the ground up. Massive walls made from the earth stretched all the way around the city, and a large building that looked like a beehive stretched to the height of the outer wall. Caves were stacked in the building, but I couldn't see what was inside the caves because the sun casted a shadow on it.

We sat there, staring outside the window in silence. We passed two more small cities, then the only thing visible were trees. We approached a large city, and I could tell it was Emor before Nax said it. I've never seen such tall and beautiful buildings. Everything was blue or white and curved in ways I didn't think were possible.

It was clear which building held the Keeper of Light. Her palace towered at the far edge of the city. It was a multitude of different buildings connected by a large base. The tallest one drew my attention not just because of its massive height, but the design. There was not one straight edge on the building shaped like the number eight with the bottom portion of the curve cut off. An elevator moved through the middle of the building without any lift or cables.

"Miller, we can let loose," Kira said from up the stairs.

Miller groaned as he stood and separated the crystals from the ship. We descended into a large patch of grass outside the city wall. The wall was a clean white color with blue triangles facing upside down and right-side up all along the perimeter.

We walked up to the top deck, and there were already a dozen guards standing on the ground below. They wore the same blue suit that all the other ones wore, but they had markings on their forehead that almost looked like a sun. Ten rays spread from the halo shape in the middle.

Sylvic was the first one to hop off of the ship with his hands high in the air. He pulled out a small badge or pin from his pocket, and the guards relaxed a little. He looked up at us and waved us down.

The guard lifted the ground up to the ship in a perfect stair-shape. We grabbed our bags but left all of weapons and food on the ship. None of the guards said a word to us as we walked towards the massive city walls.

Two more men stood at the steel gates. They pushed their hands inside the metal and slid them open. A pale blue light casted long shadows on the guards.

We walked into the city before being stopped by the guards. "Are any of you claimed yet?" he asked. He seemed to lose all the personality he had once the gates opened.

"Two of us are claimed for dark, one of us is light and the rest are still unclaimed," Nax said.

"If you are Alturus, you aren't allowed to come in," he paused, regaining what seemed to be his real self. "But Vatius has made a special request to see you all." He refused to make direct eye contact with any of us. "All of those who have Alturus markings have to cover them up."

"Is he kidding?" Foster asked. "I don't need to cover up for anyone."

"It's just for today," Nax whispered. He reached in his bag and pulled out a shirt. He ripped it towards the bottom and gave it to Foster. "I have to do it too."

Foster ripped the cloth from Nax's hand, and they wrapped their arms with the cloth. As we walked past the guard, Foster pointed at his covered arm.

"We hope you enjoy your time in Emor," the guard said.

The inner city was unlike anything else I've ever seen. It was loud but quiet, huge but tiny. It surrounded my senses: it smelled fresh and clean, it felt smooth, it sounded like harmony, even the air tasted fresh. But the sight. That was the most overwhelming.

There were no square buildings. Every building curved through the sky even if it was slight. The small apartments oscillated along the crystal-clear river that ran through the heart of the city. Marble white bridges curved over the water. The floor was white like most of the city and clear of any trash or imperfections. Light pink leaves covered the trees surrounding every building. The only thing that threw me off about this place were the people.

These people wore either white, light blue, or light pink. There were no other options for color. People already stared at us for our dark selection in clothing. I wore my maroon jacket with dark black pants. We also did not have holes in random places like they did. They would tear off pieces of fabric on their stomachs or shoulders or legs to show off their Vestrin markings.

The people were much less fit here, and a lot of them had little pets that walked around with them. Exotic creatures like deer and mongooses. The animals looked fat too. Kids our age swarmed passed us walking in straight lines without looking at us or talking to each other. They walked into a long cylinder-shaped building with large white letters on it saying *Raffia: School for Light*. They looked like robots. None of them smiled or laughed like kids our age should be doing. They walked passed us, and we continued walking through the courtyard.

"Wow," Jin said. Her head gazed towards the tops of the towering buildings.

"You could say that again," I said.

The Keeper of Light's palace was right next to the school. It was even larger than it looked from the outer city. The figure eight was a cool blue color fading into the sky above us. The sky looked artificial. Clouds were placed around the palace, equidistant apart. There was a large open square in the floor with water rushing from all four sides into a small puddle of water ten feet below. Flags mounted around the waterfalls. They were navy blue with a white ten rayed sun, like the emblem on the foreheads of the guards.

A beautiful woman with platinum hair welcomed us the second we walked inside. She had Vestrin markings on her large chest and like everyone else, she wanted to show off her markings. She cut multiple slits in her white dress making and an intricate pattern of a field of flowers over her breasts.

"Welcome to Emor," she said with a pleasing voice. "You must be the Craved."

I tried my best to keep eye contact with her as she talked.

Kira elbowed Nax in the chest as he seemed to have forgotten how to speak. "Yes," he coughed, "we're so appreciative of your hospitality."

"Of course," she looked at Kira with a smirk. "I will take you to your room and then to see Vatius. She has a very busy day."

We followed the woman to the elevator. She had the longest legs I had ever seen, and her tall black shoes only made them longer. We walked into the transparent box and a man with the Vestrin emblem on his shoulder waited in there for us.

"I forgot to introduce myself," she said staring at me. "I'm Arilna Allister, Vatius' right hand. If you guys need anything at all, don't hesitate to ask."

Her long, silver hair was held together in a large braid flowing down the right side of her head and resting just under her shoulder. The steel plate stopped rising about halfway up the bottom circle of the figure eight. We floated through the center of the building. The door slid open and Arilna walked out on thin air. When she stepped down, a colorful light held her up. She pushed her hand forward, and a path of rainbow light attached itself to the side of the curve. She escorted us across with her arms out to the side. We followed. I looked down and became queasy. It looked like we walked on nothing and could fall fifty feet at any second.

The side of the building opened towards us as we approached it. Inside the circular corridor were four different doors. The walls were a bright white, and the lights radiated a light blue tint. A magnificent statue stood in the middle of the room with the same basic principle as most of the other statues I had seen; a woman wearing a long gown entangled with a slender dragon.

"You can put all of your things out here for now," Arilna said. "Vatius is waiting for us, and she is not one you want to keep waiting."

We went back down to the main building and walked to the furthest part of it. As we continued to walk deeper, more Vestrin guards waited at the sides of the building. The hallway became brighter and brighter. We arrived at a monstrous door with floral decals protected by six guards. The guards stepped to opposite sides and allowed us to pass. Nax pushed on the heavy door until it opened.

"Welcome," a woman sitting on a white throne said with a pompous voice. Her light brown skin made her pure white dress even brighter.

She didn't stand up for us, but expected us to bow to her. We did. The room was astounding. Marble columns laced with flowers held up the large atrium. Dangling glass hung from every inch of the ceiling, taking the appearance of snow stuck in time. The large glass mosaic behind her throne made it look like a church. We walked down the extended path. The floor was cracked like we walked on thin ice.

Her throne was made of tree branches. They twisted around each other like coils and rose a couple of feet above her. The top of the throne looked like the antlers of a gigantic deer. Her black hair was separated into a hundred small braids. I spotted the Halo on her head, and remembered that was what we were here for. The Halo was not a pure white, like most things here, but a cream color with a few gray streaks along it. A beautiful necklace with intertwining circles hung low around her neck. The circle on the sides were silver and as they approached the middle one, it transformed into gold.

Standing next to her were three women and one man. They didn't speak to us as we approached the Keeper. One woman was at least ten years younger than the rest. She could've been the same age as us. They had no markings on them. Not for Alturus or Vestrin, and no ten-rayed star on their head. I wondered if they were Craved like us. I didn't ask though. I could tell that it was not in our interest to be asking the first questions

"Our Sovereign Lady." Sylvic bowed as he approached her.

"Sylvic, it is a pleasure to see you all," she smiled. "I heard there was a little problem at your end-of-year ball."

"Yes, that is why we are here."

"Aren't you glad I didn't come? If I was there, I would hope that there would've been a little more protection around the school."

"There would've been," he stuttered.

"Well, what is it?"

"I am sure you have heard about the Mallux," Kira said.

The room became silent. One of the woman in front of the chair gnawed at her lip. Kira waited for a response from Vatius, but she sat with her shoulders back and a crooked smile.

"We are looking for all three pieces, so that people will choose what they are claimed for."

Vatius laughed. "We can all assume that everyone would be Vestrin. That is why it is selected at random." The room roared with laughter. With a quick swipe of her hand, the room fell back to silence. "However, I will consider trying to make this adjustment. All you have to do is talk to Kendrax. If she is willing to make this shift, I will too." A large smile returned to her face.

She had a beautiful smile. Her teeth were perfect and a blinding white color. One of the three women walked up and whispered into Vatius' ear. She made eye contact with me as she talked. Her hair was an intense blonde color and her eyes were silver. Her skin looked too flawless to be real. It was smooth and lacked any wrinkles or freckles.

Vatius nodded and continued to speak. "Bring back the Libra Piece in two weeks, and I will give you the Halo."

"The Libra Piece, is that the sickle from the Keeper of Death," Hadlee stuttered.

"Who can know for certain?" she grinned. "That is a good place to look though."

"Thank you so much for your kindness," Nax said. "We will head out first thing in the morning."

Vatius stood up for the first time and curtsied. She was tall and had a larger build. Her shoulders were broad, and her arms looked strong. "Finn," she said.

My heart stopped as I looked at her. She pulled her finger towards her hand. Everyone continued to walk out, and I walked towards her. My hands trembled as I approached her throne.

"You are not from here are you?"

"No, I'm from California."

"Sylvic has spoken much about you, Finn."

She walked down the few steps and stood in front of me. She had to be at least six feet tall because we made direct eye contact. She grabbed the cross that hung around me and pulled it towards her.

"I would be more concerned with who the holy ones are in this world than lingering in yours." She walked back to her throne and sat with her legs crossed.

Once I passed the doorway, I ran to catch up with my friends.

"What was that about?" Miller asked.

"She wanted to welcome me to Centure."

"I'm still star-struck," Jin said. "It's not every day you get to talk to Vatius."

She did not impress me as much as everyone else. As we followed Arilna back to the rooms, everyone talked about the power and the light she expelled. I didn't see that same light.

Arilna stood in the center of our corridor. I looked more at the statue and could tell that it was Vatius. The braids blended with the dress and parts of her Halo were chipped.

The doors didn't have any numbers or letters, but different

variations of neon light came out of the crack between the floor and the white door. "It's three to a room," Arilna said with her hands connected in front of her stomach.

Miller and I looked at each other and nodded. We walked into the room with the green light seeping through. Foster followed closely behind us.

"What?" he growled. "I'm not sleeping with the girls, I'm not sleeping with Sylvic, and I don't want to sleep by myself."

Foster walked in and threw his bag on the bed closest to the door. I jumped on the bed against the wall. The blanket was soft and for once the bed did not feel like a rock. I ran my fingers through the soft fabric that stuck up all over the blanket.

Foster tore off the black fabric he had to wear around his arm. "I can't believe they had the nerve to make me cover myself up," he said.

"People in Emor are afraid of the Alturus," Miller said. "Most of them have never met one, so they base everything on rumors and stories." Miller jumped down on his bed and rubbed the soft blanket. "That is why my family left the city. They hated how others were discriminated."

"For people supposed to be pure, they sure are corrupt," Foster said. "What do you think, Finn?"

I liked it here so far, but I didn't want Foster to ostracize me more than he already did. "I don't have an opinion yet. If you could choose you would be a Vestrin right?"

"I wouldn't. If I could choose anything, I would've stayed a

Craved for the rest of my life. I don't need random markings to be what identifies me," Foster said. "But I can already read right through you. You get everything you want and you appreciate so little." He sat on his bed and acted as if his words were a fact someone read in grade-school.

"Don't act like you know me. You of all people here don't know a single thing about me," I said sternly.

"Oh, but I do," he laughed. "Somehow you come here and you are already a better manipulator than most people, the Keeper of Light knows your name, and Keegan - I have never seen her get into someone as fast as she fell for you, but you see none of these things because it isn't special to you, it's an everyday occurrence. You're a spoiled, ungrateful kid."

He remained calm as he talked, but my chest was heating. I had nothing to say, so I hopped out of bed and threw a strong punch at him with my fist in flames. He ducked down and kicked his foot to the side. A strong blade of air brought my feet out from underneath me and knocked me to the ground.

"I said you were better than most people." He pulled his hand back. "I'm not one of those people." As he threw his fist towards me, Miller jumped on top of him and pinned him down.

"Cut it out," Miller screamed.

I stood and walked towards Foster with a sharp, flaming dagger coming from my fist. Miller turned around and pushed me back to my bed.

"You stop too. You get so angry for no reason, and I can't deal with it."

"Then don't," I screamed. I grabbed my bag and stormed out of the room.

"Finn, wait," Miller said. "I didn't mean that."

I closed the door behind me and walked back in the corridor. All the neon lights outside the doors were white except for a dark blue one. I opened the door and turned off the lights. This room was a lot colder than the last. I took off my shirt and walked into the bathroom.

Angry for no reason. Those words infuriated me. I put my hands under the cold water and splashed it in my face. The cool water didn't bring down the heat I felt inside my chest. I let out a loud grunt and compiled flames on the ground. At least now I know why Foster doesn't like me. He was jealous of me. I still don't know why. I don't have Keegan, and he was a better manipulator than me.

I tossed and turned for hours. My head ran wild. Part of what Foster said could've been true. I have been ungrateful. I still lived in my world instead of this magnificent one. There was a slight creak on the floor. I assumed it was nothing at first, but another creak came closer to my bed.

"Anyone there?" I asked.

Someone stood right in front of my bed. I made a flame in my hands, and a man wearing a blue guard uniform stood over me. I projected a strong flame towards him, but I hit nothing but air. A heavy hand covered my mouth and wrapped around my stomach.

I was no longer in my bed, but flying through a white fog. There wasn't air inside this vacuum he pulled me through. Before a full second passed, he dropped into Vatius's chambers. I rolled onto the floor, hitting my face on the cold marble ground. I looked up to Vatius towering above me.

"Get up," she said. "And you get out." She pointed the guard towards the door.

I stood up and wiped my bleeding lip. The four men and women stood beside her throne. One of them couldn't stop grinning at me. It was the woman with flawless skin and silver eyes.

"So you are the one that Sylvic was so worried about," she said. "He knew you were coming years ago."

"Why am I the only one here?" I asked. I realized I still didn't have a shirt on and grew uncomfortable.

She pushed her fingers through my hair and rested her arms on my shoulders. "Finn, you have beautiful eyes my dear. Such a pure blue color like your mothers."

"You knew my mother?"

"*We all* know your mother."

"Is she-"

"I was skeptical at first, but you are strong," she interrupted. "Sylvic might have actually seen something real when he came here. Do you want me to tell you what he saw?"

"I'm assuming you are going to either way," I said.

Her body boiled with anger.

"You need to show more respect to our Sovereign," the man said with a booming voice. He had tan skin and long hair tucked into a bun. His body was large and well sculpted.

"Botak quiet," Vatius said. "Luckily, our new friend Aviva can show you."

The youngest one closed her eyes. Her thumb and pointer finger made a circle, and she touched her middle finger to her forehead. The walls morphed into a much darker palace with flames on the walls instead of bright lights. Vatius transformed into a much more slender woman. She had light skin and beautiful, blonde hair that curled around her shoulders. She had the Apex of Darkness on her head and gave it to me.

The crown cooled the palms of my hand, and something wicked fell over my body. I looked at my arms and black markings pulsed through my veins. I fell to the ground in pain and shadows fluttered from my palm. I stood in front of people, hundreds of people. The shadows passed over them all. When the darkness faded, they were all on the ground, dead. Bitter nothingness replaced the heat in them. I span around in circles and saw the world become corrupt with darkness.

Everyone I loved: my mother, Keegan, Kate, Jeremy, Miller, and even random faces I'd only seen once or twice were entangled in the shadows I controlled. It spiderwebbed around the room repeatedly until everything became darkness. The room became black, and then I was back in Vatius' chamber.

I fell to the ground; my body was shaking. I sobbed, it felt so real. For a second it was real. My arms lacked markings on them, and I couldn't manipulate darkness. There was no crown. It was like the vision I saw as I passed the bridge, but much more vivid.

"What does that mean?" I quivered.

"You are supposed to be the next Keeper of Darkness," Vatius grinned. "I don't want you to be stuck in a position like this because I see light in you. If you want to find the Mallux, I would get started before it's too late."

"Thank you for telling me this, my pureness," I said.

"Go along now. If I were you, I would stay very, very quiet about all this. Some things are better left unsaid."

I bowed towards her and walked out of the room. My legs shook. I couldn't stop them. I kept looking at my arm to make sure that there weren't any markings on it. I knew I'd messed up, but I had never felt *bad*.

When I held the crown, I felt evil. I didn't feel like myself. That wasn't me. That can't be me. The darkness terrified me, but I was even more terrified of myself. I know I lack control, but I can no longer lose control. From here on out, I will be good. I will make up for everything I have done and make sure I am light. *I'll be good.*

CHAPTER TEN
MOURNING LIGHT

The guard that came into my room waited outside Vatius' door. I could see him. He had black hair resting on the side of his face. He grabbed my arm without saying a word and transported me back to my room. This time, he held me up as we returned instead of letting me fall. When I turned around to thank him, he was gone.

The room was still dark. I curled up in my bed and tried to sleep, but a static filled the room. My thoughts became scattered. All I knew was that I hated how I felt. I gave myself a little light and then looked at the clock again. Three o'clock. I heard something fall in the lounge area. It sounded like something jumping. My feet touched the cold floor, and I crept towards the door. I heard a man whisper something in a different language.

"Lited ni hul dek," he repeated.

I creaked open the door and saw Nax walking to his room alone. "Nax," I whispered. He looked over at me in a daze. "Who were you talking to?"

"I'm not sure," he said. "I don't remember leaving my room. I must've been sleepwalking. Wait, why are you still up?"

"Couldn't sleep," I said. "But we have a long day tomorrow so I will try to sleep. You should too."

"You don't have to tell me twice."

He opened his door and crept into his room without another word. Something was going on here. I walked to the side of the building that enclosed us and tried to push it open. There weren't any doors or a way out. They trapped us in a prison. If someone took Nax, they might've taken the rest of the Craved too. I crept into Miller's room. He and Foster were fast asleep.

I tiptoed back to my room and in what felt like a blink, the sun came out. *Be good. Be light.* I repeated to myself. I got up and my head spun. I put my arm on the side of the bed for a second and walked to the bathroom to splash cool water on my face. When I looked up, I thought my mother stood right behind me. I closed my eyes and peeled them open to nothing but a towel hanging on the wall. This world was a hard one to trust. The girl from last night made me feel and see things as if they were real.

Three soft knocks echoed on my door. "One second," I yelled. I threw on a plain white shirt and walked to the door. Miller stood in front with a solemn face.

"I wanted to say sorry for everything that happened last night," he said.

Be good. "You don't need to apologize for anything." My foot dragged back and forth. "You were right. It's been hard being away from home, and I acted different. I hope we can fix this."

"You don't need to fix anything," he said. He wrapped his long arms around me and held on tight. "I'm sorry about everything."

I grabbed onto him. It was a comfort I had not felt in months.

"So we're good?" I let go of his back.

"We're good," he said. "We're about to leave so get packed up."

I saw Foster talking to Jin in front of the girls' room. "One second," I said. I walked over to Foster. I wanted to hit him, but that was a bad idea. "Hey, I'm sorry for everything that happened last night. You were right. I was stubborn, and you didn't deserve to get tackled - and burned."

"I'm not the one with the swollen lip," he laughed.

Be good. I repeated to myself. It was hard to, especially around him. I turned around and walked back to my room. Most of our things were still in the airship, but I grabbed my backpack and walked out to the corridor. Keegan and Hadlee talked near the center of the room.

"All right," Nax said with a tired voice, "we have to get going to Kordia."

"Are you feeling all right?" Kira placed her hand on Nax's shoulder.

"I'm fine. We need to go."

He walked towards the wall. Arilna looked just as confused as we were. She wore another white shirt that showed off her breasts with small lines of fabric bridged over her chest.

The glass door slid down, and Arilna glided with her hands posed in front of her stomach. She stepped out into the air and formed a colorful path of light in front of us. Miller walked right next to me on the tight path ten stories up. My stomach churned again.

The same man was in the elevator. I felt bad for him. No one acknowledged him, and he didn't speak to any of us. He brought us down, and I thanked him as we walked out. Miller elbowed my side and shook his head side to side.

Arilna thanked us for coming and invited us to come back anytime. The city didn't change at all. Every building, every banner and even the people seemed identical.

"Why can I not talk to that man in the elevator?" I asked.

"They are captives," Miller said. "He was an Alturus and sold a year of his life to be claimed for light."

"How can you change from light to dark?"

"Kendrax will have to take the dark essence out of them, and then Vatius waits until a Vestrin dies to bring the light essence into them. Those people are ostracized regardless. No one respects a captive."

"I'll try to remember that," I said.

If Vatius could control what people were claimed for, why would she not make me light? She seemed worried about me becoming the Keeper of Dark. I had yet to decide if I would tell anyone about that. It was premature because I haven't been claimed.

A loss of hope overtook me as we left the white city and fear crept through me as we walked onto the ship. The open world seemed much darker than the contained City of Light.

Sylvic stood in front of the ship, but didn't come on. I wanted to talk to him about what Vatius said to me, about what he saw, but I couldn't do it now.

"This is where I leave you guys," he said. "I need to go back to

Domister and make sure everyone is okay. Everything in that book is real, and they are trying to hide the past," he whispered now. "The Sickle from death will be in a cave just south of Kordia. Go, but be careful. The Keeper of Death is not known for friendliness these days."

"Thank you for taking us this far. I am sure we will see you again." Nax hugged Sylvic.

"Keep him safe," Sylvic whispered to Nax.

He walked back into the city and waved us off as the ship soared above the trees.

I walked to the map in the front of the ship. Kordia was in the northeast, right on the sea. There wasn't much of a view today because of the thick clouds, so I didn't care to sit near the window like I usually do.

"I'm gonna miss this place," Jin sighed.

"We were there for like three seconds," Foster laughed.

"But it was such a good three seconds."

"That's what it's like for the Vestrins. I hate them all so much. They don't understand how good they have it because of how they're claimed," Foster grunted.

It became silent after that. We stared down, out the window, at our hands, anywhere except for each other. Claiming would divide us. Half Vestrin, half Alturus, it was inevitable. We would become weapons used against each other.

"Unless we change it," Keegan smiled. "Unless we change everything."

No one moved their gaze.

"Guys." She stood up. "We are forgetting what we are doing. If we find the Mallux, everything about this place will change. We are closer to finding this than anyone has ever been because we know what the Libra Piece is."

"But we don't," Foster said. "We have an idea of what it could be, but we won't know until we get all three pieces together. This could be a total waste of time."

"What if it's not?" Keegan sat back down. "*If* this is real - *if* we can do this, there is no more light or dark. Hell, there won't even be Keepers."

"Quiet," Kira whispered. "That kind of talk gets people killed. That's what starts wars."

I put my feet up on the table and kept quiet. Miller walked down the stairs with his signature look of confusion: his left eyebrow cocked upward and he tucked his lips in his mouth.

"Why so silent party people?" he laughed.

"We're just looking," Keegan said leaning towards the window.

We soared over tall mountains, the first mountain range I'd seen here. The sky wasn't filled with fog here like it was earlier. We moved slower than normal, so I walked up to the deck to make sure Nax was all right.

He stared blankly at the sky instead of propelling us forward. I walked towards him, but he didn't respond even after calling out his name. I shook his shoulders, and he woke up from his daze.

"Are you okay?" I asked.

"Yeah, yeah," he stammered. "I zoned out. We're close. Let's get there."

We both propelled the ship by streaming fire from our hands. Before long, we flew next to the rolling sea. Nax made sure we were going the right way and used a small town as an indication that we were.

"All right, you can tell Miller to let us down."

I watched the crystals separate from each other as we drifted down into a field of wheat. The clouds thinned out, and the sun set over the acres of golden wheat around us.

Foster grabbed his sword handle and handed me my bow. "You don't want to walk through these plants."

"Thanks." I grabbed the bottom of the slick bow and threw my backpack around my shoulders.

"You guys will want a blanket," Kira said. "We will camp out here tonight."

We walked into the wheat towering to the bottom of my chin. Foster and I cut a path for us to walk through. As they fell, they shimmered with the rays of sunlight. There was a quiet whistle in each slice of my bow I enjoyed.

We got to a spot of dirt near a cliff. I didn't realize how hungry I was until Kira mentioned dinner. I hadn't eaten since we left Emor this morning.

I aimed the bow at the seagulls soaring above us. I let out a deep breath, and a spear of fire rested between my fingertips. As it shot through the air, I focused on the warmth of the flame to keep it intact. A loud cry came from above, and the seagull spiraled down. The bow was a lot more accurate than just projecting a flame from my hands. Two more crashed to the ground, and I carried them feet first to our campsite. I was not a fan of any bird, so I looked for more food while the fire was being set up.

I walked to the top of the cliff to a field of yellow flowers on the hillside. My feet danced around the delicate flowers. When I got to the top, I saw the world. I was at the end of a crescent-shaped bay and on the opposite point, a waterfall dropped about fifty feet into the ocean water. My hunger subsided. I sat there and stared. My feet dangled over the magnificent place. Although I was much higher than it, I felt so much less superior.

I could've stared at this place for hours. The cliffs integrated into the crystal blue water, and the yellow flowers covered the hills. I tried to grasp the pure magnificence, but I couldn't. I kept seeing something new. Something that made it more incredible. Keegan walked up without caution of the flowers. I didn't even realize the sun already set. The clouds turning pink and orange seemed natural here.

"This is incredible." She stuck out a cooked piece of the bird meat. "You need to eat."

It smelled appetizing enough. I grabbed it and pulled it off of the stick with my teeth.

"I've never seen anything so beautiful," she said. Her hair looked golden in this light. "Let's go to the beach." She stood up and pulled me towards an indented path down the cliff.

I didn't want to take the path. "I have a better way down." I smiled. "Just hold on to me."

"Are you gonna jump?" she laughed.

I nodded my head.

"You're kidding right?"

"I'll project fire out of my feet," I said taking off my shoes. "I did it with a glider when I first got here."

"Okay," she paused. "Have you done it without a glider?"

"Not yet." I reached out my hand. "But I never felt more alive when I was doing it."

"I swear, Finn." She grabbed my hand. "You better feel alive after we do this too."

I pulled her close to my body and looked down. It was a straight shot to the sand. We leaned over and started to free fall. Just before we hit the ground, I bent my knees and extended them. Fire propelled us forward. We were only a couple of feet above the ground.

"This is incredible," Keegan laughed.

She let out a loud cheer. I let go of her with my right hand and manipulated fire out to travel vertically again. She slipped out of my left hand, so I wrapped my right arm around her again. We headed straight for the sand. I stopped pushing fire out of my feet and braced Keegan close for impact.

Luckily there were no rocks in the sand because we slid five or six feet across it. Keegan jumped up and laughed. She slapped my arm. "Finn Lynch, you need to work on your landing."

"I'll work on it," I laughed. My arm stung. The sand scraped me from my wrist to tricep.

"You're bleeding. Let me clean it out for you."

She put her arms on my shoulders and sat back down next to me. She pulled water out from the sea. Saltwater made cuts worse, but her water was pure. She bit down on her tongue while she pulled the water across the tips of my skin. The sky was still light as the final orange rays of light disappeared behind a blanket of the sea. The crushing sound of the waterfall into the ocean created a new majesty. Water would hit the sand for a second until the next wave came. And one did, interrupting the silence between us.

"Finn," she said releasing the water back to the sea.

"Yeah," I said looking at the rhythmic pattern of the tides.

"Are you ever afraid of what you can do. Manipulating has been something so freeing for me, but this power is terrifying."

"All the time. I lose control and put other people's life in danger. I'm afraid that I will be claimed for dark because of the things I've done."

"We've all felt *dark* before."

She didn't know what Vatius showed me. I wasn't going to tell her. Not now. She tried to lie down, but her bag was in the way.

"I didn't know I still had this." She took it off of her shoulders and laughed. "Will you do something illegal with me?" she smirked.

"That depends on what we do," I laughed.

She pulled out a container of black ink from her backpack. She has had that since I first came here. "We can give ourselves Vestrin markings. They won't make us light, but we can remind ourselves that no matter what they claim us to be, we would keep a little light inside of us."

"People will see it," I said. "We always change in front of all the Craved."

"Then we can be a little more discrete. Come on, we can get them on our outer ribs." She unscrewed the bottle. "You're Virgo right?"

"Right," I laughed.

My step dad would kill me if he caught me, but he can't do a thing here. A spark of rebellion lit inside me. I can make my own choices now. This was my life. I took off my shirt and grabbed my right arm. First, she placed the dots on my ribcage; there were a dozen.

"People here believe every star is a Vestrin's soul. They are all connected through the different constellations and the essences know this." The liquid cooled my ribs. "The constellations represent the people that best represented Vestrins." She pushed it through the pores of my skin, and it became still. "All done."

"Your turn," I said. "What sign are you?"

She peeled off her white shirt. I tried not to want her. "I'm a Capricorn."

She moved her left arm and placed the dots in a concave triangle. I looked out into the water only to see a masked figure emerging from in between the orange sky and blue water. It was a seiron. I hadn't seen one in months.

"Keegan," I whispered. I nodded my head towards the water.

"We don't have to be worried about that," she said pushing the ink into her skin.

"It's a seiron," I said. "We've seen what they can do."

"Finn," she put her hand under my chin, "seirons can only take over darkness and despair. I'm only filled with happiness right now." She pointed to her tattoo. "And now we are filled with light."

Another wave crashed over our silence. I looked back, and the seiron vanished Once the orange sky became a dark purple, we walked back up to camp. I kept a steady firelight shining beneath my feet as we walked up the path in the side of the hill. We got back to camp, and the fire was lit without me. Keegan and I sat down on the opposite direction of the blowing fire. They chewed on the bird meat. I grabbed a stick with the raw bird and held it in the fire until it became charcoaled. I sunk my teeth in the leather like meat to pull it apart.

We sat there telling ridiculous stories of our past like we always did. Keegan and I talked about our wars and our guns. Hadlee said if our world had the power of manipulation, we would obliterate everything. There had only been two wars here; one's lasted since almost the beginning. Even though there was not a constant fight going on, there was still injustice. Fire rose in Hadlee's stomach as she talked about this, but something else overtook the fire. Something warmer than anything I'd ever felt.

Hadlee's chest irradiated a bright white light. She had no choice but to stand up. Her arms lifted over a ribbon of light that danced around her, and it appeared as if the stars were being plucked from the sky and brought around Hadlee. Intense white orbs that enlightened the entire hillside surrounded her. She circled around with a smile contaminating her face as she reached out to grab the light, and it reached back.

The orbs gravitated towards Hadlee's upper chest in a strict formation. I was not too knowledgeable of the different constellations, but her markings looked like a letter E. The strong illumination lived inside of her body until the white orbs changed into a black color. Hadlee fell to the ground once the overwhelming light left her body. The only thing lighting up the hill was the flame.

Her eyes lit up. She held out her hand and closed her eyes. An orb of light rested in her palm. *She can manipulate light.* She juggled the ball of light back and forth, then she covered the orb with her other hand. She sent it upwards, and it dispelled into a billion particles of light that fell over us. I kept my hands out wide and let the light pour into my skin as if it were the sun itself.

"Show off." Foster looked up at the falling light.

"That's amazing, Hadlee," Kira said.

"So are you going to go to Emor?" Jin asked. "Now that you are this powerful Vestrin?"

"Aren't we all going to Emor," Hadlee stuttered.

"But are you going to leave us? Because you can. Because now you can have anything if you ask for it. Are you going to be like them?"

"Jin, stop," Keegan said.

Jin grunted and sat back down. That started the unstoppable divergence between us all. Jin was still unclaimed and saw Hadlee as a threat. Tonight she became the most powerful. Not just because she can manipulate light, but because she was claimed for it. She was powerful because whether or not we wanted to admit it, she was what we all desired to be.

...

The morning light had the same effect on the long weeds that the sunset had. A shimmer through the golden light. The breeze blew stronger today and caused the weeds to dance in a perfect symphony.

Foster and Keegan went with Nax and Kira to get food. Hadlee, Miller, Jin and I walked the opposite way. Miller seemed on edge here. He was not the same goofy friend I knew, but I didn't want to ask him what was going on. Not because I didn't care, I just hate it when people ask me.

We followed Sylvic's directions and walked south until we reached tall, jagged rocks. We crawled through a small hole in the cliff. I shed light as we entered the dark cave. Streaks of dried blood smothered the gray stone. Hadlee gave us more light; a beautiful white light instead of a malicious looking red. I heard the scrambling of feet as we walked towards the end of the cave. We were all ready to attack at any moment. Someone scurried behind the remains of a wide tree inside the cave.

"Hello," Hadlee said. "We are wondering if you have heard of the sickle of death?"

"Heard of it?" A soothing, relaxing voice came from behind the tree. "They told me I had to cut the wheats when they would move. I didn't know a life attached to it. I had to cut at least twenty rods of wheat a day. Do you have any idea how many people I killed?"

"You must be the Keeper of Death," Hadlee said.

"Not anymore," the man said. "Technically I still am, but I no longer kill. That can happen without me. Except for me. Keepers cannot die so simply. I have tried. I have tried everything. It's ironic, huh? Keeper of Death cannot die." The echoes fleeted, and it became silent. "What are you guys doing here?"

"We are trying to find the Libra Piece," I said. We still hadn't seen the man talking to us. "We believe it is the sickle from your scythe."

"I still have it, but I want something in return. You manipulate light. You have the power to kill me. The sickle is inside this tree. If you can take me out of this miserable life, it is yours."

"I - I don't want to kill you," Hadlee whispered. She walked towards him. "You can come with us. See the world. We are living a rare and beautiful life. You can live it too."

He sat inside the hull of the tree trunk with his feet crossed over each other. Long, greasy hair split into two and rested over the side of his face. He snarled at the bright light he had not seen in years. He was somewhere between life and death; lingering on the blank canvas of a life that passed by him and a death that could not come.

"All you have to do is take the light essence out of my body," he exclaimed.

"I thought you can't remove or place essences inside someone,"

Hadlee crept closer to him.

"You can if the body holding the essence allows you to. They hook onto your soul, and I am letting it go." He grabbed his slim stomach. "I let go of it years ago."

"I won't kill you," Hadlee said.

"I won't give you a choice."

His arms and legs became long and covered with thin hairs. His mouth became two large fangs, his body enlarged into a much rounder shape, and he received four more eyes that were still human. His long, hairy leg suffocated my waist. *I hated spiders.* I couldn't even look at the grotesque thing without wanting to faint. He pulled me closer to his open mouth.

"What will it be?" he screamed.

I lost my stable vision. Miller threw boulders at him, but nothing happened. He reached another leg out and grabbed Miller.

"Hadlee do it," Miller screamed. He couldn't breathe.

"I can't," she cried.

"It's him or us, Hadlee!" Miller choked.

I saw a light being pulled out of his body as his face became human. We both dropped to the floor as his large body shrank. The light came out of his mouth. He became human and dropped to the floor. A slim, crooked smile appeared on his lifeless face.

A glowing essence flew out of the cave. It looked like a jellyfish and left a trail of light as it pulsed through the dark cave. It was mesmerizing. Hadlee went to the Keeper laying on the ground. "I - I killed him," she said.

"You didn't kill him," Miller said. "He was dead a long time ago." Miller walked to the tree and grabbed the sickle resting on it. He lifted it up high above his head.

We did it. We found the first part of the Mallux. Hopefully, everything we have done to get this far will be worth it. Hopefully, we can make up the transgressions we have committed.

We walked back to the camp, refusing to talk about what happened. The sun no longer had the golden glow that covered the wheat field. It was just light brown plants springing out of the ground. Kira and Nax still sat at the burned-out fire. She looked excited when she saw us, and even more so when Miller lifted the sickle.

"Is that it?" she exclaimed.

"Yeah," Miller said. "We found the Libra Piece."

"We found the Libra Piece," Nax repeated.

"Where was it?" Kira asked. She kept looking back at Nax.

"The Keeper of Death had it," Hadlee sulked.

"The Keeper of Death," Nax repeated.

Kira walked over to Nax and lifted him to his feet. "Let's find the others and get out of here."

We headed into a destroyed town. Charred ash covered the ground instead of the golden wheats in the neighborhood of destroyed houses and scorched ceilings. Miller stayed in the back with his head down hardly speaking. I drifted back to where he was.

"Are you all right?" I asked. "You haven't talked much since we got here."

"There's not much to say," he said. "I guess I'm just tired."

I looked up and saw Keegan standing in front of a destroyed town with vacant buildings everywhere. Most of the windows were shattered and roofs thatched off. I felt like such an idiot, Miller told me about Kordia. It was where he was born, and it was all destroyed during the war.

"Miller." I grabbed him and kept him from walking with the rest of the group. "I'm so sorry. I don't know how this feels. I don't understand what you are going through, but I am here for you. I will always be here for you."

He didn't say a word back, but he threw his body into mine. He wrapped his arms around my back and clutched onto me. It surprised at first, and then I wrapped my arms around him. He let go of me with tired, red eyes and stood at the top of the cliff side.

"She told me to wait here," he said. "She said my father would come back on ships taller than me. I waited. And I kept waiting for him, but he never came."

"Miller, I…" I didn't know what to say, sometimes sorry justified nothing.

He let go of me, wiped his eyes, then turned away from me and continued walking.

We walked over to the rest of the group. They talked under the shade of a run-down roof, excited about our next adventure and the completion of our first one. We walked along the cliff side back to the ship.

"Wait," Miller said standing still. He put his hand to the ground.

"There are people down there. There are people under us."

"What?" Foster said. "Are you sure?"

"Yes, I can feel them moving on the ground," Miller exclaimed. "They could have gotten away from the Vestrins."

He separated the earth from under him. Before long, he was at least ten feet deep. If anyone was down there, we would know soon. A loud roar came from the top of the crescent shaped cliff. Miller stopped digging and looked up at the gray beast soaring above the rocks. It dropped onto a building and crushed it under its massive claws.

It was the same creature that attacked us at Domister. Four wings stuck into the ground and massive eyes glared straight at me. It had to be the Keeper of Dark because she knew what I was supposed to be. It didn't talk like it did last time we met, but it blew an intense flame towards us. I ran to the front and stopped it, then directed the pouring flames to the sides of us. Miller stepped next to me and enclosed the beast's enormous feet with the rocks.

"Run," Miller screamed.

We ran from the powerful dragon while Kira was in the back trying to pull Nax with her. I grabbed Nax's other hand and ran with them. The creature broke out of the rocks and soared over us. When we got back to our campsite, I grabbed the bow and Foster grabbed his sword handle.

Hadlee tried to take the beast down once again, but the wheat was not strong enough. Her chest illuminated again as she manipulated a spiral of light towards the heart of the beast. This time, the light was a spectrum of color instead of white. Laughter evoked from the beast.

"So you finally have a Vestrin," she said with her raspy voice. "It's a shame you are useless fighting me."

A streak of fire came towards Hadlee, and Miller protected her with a wall of rock. The beast made eye contact with me again and spread its wings wide. I pulled back the bow and made three separate spears of fire lined on the string. As the creature reached its neck back to incinerate me, I released the three arrows at the wings. Three holes burned into them. The creature let out a loud cry, and we ran to the ship. The beast tried to fly, but it was unable to, so it ran after us.

Miller lifted all of us up to the deck and pulled the crystals back together. I watched the beast continue to chase us. We were not out of reach yet. I released a pyre towards the open door and tried to keep it all out of the ship, but I couldn't. Flames scorched the edges our ship. Hadlee screamed, but I couldn't look back yet.

We were in the air, but the beast still chased us. It jumped off of its legs and stretched its claw out for our ship. I closed my eyes and focused on the heat all around me. I released a larger fire than I ever had towards the creature. The power coming out of my hands launched me onto my back.

We lifted high off the ground, only hearing the distant and desperate cries from the beast below. Kira still had the Libra Piece in her hand, and everyone made it on. Hadlee got burned by the fire, and her left arm was already blistering up. An aurora of pinkish light was being held in her palm. She put it on her arm and the blisters faded away. A new skin covered her arm. *Light could heal.* She was just as surprised as me.

Miller looked panicked. *They were underground.* He repeated to himself.

Light had the power to heal, but it also destroyed. It destroyed Miller's home, killed Miller's people. Light does not mean good, light just meant power. They can use the power to do incredible and beautiful things, but it can also be despicable. We all have the potential to be unbearably despicable.

CHAPTER ELEVEN
BEYOND THE WALL

We needed to stop for supplies after our run in with the dragon. Our ship was falling apart, and our clothes were getting gross. We flew over the water so no one would see us.

Nax hadn't said much since we left. He had been acting strange since we left Emor. Foster and I had to switch off pushing the ship forward in short shifts. It was beautiful on the deck, but the cold breeze was torturous. We didn't fly much higher than the land because of how close Caltus was. That was one of the larger cities and one of the most lenient with how Alturus live.

We landed in another field outside the city walls just as the sun finished setting. There were more of the purple flowers rising from the grass. We brought our bags and sat in the grass while we waited to set up camp for the night.

I stuffed my dark coat inside of my backpack and threw on a clean gray shirt. Jin sat in the flowers with Hadlee, weaving a crown from the purple flowers and the forest green stems. Hadlee placed the crown on her head. The flowers made her dark black hair look even darker, and the stems brought out the slight green tint in her eyes.

There was no glow in the flowers today. I could've sworn that they were the same flowers that lit up the sky the first night of our trip.

"Why is it so dark?" I asked plucking a flower from the ground.

"It's not a full moon," Hadlee said. "The flowers reflect the moon's light, so we won't be seeing any luminous flowers for another couple of weeks."

Jin laid in the flowers and stretched her arms high above her head. She let out a loud yawn, and I yawned afterwards. Her hands pulled at the weeds in the field, destroying anything that tried to deter life from the flowers.

"Hadlee, do you think you could make them glow?" Jin asked.

"I don't think it's the same." As she lifted her glowing fist in the air, all the flowers within the light's reach shed a lavender glow.

Jin sprung up from the ground. Keegan sat next to her and sprawled across the garden. She looked like someone else in this light. The purple made her eyes look dark, and the shadows from Hadlee created even more structure on her face.

There wasn't a need for a fire tonight. We all wanted to go to bed, and it was a lot warmer here than it was near the coast. I laid down between Jin and Keegan, trying not to look at either one. I wondered if either of them were looking at me.

The morning wasn't as miserable as the others had been because of how fast we fell asleep. By the time the sun came up, we were ready to go to Caltus. I changed into a clean gray shirt, threw on my backpack, and grabbed my bow.

Nax and Kira walked in front of the group. He was a couple

inches shorter than her, but his shoulders were twice as broad. Since
we landed, Nax had returned to his normal, confident self. I
wondered if he felt in over his head, or if the dragon scared him, but
I didn't ask.

Her hand stretched down to wrap around his. They didn't seem
like a couple that would work well together. She was ice, and he was
fire. Kira was put together and stable, and Nax was wild and
sporadic. They didn't communicate while they walked except the
occasional smile.

The sun shined right over our necks, pulling sweat down my
forehead. Every time sweat formed on Keegan's face, she would pull
the small drops of dew off of her. The sun drained the energy out of
all of us.

The purple flowers became dense rock and sand as we entered
the desert. A train whistle bellowed from behind us, but there were
no tracks. The clapping of metal overtook the fading sound of the
whistle as tracks dropped from the air and connecting with the pieces
behind it. A towering locomotive sped down the track. It was only
about thirty feet long, but it stood fifty feet tall. It was a golden-
brown color with small red beams supporting it. I couldn't get a good
look at the front because of how fast it was moving. Once the train
passed us, pieces of track would soar over it and fall just in front.

We stared at the vacant desert. The train left a trail of deep
imprints all the way to the wall. The only sign of life outside that wall
was a small village with black tarped roofs. The ground was cracked
and so covered with dirt that there wasn't any distinction between the

cobblestone and sand.

A thick rope held bodies high over the village. Four lifeless men hung like artifacts. The words "you rise, you fall" was written in dark red across the tan wall. A bold smell filled the air as we neared the wall. The chemical filled water tried to cover the stench, but it only made it more notable. It was rotten, like fish baking in the sun.

No one seemed startled by this, people just walked passed it and avoided looking. The only ounce of life in the bodies came from them swaying back and forth against the wall. The rope fraying with every scrape against the wall was the only sound I could focus on.

"What is this place?" I asked.

"This is an Obrum," Foster said. "It's where Alturus live. I've never seen one this bad though."

"Maybe we could help them," Hadlee said.

"We don't have time to stay here," Nax said.

Kira looked at him with a harsh glare.

Nax looked at her and dropped his shoulders in front of his chest. "But I guess we could check it out."

The people here covered themselves with minimal amount of clothing. They wore strips of cloth around their face to keep dust out of their eyes and mouth. Living conditions got better as we walked deeper into the village, but it was still far from suitable. Cold metal plates contained the sand, and small clay homes replaced the torn tarps. Most people set up small stands around a marketplace. A pool to bathe in centered the small homes without anything to cover those needing to wash up. A water manipulator moved the clean water into an empty pool, and someone else went to scrub the emptied one.

A farm stretched far past the small village. The Alturus scattered the field, and Vestrin soldiers watched all of them. They had enough food to feed a whole city, but none of the fresh produce went to those in the Obrum.

"This is how the Aturus live," Jin said. "And the Vestrin's get to live inside the walls."

A light blue train stacked with boxes backed up towards the center. It was much smaller than the massive golden train that passed by us not too long ago. A couple men opened the boxes labeled *Brav's* to reveal hundreds of unworn clothes. People swarmed towards the train as the sky illuminated with the bright colored shirts being thrown into the air.

"Everyone calm down." A tan man with narrow brown eyes stood tall in the train. Everyone seemed to listen to him. "We will give these out to women and children first, the rest of us can survive with what we have."

"That guy must be in charge here," Nax said.

"*That guy* is my father," Jin said.

She drifted towards to him. He stood inside the train, looking out at the crowd of people. He glimpsed at her like he did not recognize her, like he had not seen her in years.

"Dad? What are you doing here?"

"Jin?" He hopped down from the train's platform and wrapped his arms around her.

Jin pushed him off of her.

He grabbed onto her shoulders and smiled down at her. "Conlin, can you take care of the clothes, I have a lot to discuss."

A large man nodded his head and got up on the inside of the train. He had the branch-like markings covering half of his face. I had seen these on arms, backs, legs, pretty much everywhere, but I'd never seen them covering someone's face.

"We stopped by to help, but it looks like you have it under control," Jin said.

"If you think this place is under control, I'm good at faking it." He walked over to the rest of us. "Welcome. You guys can rest up at my home, it looks like you have travelled a lot today."

He waved his hand towards us, and we followed him through the streets. I haven't seen a lot of kids around Domister, but here they were everywhere. Young kids played with sticks on the ground or drew in the mud. Most of the kids I had seen used their manipulation as tools of entertainment; here they played with rocks and branches. There was a perplexing sign on one of the nicer buildings. *Children's Home* was carved in a frayed piece of wood and hung over the building. Beds filled the single room and broken windows surrounded the walls.

"What's this building?" I asked although I had a good guess.

"That's where the orphaned kids go. Vestrins inside Caltus bring their kids claimed for dark to us. We have all of them stay in here so at least they can have somewhat of a family," Jin's father said. "My wife used to take care of them."

"Used to?" Jin asked.

"She's been sick. We've been running low on medicine and it goes to the children first."

Jin stared at her father with resentment. She slowed her pace and walked behind him. No one here seemed to mind all of us walking through their town. They didn't care that we were Craved. No one even turned their eyes towards us. Jin's home was a single story tall like the rest of the buildings here and the same pale color with a faded blue door. It creaked open, and a girl that looked almost identical to Jin sat at the edge of a white bed. She got up and sprinted towards the door.

"Ali." Jin embraced her.

"Jin," she said holding the back of her head. "It's been so long. Are you here with the good news?"

"Not yet." Jin showed her sister her blank arms. "We're looking for something. Something that will make all of this separation go away."

Her sister was interested, but could see Jin staring at her mother lying on the bed in the room behind Ali.

"She's doing better," Ali said with a much deeper voice than Jin.

Ali looked much older. Her cheeks didn't possess the same pink hue in Jin's. Her hair went past her shoulders, but not by much. She had the vein like markings on her shoulders.

Jin walked inside to her mother. Her father invited us to sit at the old wood table with almost enough chairs for all of us to sit. Jin told me about her sisters, but only Ali was here.

Their mother was much paler than both of them. Her hair was

turning gray and her cheekbones bulged out of her face. Her eyes opened when Jin tapped her arm. She didn't say a word, but she placed her other hand over Jin's petite fist. Jin whispered to her mom, and a tear rolled down both of their faces. Everyone in the room saw her mother's body deteriorating. Before we could say nothing, Jin's father came in with a large plate of vegetables and meat.

"It's not much," he said, "but it should carry you guys through the night."

"Thank you so much for your hospitality," Kira said. "We never caught your name."

"Bradley," he said. "Thank you guys for watching over Jin, I hope you are good influences on her."

Jin came walking back over to us with wet trails painting the side of her face. A forced smile tried to come out. She sat down opposite of me and didn't touch the food.

"Why did you leave? When did you leave?" she asked.

"When you left, we wanted to find a better life. We heard there were uprisings in Caltus, so we dropped everything we had," Bradley said.

"And you never wrote me?" Jin said. "What if I got claimed for light and didn't know where to find you?"

"Believe me, I've tried. Since the failed uprising, Vestrin soldiers have been monitoring us like hawks. We would have come to you, but there's been more talk of revolts."

"Where are my sisters?" Jin asked.

"Luckily, Caltus allows Alturus to work in the walls. Things are changing down here," he said. "Chroma might have a seat on the council if she keeps behaving."

"Revolts?" Nax questioned. "What revolts?"

"We have been trying to get all of us out of the Obrum and into the city. We can't get over that wall," he said. "Some leaders are meeting today if you would like to join. I think the Craved would be a good asset."

Nax agreed to go to the meeting and soon, they left. Bradley and Nax left us in the house with Kira. It was depressing. Jin was with her mom in the other room. Ali played with the different weapons we carried along. Her greatest interest was the two-headed sword. She manipulated steel, and she told us that her sister did too.

"I should be a little more careful with where I manipulate," she said looking outside the window.

"Why does it matter if people see you?" Foster asked.

"We have *control hours*, as they call it. We can't manipulate outside these hours." She twisted the sword once more, and the steel was pushed back into the ground. She placed the sword handle on the table.

"Is it hard for you too?" Foster asked. "Making the right choices?"

"It feels like every day I have to decide to do good," she said. "It's a lot harder for my dad."

"Do you think what you're claimed for affects your morals?" Hadlee scoffed.

"You don't understand," Foster said. He stuck his arm out and traced the different lines his marking created. "When you get claimed for dark, you can feel it inside of you. It is a small voice in your head - it's not a voice it's more of a feeling that pressures you into doing something. I'm afraid to even speak sometimes because I don't want it to consume me."

If anyone were to be dark before they were claimed, I would've said Foster. He allowed the dark to consume him before he was claimed. Maybe we had a choice, but the people living here didn't. They lived as outcasts persecuted by the world because of something in their blood. If we get to choose, what could make up for the darkness that took over when I burned down the church?

Jin walked back into the room with wet cheeks again. She stood just behind me without saying a word.

"Do you still feel the light?" I asked. My head was facing down, so I had to repeat my question. "Do you still feel pressured to do good?"

"I'm not all bad," he laughed.

"We don't just do evil things," Ali said, "but we have to try a little harder to do what is right."

"So you guys have a choice too," I said.

"Not the same choice as you," she said. She looked at Jin with remorse and jealousy.

"We can't choose," Jin said. She hadn't said a word in the past hour. "Do you think I would still be unclaimed if we could?"

"I didn't mean that. It is just going to take a little more time," Ali said.

"And what happens if I get claimed for dark? I get blamed for my family living in the dumps and my mom dying because she can't get the medicine inside the city," Jin screamed.

"Jin, we won't blame you for anything. We will be okay."

The table seemed to get a lot larger as we all fell silent. The history in this family was visible between their eyes. The entire family had always leaned on Jin. Everyone depended on her to bring them up in society, and she broke. If what I believe is true; if we get to choose what we're claimed as, then she can change everything for her family.

A girl with the same black hair that Jin and Ali had walked in the door and threw a heavy metal band off of her arm. She sat on the chair and took a deep breath before introducing herself or acknowledging us. Nax and Bradley soon followed in after her.

"My dad told me you needed help repairing a ship?" She had a deep, strong voice that carried with confidence.

"Chroma." Jin ran to her and fell into her arms.

"Little sis, it's about time you paid a visit," she laughed.

Chroma looked a lot older than Jin did. She had wide shoulders, long hands, and stood about a foot taller than Jin and Ali. Her hair had streaks of silver running through it, and her eyes were a light hazel color.

"We thought Chroma could fix your ship while you guys walk around the city tomorrow. She is becoming well known for how thin she can make and mold steel."

"That sounds wonderful," Kira said.

"How was the meeting?" Foster asked.

"I am getting even closer to becoming the first Alturus on Caltus city council," Chroma said. "If things stay in the direction they're going, I could be on the council any day now."

"I thought you guys were talking about-" Kira kicked Foster's leg to shut him up.

"You guys should find somewhere to stay in the city," Bradley said. "I can take you guys to the gate, but you're on your own from there."

We collected our things and walked outside into the dull streets. Jin didn't say goodbye to her sister. Men dressed in royal blue uniforms stood on the roofs of a few houses. They had something engraved on their foreheads, but I couldn't make out the shape because they kept their faces down. The streets were almost empty now and it couldn't have been more than an hour since people crowded them.

The wall of the city was even larger from up close. Two women wearing the same royal blue color gawked at the opening, but they did not have the markings on their forehead.

"What is your business here in Caltus," the bigger one said. She had rugged black hair and a big mole on her lip.

"I don't see any work bands on em." The little one spat on the ground in front of us. "No work bands, no entry."

"Good morning." Bradley pushed his way to the front. "I'm Bradley, leader of the Obrum." He pulled his arm up and showed them his shoulder. I could not see what he showed them, but they seemed impressed. "They are all guests from Domister, and the Keeper of Youth wishes to see them."

"Very well," the big one said again. We walked towards the wall until a strong force pulled me back. "You will have to leave these outside," she said grabbing my bow.

"I can take those back to my place for you," Ali said.

"We can't be letting weapons in from the Obrum, especially when there's been more talk of a revolution."

CHAPTER TWELVE
SMOTHERED

The inside of the city was even more miraculous than the large gates surrounding it. As the doors pulled open, the harsh sunlight reflected off of the towering buildings. We walked at the absolute lowest point of the entire city, underneath bridges that connected everything above. Clear bridges staggered along the inner skyline. Some arched between the third stories of the buildings, others at the roofs.

About half a mile down the main road, a towering octagon shaped building stood high above everything else. It was a vibrant silver color instead of the bronze that coated all the other towers. The buildings here didn't just reach towards the sky like they did in Los Angeles, they spread themselves wide. Everywhere we looked there was life. Men wore large, blue button up shirts with white collars and gold buttons, and a couple men had top hats that were much too tall. Women were raised by tall shoes and covered with expensive dresses. Their dresses were short, ended with perfect circles, and kept the same blue and gold color pallete that the men wore.

Those with Alturus markings stayed at the bottom while high above us, I saw glimpses of Vestrin imprints on the citizens walking on the bridges.

A massive gold ship left traces of gray smoke behind it as it soared through the sky. It resembled a blimp, but with crisp edges. The front came together at a sharp point, and the back was the shape of a whale tail. A steel basket hung underneath, like in an air balloon, with silhouettes of at least a hundred-people standing in front of the large glass windows.

On the sides of some street corners, tall, spiraling staircases stretched to the bridges. A man dressed like everyone else stood at the entrance to the staircase. He had a marking on his forehead that looked like it was engraved there on purpose. It was a skinny crescent shape with a small dot just above it. Before people could go up the stairs, he would make sure they were claimed for light.

"What are we going to do with Foster?" I asked. "Bradley said that the Alturus have to return to the Obrum after sunset."

"We need to find someone willing to take us," Nax said. "If not, we need to find supplies so we can make camp."

"Let's split up, we don't know how big this city is," Kira said.

"Meet at that building at sunset." Nax pointed towards one of the taller buildings around us.

The bottom half was a large triangle but as the building stretched taller, it became slimmer and slimmer. The top was a clear globe with a large ring surrounding it at an angle.

"I will find the council leader of the city." Nax kissed Kira and walked into the city.

Miller nudged me, "let's go check out the city."

I nodded my head. It was interesting to see who looked together. Foster went with Kira and Keegan, and Jin left with Hadlee. I would've wanted to pair up with up with Keegan, but Miller would have been my second choice. He was kind of like the opposite of me. I was shy at first while he talked to anyone and did anything. But when I was with him, I liked who I was.

We walked towards the large octagon building. People were accustomed to the style of the city and saw that we were not practicing those customs. I wore my dark maroon jacket and light brown pants. Miller had a light gray shirt and black pants. The city infatuated him, and he didn't even notice how different we looked than everyone else. He hadn't seen buildings like this before.

"Are you doing all right?" I asked. "Seeing Kordia must've been hard."

He watched the large blimp above us. It soared above the large octagon building and dropped into the center.

"You see those ships," he said.

"Yeah, they're incredible."

"Not hordes of them. It was about five years ago, twenty of those came out of nowhere. They used everything against us. Fire first. Fire shows no restraint. My mother told me to run. I didn't want to, but she specialized in minds so I had no choice. When I regained control of my body, I assumed that my mother died."

"I'm sorry, Miller."

"Don't be sorry. My mother was claimed for light so she is still around me. In the stars and the flowers."

"Where do the Aturus go?"

"Not in the same place I assume. I only know about where Vestrins go because it was in a poem my mom would always read," he said. "It must be so different from where you live. I could not imagine not being able to manipulate."

"I couldn't imagine ever having this power. It's like we're all superheroes here," I laughed.

"It was strange growing up where I did. We didn't follow the standard of lights and darks. We were just one people."

A dorky little kid came out from behind one of the small cracks between the buildings. He had long blonde hair pushed to the right side of his face. His front teeth were big and crooked due to the huge piece of candy he kept sucking on.

"You guys don't look like you're from around here," he said with a high-pitched voice. With every word, his saliva made a soft clicking sound.

"We're not," Miller said and kept walking.

"Well where are you from?" He was out of breath due to the long strides needed to keep up with us.

"We're from Dom-"

"Not around here." Miller nudged my ribs with his elbow.

The kid circled around us once and then ran to catch up to us. "Where are your markings? Most people show their markings, but you don't.

"Trust me, you won't want to see them," Miller said.

"Wait, you guys are Craved!" he shouted.

"Quiet kid. Don't tell the whole city." Miller bent down and stopped the boy from walking further.

"They've been talking about you. We all saw the sails on your ship," the boy whispered. "Why are you in Caltus? Are you guys going to the Octagon?" the kid asked.

"No," Miller said. He walked faster than I could keep up with.

"Sorry kid, we need to find somewhere to stay tonight," I said.

"You can stay with me," he shouted.

The kid was relentless. We jogged now, but he kept pace with us.

"I live at the Octagon."

"Is your dad part of the council or something?" Miller laughed.

"No. Let's say I am close with the man who is." He held a crooked smile for a couple of seconds.

We stopped. I looked over at Miller, and he looked back over at me then shrugged his shoulders.

"How about this? We're meeting at that building at sunset," I said pointing to the tall building with the ball on top. "If we can stay with you, get your friend to meet us there."

He pulled his fist down to his side. "Awesome. So Spaceport at sunset. I'll see you guys there." He ran towards the center of the city. We were not far from the Octagon now, but there was not a point in going there anymore.

"That was a strange little kid," Miller said.

"Do you think he was being serious? About living in the Octagon and letting us stay with him?"

"Who knows?" he laughed. "I guess we'll find out tonight. I don't know about you, but I am starving and heard Caltus has even better food than Anador."

It looked like we were at the heart of the city. The silver octagon building was just past a small moat. An even larger octagon surrounded it. Eight different streets met right here. There were no more pathways above us. It looked like only Vestrins entered this area of the city.

The surrounding buildings were not as plentiful as they were on the outer ring, but this area was stunning. Bright green grass with intricate steel structures circled the moat. A large statue of a woman with the wings of a gigantic beast stood tall in the center, like the one in the middle of the courtyard at Domister.

Peculiar animals walked around the large center. Two middle-aged women carried their kids in one hand; the tall blonde one had a goose attached to a rope, and the red-haired woman had a peacock.

Small shopping stalls scattered around the slim streets. They were not like the wooden stands in the Obrum. Large glass windows bordered the stores, and pastel colored steel covered them. The fruit in the stands was vibrant and organized by color while the fruit in the Obrum rotted away.

Just a couple stores over, a big blonde guy with wavy hair looked in the store windows. "Is that Nax?"

"It looks like it," Miller said. "Isn't he supposed to be in the Octagon right now?"

"Nax?" We walked towards him. He looked over at us covered with sweat.

"Finn. Miller. Just the guys I need," he said. His eyes were opened wider than usual, and his voice sounded stripped of all pride.

"What's up?" Miller asked. "You seem all antsy."

"I was planning on asking Kira to marry me tonight." He twiddled his thumbs. "I can't find a good promise bracelet. It has to be perfect, but I can't find anything. I mean we should wait, anyway. We're still young still got time. I mean we've only been dating for a few years. It can wait. Right, if you were-"

"Hey," Miller put his hand on Nax's shoulder. "You can do this. She talked with Keegan the other night. She wants this to happen."

Nax took a deep breath and collected himself for a few seconds. "Could you guys help me?"

"This is my area of expertise," Miller said as he wrapped his arm around Nax's shoulder. "I'm like a love manipulator."

"Teach us your ways O great *love manipulator,*" I laughed.

"First, think of something sentimental. Any remarkable dates? Any special flower or song?" Miller asked.

"We met during a Gimbat match, but we hated each other."

"That's a start, but maybe some positive things," Miller said.

"She took me sailing." He smiled. "The water was rough and somehow we stumbled on the crystal caves. The ship floated up, and we both freaked out. After that, we went there every month."

"We need to find crystal bracelets, that's perfect," Miller said.

We walked inside a *fine jewelry* shop. Diamonds studded across every piece of jewelry. Colorful lights struck every corner of the store. Inside a glass case were about fifty promise bracelets with a wide assortment of colors, but each one of them had something in common. All of them were one bracelet that separated into two different ones. Three were made of crystal: one of them could be clicked together to form a large circle, another were two jagged bracelets that reflected each other, and the last was a fat bracelet that split through the center.

"This one nice Finny boy," he said with a strange accent. He had these big gold glasses on his face and examined it. "How much you reckon?"

"Stop messing around," Nax laughed. He sat there for a minute or two staring at them.

"Well," Miller said, "which one?"

"We can only take you so far," I said.

"I'm with Finn. You make the final decision," Miller said crossing his arms and putting the stupid glasses down.

"You guys are no help," Nax said.

He grabbed the fat one and put the black outlined bracelet on his wrist. He looked over at us, and Miller shook his head. He picked up the jagged one. It was the purest looking, almost clear until he pulled it apart. One half gave off a purple tint and the other one was almost a black. When he brought them close together, it changed back to the original shade.

"This is the one," he said. He looked up towards the slender woman selling the jewels. Her lips were small and black as her hair. She did not put the effort in to stare at any of us.

She placed the bracelet in a brown sack, and he handed her a good sum of money. He gave her a warm smile, and she wiggled her long purple nails towards him.

"She was a ray of sunshine," Nax laughed.

It cooled down. Clouds rolled in once again. The aqua sky faded into a cool blue. Nax strolled to the thin cut grass and sat with his legs crossed. Miller and I followed.

"Did you end up finding a place to stay?" I asked.

"I didn't look," he laughed. "I got so distracted but I should get on that."

"Don't sweat it," Miller said sitting down. "Finn and I found some kid who lives in the Octagon. He said we could stay with him."

"That doesn't surprise me. You both can get anything if you tried," he said. "Kira tells me you and Keegan are sparking up a little romance."

Keegan was talking about *me?* My cheeks were painted pink. "I mean not really. We're just-"

"Oh please," Miller said. "Keegan hardly talks to me. The second you showed up she became a whole different person."

"She just connected with another kid that used to be *normal,*" I said. *Maybe she does like me.* "What was she like before?"

"She was quiet," Miller said.

"Her confidence never changed. She is the only Craved that I think knows who they are. I can see her learn from every single mistake she makes," Nax said pulling out a bag of food.

"She's strong," Miller said, "but I think it might just be a show. She has this massive wall built around her, like she wants to be this mystery." Miller looked above his head to the right. He pointed to the large wall that surrounded us and grabbed some of Nax's food. "You and Foster are the only people she lets behind the wall."

I picked the grass below me. Whenever Keegan was brought up, I forget about home. I forget about Kate. I forget about the fire. There was something not so bad about this place. In fact, there was something here that I found more captivating than anything back home. When I think of her, this place is not foreign.

"Finn." Nax hit my knee.

"Sorry, I'm super tired. What's up?"

"I asked how you liked it here. Are things making sense?"

"It's getting a lot better," I smiled. "There are things here that I wouldn't even imagine back home."

Nax was too busy looking at the sky to continue our conversation. "It looks like we only have about an hour until sunset," he stood up. "I'll go down to the restaurant and make sure we get seats."

"Make sure you get one for our friend. The one who said we can stay with him," Miller said.

Nax stuck his thumb up in the air and continued walking. Miller was in a weird mood now. He continued to ask questions about Keegan and me.

"Did you ever like her?" I asked.

"Every guy does," Miller laughed. "I'm just wondering how you ended up with her."

"We aren't even together like that. She has said nothing that would lead me to believe she was interested in me like that."

"She doesn't have to," he said. "You need to make your move."

"Is this more advice from the *love manipulator?*"

He pushed the ground up from underneath me. "Yes, you jerk."

"Ow!" I yelled as I jumped to my feet.

He pushed the floor against his back to lift himself back up. "Tonight, at the spaceport, you need to get her alone, give her a little necklace or something, and kiss her. Girls swoon over random acts of romance."

"I could get her that loaf of bread I can afford," I said.

"Who said we had to buy it. When I was being raised, we didn't have any form of currency. You took what you need."

"So, we're stealing it," I said.

"No, I'm stealing it. I will take it for you because I'm an awesome friend," he said.

He walked into a jewelry store on the opposite end of the circle. It was not as nice as the other one, but I still felt sick. I waited just outside the store and saw him put a gold necklace inside his pants. He put a ring on the table, and the woman told him he could not afford it. As he walked towards me, the necklace flew out of his waistband and into the cashier's hand.

"Guard," the woman screamed, "these kids were stealing."

About five adults with the crescent moon marking on their forehead ran towards us. I put my hands up, unsure of what to do, and Miller took my arm and pulled me away. We made our way through the alley with a sign stating *Caltus Circle*. He pulled a large stone wall up from the ground, and we continued to run. The wall was blown into small pieces. A slender woman ripped water off of the storm drains and whipped it towards us. I yelled and fire came out of my mouth evaporating the water. *That's a new one.* My throat itched. I coughed and more flames came out of my mouth.

Miller turned around and sent a dozen skinny pillars of earth upward. The girl slammed into it, but there were still three guards right on our tail. One of them snapped a long vine from the wall to grab Miller's wrist and entangle his entire arm. I engulfed the vine with flames until it was nothing but ash. We reached a construction site at the top of the city. There were fifty feet of nothingness below us.

"Hold on tight," Miller said.

He loosened the edge of the cliff into a long, board-shaped rock. It teetered back and forth as half of it hung over the edge.

"You're insane," I screamed.

He pulled me onto the board, and we sped down the steep cliffside. I let out a big laugh, but it was silenced when I noticed one more guard still following us. She had steel shoes on and skated down the hard earth like ice.

"We have company," I said.

Miller looked back with a slight panic. He gripped our feet so rock attached to the board. "I need some serious firepower," he said.

He created a steep ramp a couple yards in front of us. We barreled down the hill. When we reached the jump, Miller screamed "Now!"

I turned my torso and jetted flames out of both of my hands. The guard slowed down because she thought we would kill ourselves. I looked forward again, and we headed straight for the roof of a building. We crashed onto the roof but continued to slide across it, tearing every tile on the way. Miller covered his hand with the hard stone and pressed it to the roof to slow us down. We would not stop in time. Miller let out a loud scream as the rocks on his hand scraped off his skin. He continued to slow us down using his bare hand while I made a steady stream of fire in front of us. The half-chipped board stopped at the edge of the roof, it tilted back and forth. Rocks still clenched my feet, so I could not step off. Miller stood up with relief, and we nosedived off of the building. A teal awning slowed us down, but it's the wooden barrels that broke our fall.

Miller pulled me up to my feet. His hand was scraped and covered in blood.

"Are you okay?" I asked.

"It's just a scratch," he said clutching it.

I bit a small tear at the bottom of my shirt and ripped it off. The dark shirt became darker when I wrapped his hand with it.

"Thanks," he smiled.

No one saw what just happened. Nobody was even around us. The streets were barren. The buildings were not the tall, intricate towers we had seen. These were one or two stories tall but spread long. Houses split up into small sections. The rooftops were flat and made up of small brick blocks.

"Do people still live here?" Miller asked.

"It doesn't look like it," I said. I peered through a window. Cold steel made the immaculate homes. "Where did everyone go?"

The whole street was like this; a street of empty houses fully furnished. We were somewhere we weren't supposed to be. A large bolt locked a cellar door shut. Miller walked over to it and tried pulling it open until I pointed to the sealed top. He looked at me with a grin and pulled a chunk of the ground up. He lifted it above the wooden doors and smashed it open. Just as I was about to shed light into the cellar, someone called out to us. We ran as fast as we could towards Spaceport.

We made it back to a main street in the city. Spaceport was not too far away from us, but hordes of people walking towards the gate made it hard to get through. "Come on," Miller said looking back.

We got lost in the flood of bodies. The Alturus walked out of the city because the sun had set. Men with the crescent marking on their forehead stood at the intersection of every path, making sure they did not stay in the city. We walked with the hoard until we reached a path that led towards Spaceport. One guard stopped us.

"Can I see your markings," she said with a soft voice.

"We're both Craved," Miller said.

"Why would two Craved be here," she snarled.

"We're staying here for the night," I said. "In the Octagon."

"Yeah, and I'm the Keeper of Light," she laughed. "You guys need to make your way to the Obrum."

"They are with me," the young man that was calling for us said. He had long blonde hair and crooked front teeth.

"Camben," she kneeled to the ground. "I'm sorry I-I didn't know."

He nodded at her and told us to come with him. "You're friends with the kid we met earlier today?" Miller asked.

"I *am* the kid you met earlier. Sorry, I didn't introduce myself last time." As he walked, his body shrank. He transformed into a teenager. "I'm Camben. Keeper of Youth."

"Do you manipulate time?" I asked.

"No," he laughed. "Just my age. I think being a kid is way more fun than some high-strung adult."

"It's an honor to meet you, properly meet you, Camben," Miller bowed towards him.

"It's an honor to meet you guys. I've heard a lot about all of you," he said.

Everyone stood around the large fountain outside. It was a large ball with a ring of water circling around it. It looked like Saturn.

"Who's this?" Foster said.

"I'm Camben. Keeper of Youth. We have all heard so much about you guys," he said.

All of them tilted their head down. "It's a pleasure to meet you," Kira said. "Nax is waiting up there, so we should get going."

"I can't believe we met another Keeper," Miller whispered.

"I heard he can change to whatever age he wanted, whenever he wants," Jin turned around and joined our conversation.

A man wearing a platinum suit peeled the large, glass doors open for us as we entered the pearl building. Two women greeted us from a small silver desk in the center of the bright white room

"Welcome," they both said at the same time. "Your table is ready, please wait for the lift to come."

The triangular roof opened, and a glass box settled onto the ground. The clear box emptied, and we walked towards it.

"Enjoy your stay here at Spaceport," they said without breaking eye contact. Their voices were in a perfect harmony.

A man stood in the glass box. Alturus markings covered his arm, but a circular symbol tried to cover them. It was a halo with ten different sized rays coming out, like a sun. He did not say a word to us while he raised the glass up to the top.

The sun rested behind the walls, leaving the sky with pink and orange tinted clouds. Rich looking adults with an abundance of jewelry covering their necks and arms filled the restaurant. Candles centered every table releasing a white flame that illuminated every inch of this place. I couldn't control this white flame, so it couldn't have been fire. The entire city glowed through the clear panels that covered the circumference of the walls.

Every building illuminated with candle light, shrouding the city with a red glow. I felt the life of the city. I took a deep breath in and let it out. Every single flame flickered with the beat of my breath. The flames were alive with me. The city was alive in me.

There was a single pink lily lying on the table and a small note attached to it reading: *Come find me where the world meets the sky at the top of the Spaceport.* Kira smelled the lily. Her eyes were pushed up by her smile hidden behind the flower.

"I'll be right back." She blushed.

"What's happening?" Keegan asked.

Miller and I both shrugged our shoulders. We sat down at a long gold table. I sat next to Miller and Keegan. The toasted rolls of bread on the table were devoured by the time we sat. Eating it made me realize how hungry I was.

"So," Camben said, "you guys are all Craved?"

"Yes sir," Hadlee said. "Foster and I are the only ones who've been claimed."

"Dark or Light?" he asked.

Foster pulled up his sleeve to show his markings while he shoved more bread in his mouth.

"I've always wondered how it feels."

"It hurt," Foster mumbled swallowing his food. "For a second you don't. You're numb. It's like it paralyzes you and the energy builds up. When it's released, it felt like a thousand pins digging in my arm and chest."

"That sounds excruciating," Camben grabbed his arm. "Finn, you were born outside Centure, right?"

"I was born in Centure, but my mother left before I was old enough to remember anything," I said.

Kira and Nax walked down the long staircase. She had tears in her eyes and a huge smile on her face. She leaned on Nax's shoulder. While they held hands, the bracelets were the crystal color. She lifted her hand up and showed her now purple tinted bracelet.

"Shut up," Keegan screamed.

"Oh my." Jin covered her mouth with her hand.

"It's about time," Foster laughed.

"We will make a small pit stop on our way to Emor," Nax said. "We're going to get married at Sapphire Bay."

"I'm so happy for you guys," Keegan said as she hugged Kira.

"You have to check out the roof Keegan, you would love it up there," Kira said.

Keegan walked towards the staircase. Kira nudged my back as she walked towards her chair. I looked over at Miller who pretended to cough. He nodded his head over towards the staircase.

"I hate to ruin this joyous moment, but we need to talk about staying with me," Camben said.

I stood up and followed her towards the roof.

"If you guys have seen the Octagon, that is where-" his voice faded to nothing as I walked up the marble stairs.

Her silhouette was just as beautiful as any other part of her. The view was spectacular up here, but I couldn't take my eyes off of her. I couldn't even see her, but the idea of her compelled me. The wind pulled on her hair as she leaned on a dark railing.

"It's beautiful up here," she said.

"It is." I walked up next to her.

A potent silence walked the thin, steel railing between us. Her hair flickered over her face in waves from the changing winds.

"The city is alive." She tucked her hands in her long sleeves.

She made a quick glance towards me, but it felt like she never turned her eyes back to the skyline below us. Her eyes were piercing.

I couldn't even look at them without feeling hypnotized, so I kept looking out at the city.

"Watch this," I tapped her with my elbow.

I felt the heat from all around me. All the windows, all the buildings, and from her. I breathed in once again and synchronized the beating of the flame's heart. Every flame moved with the same speed and the same strength. Darkness covered the sky one second only to be consumed by an orange glow the next.

"Someone has been listening to Nax," she laughed.

"You have a good memory." I moved closer to her.

"So fire comes from the breath. From oxygen?"

"Yeah, you have to concentrate on the breath of the flame. It's like a beating heart." We stared at the glowing city in silence. "When he first said I needed to think of *my oxygen*, I couldn't help but think of you."

She hesitated looking at me. "I'm flattered, but you have me all wrong, Finn." She turned her head back to the city. The orange glow outlining her from the city dimmed. "I don't start flames, I only smother them. That's all I've ever done."

I grabbed her hand that rested on the railing. "It doesn't have to be like—"

"It does. It's always been like this." She sighed and pulled her arms towards her body. "I've tried to make things work, but every time I let someone get close, I mess it up. I don't know how to act when someone actually cares about me." She turned back towards me and grabbed my hands. "I like you, Finn, but I'm not ready for this."

She stared at me again with her silver-blue eyes. I leaned towards her, and her hands pushed against my shoulders.

"Did you not hear a word I said?" she stuttered.

I am such an idiot. "Keegan wait." She ran towards the stairs. "UGH!"

I threw my hands towards the ground and flames erupted from them. If I was ever inside her huge wall, I built a bigger one. I followed her down the stairs. Jin took the seat next to Miller and Keegan moved to Kira. Everyone laughed around the table. The food came and so did the wine. I wasn't hungry anymore. They were celebrating the love of Kira and Nax while I ruined the one thing I liked here.

I sat down next to Jin. Keegan was still across from me. I stared at her without saying a word, but she did not look back at me. She acted engaged in conversation with Camben. Kira wrapped herself around Nax's arm. It would have been a perfect night, but I was selfish once again. I let darkness win again.

"You need to give her up, Finn," Jin said quietly grabbing my hand. "It'll only hold you back."

She took her hand off of mine and whatever warmth I felt disintegrated into nothingness.

CHAPTER THIRTEEN
CATALYST

Back at home, we would go to my uncle's cabin in the woods for a night every other weekend, but I had never appreciated these weekends. We'd started this tradition years ago, but I would always try to get out of it. He lived on a big hunting property and "the men" had to go hunting every time we went down there.

My step brother, Jeremy, loved to hunt. He would bring his kill up to the house just to show me. I had always been able to come up with excuses why I couldn't join them. Homework or college applications worked, but last time it didn't convince them. They handed me a large rifle and pushed me out the door with them.

It was a waiting game for a while. They didn't bother to shoot smaller animals like squirrels and rabbits, they looked for deer. We sat in the bushes by a small pond and waited. There was a charm to it at first, like I was becoming a man, but that soon faded. A beautiful deer and one of her fawns were at the pond. Jim nodded at me.

I stuck my eye up to the lens and peered at the innocent animal. My finger rested on the trigger but I couldn't pull it. I could not kill it. I didn't want to make a fool of myself in front of my step-dad so I looked around my feet and stepped on a nearby branch. Once it snapped, the deer sprinted into the woods. I fired the gun and let the two creatures live. The only person who knew I purposely missed that shot was Jeremy.

Animal hides covered the inside of Camben's home. The dark browns contrasted the shining gray steel that had surrounded much of the city. The only color were small hints of yellow. A few stairs led to a large table surrounded by yellow booths and a large animal covered half of the couch with its green tail. I walked towards the scaly creature as it snored on the cushions. Its sharp teeth stuck out of its long snout.

"That's Trixie," Camben said stroking the alligator's snout. Its yellow eyes radiated as they opened and looked towards us. "She won't bite." Camben's big mouth opened with a smile. His eyes matched that of the alligator's skin, a dull green with splotches of yellow.

"Nice place you got here," Foster said as he walked deeper in the house. A charming chime came from his hand pushing the dangling glass from the chandelier.

"That's just one perk of being a Keeper." He kissed the spikey head of Trixie. "You're treated like royalty." He walked towards us. He was tall when he was an adult. A couple inches taller than even Miller. "There are only six rooms in here so some of you will have to share, but you will find everything you need on this side of the building." He lifted his right hand towards the single hall across from us.

"Thank you so much again for letting us stay here," Kira said.

"It's my greatest pleasure." He bowed towards her. "You guys deserve a good night's sleep. I'll see you in the morning."

Miller looked over at me. "Let's go find a room."

We walked through the reflective steel hallway with huge rooms on both sides of the hall. We took the third one down on the left. I threw my bag on the ground and fell into the bed. I didn't think I could miss an actual bed so much. I pulled the feathered blanket close to my body and exhaled all the oxygen in my lungs.

A light turquoise paint covered the walls. Paintings of mountains covered the walls. Streaks of white made up waterfalls dropping into an abyss of mist. Dull, green grass that looked as if it swayed in the wind covered the bottom of the painting. Miller closed the yellow door. About fifteen candles rested in small orbs above us, and a small rope dangled underneath. I pulled it down and the orbs closed, causing the flames to dissolve into darkness.

"So," he said, "how did everything go with Keegan?"

"Ugh," I shoved the pillow over my face. "I ruined everything," I mumbled through the pillow.

"What?" he laughed.

I threw the pillow off of my face. "I ruined everything."

"I'm sure it wasn't that bad." He sat on the small couch to the right of my bed. "Tell me what happened."

I sat up and crossed my legs over each other. "I can't tell you everything, but I tried to kiss her at the worst time. She said she liked me. I was so fixated on that, I didn't hear another word she said."

"Keegan admitting to any feelings is unheard of. She loves being chased, that's why she likes being a Craved so much," he whispered.

"What did you love before you came here?"

"I had a girlfriend, her name was-"

"I'm not talking about girls," he interrupted. "What did you do? What did you want to be?"

"I was going to study architecture," I said.

"Why?" Miller asked.

"I'm not sure, I always found it interesting."

"Oh, come on," Miller said. "There's a reason everyone wants to be something."

"Well, I have this fear of just passing through this world. If I designed a big building in New York, I would live in the skyline forever, or at least as long as that building is there." It's been forever since I had talked about this. It was refreshing. "What about you?"

"I want to be a teacher. I change what I want to do every month, so it doesn't really matter," he laughed.

I didn't even feel tired. We kept talking and talking. We probably talked for three hours. My eyes became heavy, but I didn't mind. We went back and forth about facts about Centure and California. Pulurves, the half creatures, used to roam around everywhere and so did dragons. People made game of fighting these creatures as a test of strength.

Miller laid back down. My head spun as I laid on my right side. "Finn, I wanted to tell you that I-"

Bright lights shined in my eyes. "Don't say a thing," Camben's familiar voice said.

He was older than I'd seen him so far. His shoulders were broad

and hair went down towards the middle of his back. He stood at the
open door with two women wearing a gray suit. There were logos on
both of their shirts that looked like the one I drew for our ship. The
sharp C covered half of the Halo of the same size with the same
sharp triangle resting in the middle.

"You both need to come with us and keep quiet."

I looked over at Miller. He squinted his eyes and looked towards
me. He nodded, and we both got out of our beds. We followed them
through the dark hallway and to the other side of the Octagon
shining with a dark red color. The two women twisted the gears
hanging on the steel door until the spokes made a triangle shape. The
door released air that kept it shut, and Camben pushed it open. The
room was black except for the white table in the middle with a model
of Caltus and the Obrum. Nax and Kira sat with their shoulders back
at the table next to Bradley.

"Good choice," Nax said. His feet rested on the table right next
to the model.

"Can you put your feet down," Camben said. "I mean seriously,
I spent hours on that model."

Nax put his feet down and grinned over at Kira.

"Yeah, hilarious you stained this porcelain table," Camben said.

"I'm sorry," Nax wiped off the dirt from the table. "Finn. Miller.
Sit down."

"What's this about?" I sat down on the smooth white stools.

"Kira told me you drew the sail on your ship," Camben said.

"Yeah, I drew the whole thing."

"That is a dangerous symbol my friend. That is almost identical to the symbol for the Slate Ward."

"I just drew the Mallux."

"That's what Kira said. I understand where you got the base for the dark and light emblems, but where did the triangle come from?"

"I heard it in a story I read. The one about the Keeper of Death. Is there something wrong?"

"No, just the opposite." He got excited and became younger. It seemed like he couldn't completely control his branch. "You see, the triangle is the symbol for balance. The Slate Ward believes Light and Dark should be treated equally. People saw your sail and thought it was a symbol for balance. Word is traveling around fast about *the Craved.*" Camben walked towards me and Miller. "You guys are bringing strength and more importantly hope."

"So what we want is for you guys to start an uprising in Caltus. We need you to get the Alturus inspired," Bradley said. He spoke with the emotion of a rock. "They all believe you guys are a part of the Ward."

But we aren't.

"An uprising in Caltus," Nax said quietly. He stared off at a wall and didn't seem to have any attentiveness to the conversation.

"How are we going to get them past the wall? I have seen the guards on top of the buildings," Miller said.

"We need to cause a diversion. A fake riot," Kira said.

"We will have a few citizens who are a part of the Ward over here." Camben moved a flag with the Slate Ward emblem towards the west of the wall. "They will cause a fake riot and attract the guards towards them. Then we will come from the north and get through that wall. If there are any guards, we can take them out."

"What happens to the decoys?" I asked. "Are we going to let them take our hits?"

"They know what is at stake," Camben said. "Getting a big city under control of the Ward will be a huge stepping stone for us."

"What about the Mallux?" I asked.

The Mallux was the reason we left Domister. We only went to Caltus to repair our ship and get supplies, not to start a revolt.

"This is just as important." Nax made eye contact again. "The Mallux might not work, but this can. This can be a major step in the right direction."

"We need you guys," Bradley said. "You don't understand what the Craved mean to us."

"I will tell the others about this if you two are in," Nax said.

"I'm in," Miller said. "This is what I was raised for."

I was never one to result to violence outside sports. They were using us as faux heroes, but maybe that was what I needed to be. For once, I could do something good.

"I'm in too," I said.

"Okay, I will inform the rest of you tomorrow," Nax said. "Get sleep, tomorrow might be a long day."

The two guards pulled the door open for us. I looked back, and they remained staring at us until we walked out once again. There was something wrong about all of this, but I couldn't stop it from happening. I didn't sleep again that night, how despicable would it be if I could; if I went to bed knowing in a few hours innocent people would die, and I could be the cause.

The smell of breakfast came as the sun rose and plates of food covered the table. Everyone was already awake and waiting around the table with plates in their hands. Two identical women wearing shining, tight silver dresses welcomed us to the table. Camben told us to eat light, but I hardly listened.

Camben came out to the table looking about the same age as Nax. He wore a silver suit with long, steel shoulder pads. A sword hung from his belt.

"Good morning." He waiting until we stopped eating. "I know that you guys did not expect to do anything more than find the Mallux, but I wanted to say thank you for fighting with us. You understand what is at stake, and you understand the effect you can have on people."

He already told the rest of them. None of them were deterred by what he said.

"You will help us rise today. If we can get into the city, Caltus will change for good. I want to make sure you are all ready and willing to do this."

"Absolutely," Jin said standing to her feet. "We're with you."

Hadlee stood up next. "We will rise."

Foster and Keegan rose at the same time. Then, Miller stood. Finally, I rose.

"Things will be different. They're going to be better because of you."

We left the Octagon and there was an indisputable tension in the air. The city was not as busy as it was yesterday, and it was mostly Vestrins walking around. None of them seemed to have any clue about what was about to happen.

We walked out of Caltus and into the Obrum without saying a word. Everyone felt warm: in their stomachs, or hearts, or head. We walked passed the bodies hanging on the wall. I tried not to look at them. I tried to stay hopeful, but I only feared the possible losses we might encounter today.

A man wearing gray from head to toe guarded Bradley's door. Nax walked up to him and whispered, "the shadows only show when the light shines."

"The Slate would like to thank you for your commitment," the large man responded. He opened the door, and we walked inside.

A huge basement hid underneath Bradley's house hidden from anyone who didn't know where to look. A hundred-people wearing dull clothing squeezed within the walls. Some people had Vestrin markings, but most had Aturus markings. Our ragtag group was not even the youngest. A few kids who looked no older than twelve put on the face of a soldier.

The door closed above us, leaving only the light scattering through the broken wooden panels. Nax shot fire towards the front of the building and ignited a contained pile of brush that created an orange glow around the room. The smoke rose, but the ceiling enclosed the smoke above the crowd.

Camben stepped up on a raised platform with Bradley standing just behind him. "Good morning." Camben lifted his hand and people quieted down. He looked around twenty right now and was in better shape than I had seen him. "In just a few minutes, we will become known to Centure. The Slate Ward has been growing in Caltus, but we have been unable to further increase our numbers. We have discovered a group of kids who want balance just as we do. They are a few of the Craved, and they have come to Caltus to help us win the city!" he shouted.

Everyone cheered for us, which felt different. It felt good.

"We found something. We found a piece of the Mallux." Nax lifted the sickle high above the crowd. "We have leverage and we are trying to make things right, but we need your help. We have the capacity to do this."

"With their help, we can take this city," Bradley said.

Everyone cheered once again. I couldn't help but yell with them.

"I didn't think my dad would ever be a leader of a war," Jin whispered.

A war. This could cause the next war here, and we would be stuck right in the middle. "This isn't a war," I stuttered to Jin. "War causes chaos, we are doing this for order."

"What do you think the Vestrins said when they started the last war?" she said. "Everyone who starts a war thinks it's justifiable. Even if it is, that doesn't make it any less of a war."

"Courageous men and women are risking their lives to cause a diversion for us," Camben said. "In a few minutes we will risk our lives for a balance that will last."

A small man opened the hatch above us. "They sent the signal fire. It's time," he said.

"Okay, we only have a few minutes to get through that wall and take the heart of the city. We need those who branch in earth to take their fortress down. Everyone else needs to watch their backs," Bradley said.

Everyone walked up the large staircase and out the door. The sun was blazing hot and a bright yellow. I looked towards the wall and there were no guards at all, there were no guards anywhere. Someone let out a loud war cry, and the crowd charged towards the wall. I stayed towards the back with Jin.

"It's too quiet," I said.

"There would at least be one guard," she said.

I heard the loud clanking of metal. A large silver train sped parallel to the wall. Smoke drifted high above us as a signal of what was coming. Banners with the ten-rayed star trailed behind the train.

"They knew this was happening," I said.

But it was too late.

CHAPTER FOURTEEN
ENDINGS

We had already made contact with the wall and large cracks traveled across it. In the middle of the thick rock was a dense coat of steel. Foster and a few others headed towards the front of the line. One person pointed towards the train bellowing towards them, and everyone erupted into panic. Those who broke down the wall now clung towards it. Everyone behind them ran the opposite direction. Foster didn't move however, he bent his knees and fixated his vision on the steel train.

The train was not stopping to spare him, but he refused to back down. He stretched his hands towards the steel giant, and his veins pulsed out of his skin. The train slowed down and the pointed front of it impaled the side of Foster's stomach before it came to a stop.

Foster stepped back and waited. He stared at the train relentlessly waiting for anything to happen. It was silent for a while. Everyone stared at the shining silver beast that looked over them. It was as tall as the one we saw delivering supplies to the Obrum, but ten times as long.

There was no gap of time between the large doors swinging open and hundreds of guards wearing navy blue suits running out of the train. Large pieces of the wall were stripped off and tossed towards the men, but Vestrin guards were being led by a giant steel wall that five men manipulated. Foster darted toward the shield with another girl who branched in steel. As they wrapped the steel around their arms, streams of fire were being hurled at them. Foster punched his left arm, and a gust of wind destroyed the fire and scattered the assembly of guards. I heard them shouting that he was a Craved, and soon a pillar coming from the ground entangled his arms and pulled him towards the Earth.

"Are you guys just going to watch?" Keegan screamed. She threw me her whips. "Let's go!"

Keegan ran towards Foster. The frequencies created by another guard who manipulated sound pushed Keegan to the ground. Chaos exploded from the center of it all. It kicked dust up and surrounded everything.

Jin turned her head towards me and kissed me for only a second, and then she ran towards the forest. She looked back at me and nodded her head. It was too late for me to say something to her. She left the fight and everything in me wanted to follow her, but I didn't. I looked down at the thin strings attached to the gray handles and ignited them.

I sprinted to the chaos. Both sides were out of order, and everyone fought to kill. They pulled Foster into the train, and a dozen guards stood with heavy shields in front. Keegan was by one of the bathing pools outnumbered three to one. One man manipulated earth. He had the crescent marking on his forehead, but instead of a circle there was a diamond over it. She had the entire pool of water under her control.

They all remained still, ready to attack. Keegan had two hands sticking out towards the women on the sides of the man, but kept eye contact with the large man. The dark-haired girl sent fire towards Keegan. I ran towards her. Keegan enveloped the fire and the girl's arm in water, causing steam to rise. The ground rose and hit Keegan in her left hip. She lost control of the girl's arm, and the guard shot fire towards her again. I jumped in front of the fire and roused it back to nothingness.

Keegan pushed her back with most of the clean water left from the pool. I had not used the whips of fire before, it was different from the bow and arrow. It was much less contained. I swung them towards the man and left a large tear in the center of his shirt. His skin became red and covered in blisters, and his eyes became filled with anger. He swung his arms up and directed a wave of the earth towards me. I fell onto my back and lost the air inside of me. He was about to land on top of me with dense rock covering his fists, but I rolled onto my hands and pushed myself back to my feet.

Keegan was still engaged with both the other girls. The other one had cream colored hair. She pushed Keegan back into the empty pool by clapping her hands and sending strong vibrations every time her hands would touch. Keegan was all out of water and had no more room to back up. The dark-haired girl stood above Keegan with her hand held high. She projected flames out of her hand and into the air and then brought it towards Keegan. I slashed my whip at the girl and her leg bled.

"Someone's protecting his little girlfriend," she said with a hoarse voice.

She pulled her arm back and had a cynical look on her face. As she brought her hand toward Keegan, I wrapped the thin whip around her wrist and yanked it back. Her right arm became limp, and she let out a loud scream. The pale girl let out a screech, and the vibrations sent me flying back, but I didn't loosen my grip on her wrist.

"I don't need protecting." Keegan pulled the water out of the ground. She pushed it over my head and caused it to crash on the large man right behind me.

Both the girls teamed up on Keegan while I was down. Her water evaporated from the flames of the girl with the now dislocated arm. They pushed her back towards the buildings. I pushed myself up to my knees and rotated the whip towards the girls. The fire broke off of the whip and brought the wooden building to flames. The one who manipulated sound kept pushing Keegan towards the fire. I was dizzy as I stood back up on my feet. All of Keegan's water turned into steam, and she had nowhere left to go. I stumbled as I walked towards the inferno.

It felt like the church. It felt like I was back, but this time I was not running. I stripped all the flames from the wood and pulled it towards the two guards. The pale one ducked below it, but the flames enveloped the other girl. It knocked her back into the bathing pool, and she screamed as she tried to smother it. The other girl ran back to the rest of the guards.

"Are you okay?" I put my hand on Keegan's shoulder.

"I'm fine," she pulled her shoulder away from me and jogged back to the Ward.

Blood mixed with clean water dripped out of the now broken bathing pool. The girls dark skin was covered with even darker spots. Her chest was still as blood rolled down her neck. She manipulated fire, but it still killed her. Her blood seethed inside of her veins and cooled as it poured out of her.

She was not the only person who died today. Blood-stained gray uniforms scattered the floor. One of the twelve-year-old boys cried over his twin on the ground.

There were three Vestrin guards for every one of us. Hope for our victory was destroyed.

Loud screeching of birds and stomping beasts came from behind me. I turned around to a hoard of different animals coming out of the dust. Jin sat on a large mountain lion running towards us. Condors dove and grabbed the shoulders of the guards. Their wings manipulated air as they flapped them. Lightning sped towards the birds, and they twitched as they fell to the ground. Large snakes slithered right over my feet and towards the army of blue. I couldn't see what was happening, but guards dropped like flies. They saw Jin coming towards them. She pushed her hands forward and more terrifying beasts came flying overhead.

"It's the girl," one guard yelled.

He pulled the roots deep beneath the hard clay as he ran towards her. He swung a long vine at one of the gigantic birds and pulled it back to earth. Dozens of guards ran towards Jin, and Keegan and I followed. A plant wrapped around my body and pulled me to the ground. I hit the back of my head straight on the ground and tried to stand back up. Everything looked blurry.

An intense cold rolled underneath me as shadows raced past me. Roots entangled Jin high above the ground. She had lost control of the variety of beasts fighting on our side and most of them were dead, anyway. There were at least fifteen Vestrins closing in on her. The black shadows rose through the vines and turned the light green color into a dark forest green. Jin let out a loud cry as her legs became engraved with the Aturus markings. She broke the vines tying her hands up and threw her arms down. A surge of dark shadows rose over the guards. When the light overtook the darkness once again, Jin laid on her side.

Every guard that stood so strong now fell on the ground, frozen. I expelled flames out of my feet until the hard ground cracked open. I swayed left and right as I tried to run to Jin. *She controls darkness.* A warm liquid dripped down my neck, but I didn't stop heading towards her. I picked her up with shaky arms. Her slim eyes were closed shut. She was still breathing, but I had to get her out of there.

This battle was over, and we lost. There were almost no members of the Slate Ward left. Bradley screamed at the remaining while throwing his arm in circles back toward the village. The Vestrins chanted at their victory, although I couldn't hear much over the buzzing in my head. Keegan was no longer lodged into the ground. She waved her hands towards the wooden door of a white building. I sprinted inside and put Jin on the table.

Keegan mouthed something at me, but I still couldn't hear. She tore off a little bit of her shirt and pulled water from a small plant. She put the wet cloth to my left temple, and it stung. The room looked grainy. Keegan's ripped cream shirt absorbed a dark red color.

"Jin. Is she okay?" I stuttered.

"She will be fine," Keegan said.

My eyes could not focus on her face like they normally did.

Jin had bulging markings on her left leg. They were the ones that looked like tree branches, except now I could tell they were veins. Darkness replaced the blood that traveled through her.

Keegan sat me down on a long chair and said something about me having to stay straight up. She put the warm and wet cloth in my hand. I kept it up to my temple. Blood stained my hand as if there had not been enough already. I killed someone today. I helped plan something that killed even more innocent people. I pictured the bodies crashing into the floor.

Keegan brought a bin over towards me and held it beneath my face. Everything I ate this morning came pouring back out of me. The vomit didn't stop, neither did the dizziness. It was hard to keep my heavy eyelids from blocking my brain, and I dozed off into a cold darkness.

When I opened my eyes again, I was in a different room. Jin sat up at a table across from me. We were back at her family's house. It was just Jin, Nax, Kira, Bradley and me. Kira sat next to Jin and Nax. Bradley sat next to me, not saying a word. Kira looked at me with a wide eyes.

"You're okay," she whispered.

"What happened?" I asked.

"They knew we were coming," Bradley said with his hand almost covering his entire mouth. "I can't figure out how though." He rested his head on his hand and stared at Jin across the way.

"It wasn't me. You didn't even tell me about this plan of yours," Jin said.

"I didn't think it was you," he scolded.

"Whatever," she responded.

"I think I might know how," I said. I tried sitting up straight. "When we were in Emor, someone kept whispering to Nax late at night. They spoke in a different language, but Nax remembered nothing."

"What did they say?" Kira asked.

"I don't remember."

"Try," she screamed.

I didn't respond. I tried to think, but my mind was blank.

"*Lited ni hul dek,*" she said.

"That's it," I said. "He said it over and over again."

"They tainted him." She grabbed Nax's hand who looked just as confused as I was. "They can see what he sees, hear what he hears."

"That's perfect," Nax said.

"How is that a good thing?" I asked.

"We can divert them with a fake meeting and try to take the city again."

"And put more people's lives at stake?" I screamed. "We won't do this again." I plummeted back to my seat. My head spun.

"Finn, you don't understand. The Aturus have lived like this for decades. There are few options for people like us to climb up this social ladder," Bradley said once again looking at Jin.

"I'm sorry!" she screamed. "I tried everything to be claimed for light, but I wasn't." She choked up as she stormed out of the house.

Her father stood up to follow her. I put my hand on his shoulder and pushed him back into his seat.

"No offense sir.," my brain rattled as I stood up, "I think she needs to talk to me right now."

His eyes looked unconcerned. I walked out of the house and saw her dark black hair walking towards the desert sand. I ran after her. She sat on a broken concrete wall. The wind picked up, carrying a light dust around us. The sun was bright and made me nauseous. The sun was almost setting already, so I was knocked out a lot longer than I thought.

"You don't have to be here, Finn," she said. "Go find Keegan and Miller."

I sat next to her. Her feet didn't touch the hot ground below like mine did. Silence sat right between us. I covered her fist with my hand.

"Everything will turn out all right," I said.

She looked at me with her small brown eyes and shook her head. "No it's not," she whispered. "My family depended on me for this. My mom needs the medicine from the city. My sisters can't keep working for my father. My dad has to-"

I wrapped my long arms around her and pulled her into my body. "This is not your fault," I kept repeating.

I felt her trying to catch her breath. Her back kept moving up with big gulps of air. Her eyes were red and bloodshot, but not wet.

She breathed for a little while. "My dad just started another war, and no one will benefit from it," she said.

"I don't think a war will happen again," I said. "Wars don't start when power is kept. If it does, we're strong enough to stay alive."

She laughed. "We all think we are so strong because we have control over something. We are blind. We can't even control our own fate or our own morals. We are the ones being manipulated."

"So you don't think our actions define what claims us?"

"Don't be ignorant, Finn. We don't work for anything in our life. Everything is planned out from the second we are born. We are a part of this never-ending cycle that no one can break."

"We always have a choice, Jin."

"I didn't. You didn't either," she said. "Do you think you would have come here? That you would've chosen to control fire. You wouldn't have. If you had a choice, you would be back home, but you're not."

There was a harsh truth in that. My life was perfect before I lost control. My worries did not even graze the surface of what I deal with here.

"You still have a choice you can make. You can choose to ignore what your family says and what that stupid marking says you are."

"I do have a choice. I chose you. You chose Keegan. Keegan chose Foster. Even when we want to choose something, we can't have it. You don't get to ask anything from this world."

I put my hand on her slim knee. "Jin, I didn't choose Keegan."

"Finn, go back to my house."

"You always do that. I try to talk to you and you shut me out," I said.

"Go!" She turned around and pushed me back with a wave of shadows.

It was cold and overwhelming. For a second, I couldn't move. The shadows held me down and decided when they wanted to give me control again.

I let out a grunt as I threw fire towards the dry roots beneath me. I stammered back to her house. My head still spun, but I didn't know if it was because of Jin or my injury. She thinks I don't understand what being claimed is like, but I was claimed since the second I got here. I was still just the kid from another world, the kid who ran, the thing that killed someone today. *I am Craved.*

My feet shook as I walked. I sat down on the floor and leaned up against a brick wall. The sun was almost behind the huge wall. I closed my eyes and felt the heat on my neck. The bodies hanging above the Obrum weren't as ominous anymore.

We rose. We immediately fell.

My eyes opened to an orange sky. The sun was almost gone. My head felt better until I stood up. The dark blue uniforms of the remaining guards looked black in the silhouette of the setting sun.

They didn't seem to mind me out in the village although everyone else was locked away in their shanty houses. I walked to Jin's house again, which wasn't too far from where I was. I felt less dizzy when my hand pressed against my temple.

I opened the door and everyone was in there. They surrounded Jin, who laid on the cold table. People had trouble catching their breaths over the heavy cries. Kira's red hair spread along the table. She held Jin's hand. Two holes pierced Jin's neck, and the heat she once carried was a bitter cold. She was dead. I looked around at everyone standing around the table.

Wetness stained everyone's face. I was just with her. I just left her. The guards left right when we lost. There's no way they could've killed her. There's no way.

My eyes filled up with tears, and then they let them go. My hands plummeted down to the table. My lungs scrambled for air as my chest heaved. Tears wouldn't stop falling on the table below me. I was just with her.

"What happened?" I stuttered.

"She sat on the ground by the sand, and a snake bit her neck. The poison killed her instantly," Bradley said. His voice was still. His eyes were dry.

"The poison didn't kill her. You did," I screamed.

"Finn, you need to understand-"

"Understand what? You needed her to be claimed for light so you could be in the city. I'm not as ignorant as you all think I am. She killed herself with that snake, and she did it because of you." I shouldn't had said that, but I had no control of my words.

No one responded. Did none of them realize she put this on herself? I threw my face in my hands and cried again. It seemed like the crying never stopped.

We took her body out to the small field of wildflowers that grew among the sand. We laid her down in the dull yellow and green patch. Hadlee still had the crown of glowing flowers that Jin made for her. We stood around her for a while. She looked beautiful right now. I didn't realize how much I cared about her until I couldn't tell her. The sky was just blue. A dull, gray blue. I romanticized this new place, but that did not last.

Hadlee bent down, grabbed Jin's hand, and held onto it tightly with both of her hands. All of Jin's sisters were here. I didn't introduce myself to any of them though. They all looked similar to each other, but none of them were her. Bradley stood at the feet of Jin's corpse. He seemed just as emotionless as before. He said a few sentences about her, but I couldn't take anything he said to heart.

"Jin was light, whether her markings said that or not," Hadlee stammered. "She had a contagious spirit and the brightest smile you could ever feel. She was the most innocent of us, and the first to die. That proves that life holds no pity." Hadlee picked up the halo of flowers on the ground and placed it on Jin's chest. "She was my best friend."

For just a second, the flowers glowed the bright purple color they had when they attached to the stem, but like most things, that did not last.

Hadlee sobbed when the glow faded. She fell into Miller's arms. He wrapped his long arms around her and held her close. He kept repeating everything would be all right, but it wasn't.

Camben walked us back to our ship. I didn't say goodbye to Bradley or anyone for that matter. We needed to leave. We needed to fly through the night and try to find Foster. The guards took him and a lot of others to Emor as prisoners, but I felt beyond apathetic for him. It was hard to leave so quickly because none of us had time to process a thing.

"I'm so sorry," Camben said. He looked the same age as us now. "I'm so, so sorry."

"This isn't your fault," Nax said. "If anything, there's hope now. People know about the Slate Ward."

There wasn't hope. Not now. We lost today. We lost a lot more than I prepared for. It was a lot different when my mother died. I was heartbroken, but we knew it was coming. No one expected this, especially from Jin.

"I know that they took your friend. You won't be able to find him in the city, but there are secret entrances to the undergrounds all around the forest."

"Thank you again," Kira said as she hugged him goodbye.

We walked up the steps to the ship. I stayed towards the back of the group. Before I could take a step, Camben pulled me back. I didn't look at him until he put his hands on my shoulders.

"Finn, I need to give you something," Camben said.

"I don't need anything."

"I've had it since I was a kid." Camben reached in his pocket and grabbed a black necklace. "I've been a kid for a long time, Finn. You need to keep this safe. They might take me to Emor. They might do awful things to me."

He turned the black circle until it faced heads up. In the moonlight, a couple numbers shimmered out of the design. The emblem for the Slate Ward was on this clock in a dark black color with glittering gems inside the paint. I flipped open the sharp "C" shape and the half circle on the other side.

Camben pressed on the curved triangle in the center of the emblem. The white clock slid into the edges of the necklace revealing a compass underneath. A red arrow swayed between west and east.

"It's a compass too. The arrow is moving like this because the compass can manipulate desire. If you focus on only one thing you want, the arrow will point to that thing. You need to decide what you want, Finn."

"Why are you giving me this?"

"I know you don't see it, but you are so important. We need you. They need you." He put the chain around my neck. "You need to stay safe. You should get going. Use this to find your friend." He walked away.

"Wait," I said.

He turned around. I looked at his bright green eyes. I hardly knew him, but he was one of the first people who seemed to care about us. I wrapped my arms around him.

"Thank you, for everything."

He nodded at me and walked back towards the city. I looked at the compass around my neck. It swayed back and forth because I didn't know what I wanted. I didn't know what I *craved*. I could desire the world or nothing at all.

I slid it closed to see the clock again. I didn't want to think about what I desired right now because all I wanted to do was sleep. I walked up the stairs, and we soared over the skies.

The city looked just like it did when Keegan and I were on the roof, but it didn't strike me as beautiful anymore. The people living in those golden rooms shrouded with a warm flame had no idea what just happened. I'd be surprised if they ever did. They had the freedom to live where they were, in a world without war and without a real threat.

That was until now.

The threat was coming, and we're shaping up to be one hell of a storm. We rose, and we fell hard. Now it's their turn. They had already risen to the top. They don't need to fight for a thing to get what everyone deserves, but they will have to fight if they want to keep it.

We are finding the Mallux, we are leading the Slate Ward, and I am making sure that no one is ever hurt the way Jin was hurt again. We may be the Craved, but what we want is a lot more dangerous than anything that desires us.

Part Three

CHAPTER FIFTEEN
TRUST

Hadlee restored Nax using her own light. Kira seemed all too familiar with tainting, but she never said why. She told Hadlee to fix it by placing both hands around his head and pulling a halo of healing light around him. He remembered the face of the man who did it, but he didn't remember where they took him.

"Camben gave me this so we can find Foster." I showed them the compass. "It's a mentibus and can point you toward what you want."

Nax reached out to grab it, but I ripped away from him.

"Awesome," he said. "This will be very helpful."

"You guys need to sleep," Kira said. "We have a long day tomorrow." She walked up the stairs, but turned before she left the room. "I love you guys, no matter what becomes of you. Remember who you are, not who they make you out to be."

It wasn't hard to fall asleep. Everything was dark when Hadlee stopped exposing her own light. I laid on the couch and none of us spoke a word. This still didn't feel real. Now, there are only four of us on this small couch. I wish I didn't have as much room as I did. I wish we had to all squish and roll into each other.

We landed outside of Emor well before the sun peeked over the horizon. It was 4:30. I pressed on the center and focused on Foster. To my surprise, the arrow moved to the east. We got up and walked through the woods, following wherever the compass led me.

We weren't looking for Foster yet, first we needed to find the entrance. The arrow moved to the west as I changed my thoughts to the entrance. We walked through more trees until the arrow moved east again. It seemed to be pointing towards a thick tree.

Hadlee placed her palm on the tree and closed her eyes. She dug her fingers in a thin crack and peeled open a small door. Metal stairs spiraled down into nothingness. She stepped inside the staircase, and we followed her down.

Despite having three sources of light, the tunnel was still dark and filled with a strange scent. A gray liquid with a putrid stench dripped from the ceiling and onto our heads. We kept walking downhill while our hands shook. The heat inside of everyone was sporadic and unnerving, like the flicker of a burning match. I was alone in the back holding the fire up behind us.

Scampering feet crept from behind us. I looked back but couldn't see anything. It was getting closer. "Finn!" Miller shook my back.

I just about hit him in the face. When I turned around, he cracked up. I actually hit him in the stomach.

"You seemed a little scared back here by yourself," he said.

"I wasn't scared," I said. "I just heard something behind us."

"You should've seen your face." He made a dumb face with his mouth and eyes wide open.

"You guys need to be quiet," Hadlee whispered. "If guards hear us, we might not even make it to Foster."

"I'm not too worried about them," Miller said. "We have four of the most feared manipulators right here."

"It used to be six," Nax said.

It became silent when Nax realized what he said. I looked down and tried not to think about her. Miller wasn't laughing or smiling anymore. Jin should've been here with us. Every time I thought about her, it hurts just like it did when I first saw her lifeless body.

"We need to quiet down," Nax stuttered. "I can see the end up ahead."

We reached a dead end. Hadlee's light bounced off the rigid rocks. Miller squeezed his way to the wall on the left and dug his fingers into the dense rock to drag it down. The path behind the wall was no longer rock and dirt, but steel surrounded with fluorescent lights. Walls illuminated a green tint, and it no longer smelled like rotten eggs.

Everything echoed in here: every footstep, every whisper. The path diverged into two identical ones, and Nax split us up. He pointed towards me, Miller and Hadlee and then to the path on the right. The others went down the other path.

As we walked, cautious footsteps came closer to us. I turned around with a fire ready in my fist, but in the distant light, Nax jogged towards us.

"I promised Sylvic I would keep you safe," he whispered to me.

"Check this out." Miller stretched his head to a small window through a door.

Two men were locked inside; one was tied standing up. A ring of light circled above his forehead and skinny strands of light stretched down his forearms. The other man wore the blue guard uniform and circled the Halo of Light.

"This is what they did to me," Nax said. "This is how they get inside you."

"We need to do something," Hadlee said pushing her way to the front.

"No," Nax pulled her back. "If we do anything they will know where we are."

Hadlee lingered at the door trying not to do anything and eventually followed us. There were more of these rooms and at every single one, Hadlee would look into the room and want to do something about it.

Two guards walked towards us. One of them wore sharp shoulder pads that stuck out at least a foot on each side. There was nowhere for us to go.

"Who's there?" a woman said.

Without a second thought I ran over to her. She pulled her hand down towards the sword in her belt until I covered it and grabbed onto her wrist. I spun my body around and threw her into the steel wall. She collapsed to the ground. Nax grabbed the man's shirt and pushed him against the wall

"You killed dozens of innocent people," Nax said.

"What are you talking about?" he responded.

Nax pulled him towards his body and pushed him back onto the steel. "In the Obrum outside Caltus. You tainted me and listened to everything we said." He held a growing flame in his hand.

The guard didn't respond.

He was the reason Jin died. I pulled a thin flame from the air and pressed it towards his neck. I pushed him further into the steel. He stuck his hands out to the sides of his head.

"Where are the prisoners kept?" I growled.

I let go of his throat just for a second to let him scrape oxygen into his lungs. He had the weakest face I had ever seen on someone. He looked afraid, terrified of me. *He should be.*

"I don't know. I swear. I have not been here long."

"You're a liar." I stuck my forearm against his throat.

"Finn stop." Hadlee pulled me back. "He doesn't know."

"You're pathetic." I swung open one of the empty rooms and threw him in it. I dragged the female guard in there with him and slammed the door shut. "Miller close it up."

He stared at me. Frozen.

"Fine," I said.

I made a small flame on my fingertip and melted the steel into the cracks on the door. Once I was sure the door was sealed, I walked through the path again. I looked back, and no one moved.

"Are you coming?"

"Who was that?" Miller asked.

"That was the man that tainted Nax and sent hundreds of guards to the Obrum. That's the man who killed Jin."

"Finn," Miller walked towards me. "Jin killed herself."

"She wouldn't have had to if it weren't for him." I kept walking.

The loud screech from moving steel pierced the halls as the door ripped open. The two guards walked out of the hole in the door.

"You should've seen what we branched in before you locked me up." He had the dumbest smirk on his face. "Your friend should be just ahead. Once the paths meet up, it's the second door on the left. I'd hurry, unless you want your friend to end up like Nax."

A bright light surged from Nax's hand. It crackled and left his body once he clapped. A streak of lightning hit the sheet of steel covering the woman's body. Although the bright, burning white light was astonishing, the booming thunder that came afterwards amazed me. A dense layer of rock crumbled underneath the steel from the wall. Miller penetrated the metal underneath us with sharp rocks.

"You guys go find Foster. I'll hold them off."

Before I turned, a streak of fire emerged from my wrists and knocked the guard backwards. I turned for a second, and Miller enclosed a wall of rock around the woman. We kept running. I heard the wall shatter as small fragments bounced off the steel, but I didn't look back. As much as I wanted to help my best friend, finding Foster and getting the Halo were more important.

We reached the point where both paths met, but the other half of our group was gone. We waited to catch our breath and listened for echoes, but there was nothing.

"How do we even know we can trust what he said?" I said taking shallow breaths.

"We can't," Nax said. "We have no other idea of where he can be, so we have to try."

We walked further until a large white door appeared on our left. There were no windows to peek through. If we were going in here, it would be blindly. Nax walked up to the door and pushed it open. We walked through the room filled with different cells. Most were made of steel, but for those who branched in metal, there were stone ones. Foster was not in any of these.

Something wasn't right about this. There were no guards anywhere. If we wanted to, we could release every prisoner in here. "Where are all the guards?" I whispered.

"I was just thinking the same thing," Nax said.

We turned around and walked back to the door. The lights shut off one by one until it was pitch black. Hadlee raised her arm up, and light trailed over us. If five guards wearing white uniforms didn't surround us, I would appreciate the celestial lights swirling above us. Arilna walked through the door, and with every step a square box of light illuminated on the floor.

"We need to have a word with you, Finn."

"You aren't taking him anywhere," Nax said.

"You guys don't look like you are in a very compromising position." Her fingers laced together in front of her stomach. "Take him to Vatius, but don't hurt him." A guard grabbed onto her and transported her out of the prison.

Within seconds, the guard transported back into the room. We stood little chance to win this fight. It was three against five.

"You take the ones on the left, I got the right?" Nax stuttered.

"Sounds like a plan," I said.

Hadlee grabbed the light from above us and whipped it at the guards. Every time the light moved, it became harder to see. A guard knocked me into Hadlee with a loud clap.

"If you could keep some of the light up, that would be great." I swung my arm downwards, and a blade of fire knocked one guard to the ground. "It's getting a little hard to see."

She threw her hands up and the beautiful spectacle of light shone above us again. "Is that better?" Her chest glowed as she created more light. "You going to use this?"

She grabbed the bow hanging around my shoulder. She created a piercing arrow with a burning white glow and pulled the string back to her chin. An intense heat came from the light on the arrow. It was like nothing I had ever felt. When she released the arrow, the entire room illuminated. She hit a woman in the ribs and knocked her to the ground.

Another arrow flew through the air and just before it hit another guard, he vanished. I heard his feet hit the ground right by Hadlee. He grabbed onto her shirt, but before he was able to move again, I sent a constant flame towards him. He stepped back and vanished again.

"Nax, there's a distance manipulator! Don't let him get too close." There were only four guards in the room now, and one laid on the ground.

Two of them fought against Nax. One branched in fire, so she had no chance against him. Every move she made, he redirected it towards her. The other guard branched in steel, so he had the upper hand. Pieces of steel rose towards Nax, and he jumped on one of the large plates then crossed to the other one. He ran to the top of the speeding steel and jumped towards the other guard. His foot circled around the guard's body, and a bright orange flame knocked the guard into the steel bars.

There were prisoners in the cells. They didn't respond to anything happening around them. They were tainted just like Nax was. I turned back towards Hadlee just as the guard grabbed onto my shoulder.

"Finn, look out!" Hadlee screamed.

Before she pushed him off of me, she grabbed onto me and we travelled through a white atmosphere.

I rolled onto the cold marble floor while the guard held Hadlee upright. I looked up and saw Vatius walking over to me.

"I'm sorry your pureness," the man trembled, "she grabbed onto the boy. Do you wish for me to take her back?"

"No."

Her white dress dragged along the discolored floor. I stood to my feet. Her slim hand dragged down the side of my face until it hung from my chin.

"She is a bonus." She dragged her feet back towards her throne. "You are the Craved that can manipulate light. I can feel it. You're very strong young lady. With this power, you could be one of my highest ranking officials."

"I'm not interested," Hadlee snarled.

"Suit yourself. A life without worry or condemnation is one that sits well with most."

The same four people stood at the side of the throne. The young one, the reality morpher, stared at me with a smile. She was not hard to look at. I nodded my head upwards toward her, and a pink tint filled her cheeks.

"You have got to be kidding me." Hadlee hit my shoulder. The guard grabbed the bow from Hadlee's hands. "Give that back." She reached her hand to grab it from him, but he was already at the side of Vatius's throne.

"We found them underneath the premises. She injured one guard with this." He handed her the black bow.

She examined it for a while; sliding her hand down the smooth center portion. Arilna came to the side of the throne and took the bow from her.

"This is a sweet homage to me." She put her hand on the dragon head engraved at the top of the bow. "I do not know if you are aware, but the spirit of the Keeper of Light is a dragon."

Her left eye twitched as large wings spread out of her back. They were a dull gray color with three holes pierced in the left wing. The same three holes I shot into the beast that attacked us at Kordia.

"It was you the whole time," Hadlee said.

"You will have to be more specific," she grinned.

"It was you at Domister. It was you at Kordia. You tried to kill us and blamed the Keeper of Darkness. Why?"

Arilna looked at Vatius and then back at us. She longed for an answer from her Sovereign Lady. She was just as shocked as us.

Vatius retracted her wings. "Arilna, we have a breakout in the third quadrant. I need all guards there immediately."

"What do you mean?" Arilna replied.

"Did I stutter? I need every guard here to go to the third quadrant now. No questions asked. Can I count on you for this?"

She nodded, put the bow in front of the throne, and left. Two other guards in the room also walked out. When they left, I saw someone standing up against the wall. It was Foster.

"Did it take you guys that long to figure it out?" Vatius laughed.

"What did you do to Foster?" I asked.

"Him?" She looked over at Foster. His shirt was ripped at the shoulder, with the ten-rayed star marked on it. "He did this to himself. He came asking to be a captive. Begging me to be a Vestrin."

"You didn't," Hadlee said.

"I did," Foster walked out from behind the throne. He stepped between us and Vatius. "You don't understand. I had to be with my family."

"Your family shouldn't love you only if you meet a certain expectation for them. They left you. Alone. We didn't. Your family is right here," Hadlee said.

"That is adorable, but I hate getting blood on my hands," Vatius said before he could speak. "Foster would you take care of them? It should be hard for you to fight your family."

"Trust me, it won't be much of a fight." Foster swung his hand down to grab his sword.

He ran towards Hadlee, throwing wild punches of wind towards us. He pulled steel from the walls and reached back to slash it at us.

A pillar of light came from the ceiling and covered Foster. He rubbed his eyes after the light scattered back around the room. A small green plant hung on the side of the wall. Hadlee wrapped the long vines around Foster's legs and pulled him to his face. Hadlee pulled the vines back to the steel pot and wrapped Foster around the pillar.

Vatius began to clap her hands. "Well done. Being one of my advisors means you will have to protect yourself even if it means hurting your friends."

"You never answered my question," Hadlee said. "Why did you attack us?"

"You guys are dangerous to yourselves and to this society. I've created order, and every generation of Craved have tried to ruin it." She walked over to me and stared into me. "And then Sylvic told me he saw you becoming the Keeper of Dark. I told you all this, but when I first met you I felt a strong light inside you. Even now, I can feel it. You are the only one that has harmed me."

"Finn, did you know this?" Hadlee looked over with big brown eyes.

"I was going to tell you guys," I said. "There was just never a good time." I was never going to. Fear already grew in her eyes. She turned back to Vatius.

"So why are we here? Are you not afraid that we will try to kill you right here? Right now?" Hadlee asked.

Vatius walked towards the throne and stopped next to the four henchmen that stayed by her side.

"If I was afraid of you two, you would not exist."

She looked to her left and right. The girl with platinum hair pulled pieces of glass from a necklace and twirled them around. An opening in her skin spread on her wrist, almost a perfect triangle shape with no muscle or blood underneath her. She was hallow.

"I still need something from you guys."

"What is it?" Hadlee stepped towards her.

"The Libra Piece." She clicked her long white fingernails together. "My friend Nax told me you guys have it. I know that you have this fascinating fixation on the Mallux, but believe me when I say you do not want to continue your quest. If you want to be the next Keeper, I need the Libra Piece."

"So the Mallux is real?" Hadlee smiled.

"Very real. Very dangerous. I understand that you found the story about Gentry searching for *the thing that can save them*. I also understand that you do not know how it ends, but she was not successful. You won't be either." Vatius stuck her hand out towards us. "I need the Libra Piece so I know you are on my side. So I know that you are light."

Hadlee looked over at me. I nodded my head. "I understand that you know we are Craved," I said.

"And I also understand that even though I may be claimed for light, I don't want what people are marked with to determine their own life," Hadlee smirked.

The fake smile faded off Vatius's face.

"Finn, don't make the same mistake your father did," Vatius said cynically.

I stared at Vatius, but no longer with a straight back and broad shoulders. She knew my father, she knew my mother, and she had always known about me.

"Me and your father were so close. It's hard to forget a name like Finn Lynch; that sticks."

"Finn," Hadlee whispered. "She's toying with you."

"Where is he?"

"He was one of my most trusted guards, and when he found out about the raids on Kordia, he wanted to tell the world. He used the quick minute that the storms had to be settled for a time your mom could escape. He tried following your mother, but he must have not made it." She shrugged her shoulders and held her arm out. "Give me the Libra Piece," she said.

I wasn't sure what the plan was, but I knew we had to get out of here. I might not have another chance to learn more about my father, but this was our only chance to get the crown.

"Go," I screamed as flames scattered to smoke covering the room.

Two long vines came from the side of the room, one wrapped around her crown and the other grabbed my bow. Hadlee grabbed the Halo, and I caught the bow. Vatius screamed. The plants came tumbling down to the marble and stretched like a web towards the ceiling and every wall. The scream became a loud roar.

Her mouth stretched out until it was a couple feet long and filled with massive fangs. Her legs became thick as she fell onto all fours. Hadlee continued to wrap the room with plants while Vatius transformed to a dragon one painful limb at a time.

"Ignite it, Finn," Hadlee said.

I burned every inch of the green plants.

We ran towards the door with bellowing footsteps chasing us. The beast ripped the vines as if they were strings. Hadlee stopped and stood with her arms out to her side. The brightest light emitted from her, and it kept growing. The woman who manipulated glass ran towards Hadlee, and I incinerated the sharp shards of glass pursuing her. I grabbed her arm, and we continued running. Vatius continued to chase us, but the bright light dazed her. She rammed into the pillars and the room crumbled. We got out of the door before the crashing of stone.

We ran out and straight towards the wall. The large man that stood by her throne walked out of the building, but we were already lost in a crowd. Arilna stood at the wall, waving her hands to go towards her. I walked to her.

"What are you doing?" Hadlee pulled me back.

"We don't have anywhere else to go!"

"You're feeling very trusting today," she said. "If this is another trap, I'll kill you."

Arilna was right up against the wall trembling with fear. "Your friends are already in a safe place. There will be an alokrite waiting near the forest, follow it. You need to stay safe, it is long past time

249

for a new keeper. I believe you can make things right again."

A piece from the wall slid up. The dark head of the man towering above the crowds came even closer to us. Hadlee shook her head at me and walked through the small slit.

"Thank you," I said as I crouched through the hole.

She nodded her head and closed the wall. Just outside, a foxlike creature wearing a white mask stared directly at us. We ran towards it. It had soft gray fur and the same mask as the one that approached me in the forest; two oval eyes and a slim black smirk. We followed the alokrite through the trees until we reached a circle of open snow.

Nax, Miller, Kira, and Keegan stood near the trees. They made it out.

"We need to get to the ship," I said. "Vatius has been after us this whole time."

I could see the top off the ship peeking through the trees sprinkled with a white coat. Clouds were being pulled above it, and I knew we did not have a ton of time. I ran, but the alokrite pulled at my jacket. Four incredible bolts of lightning connected with the ship. First, we heard the strong explosion that broke the ship into pieces, then we trembled with the thunder.

"Find cover," Nax said.

He sprinted into the woods, but the alokrite dragged me east. I was still unsure if I could trust this thing, but there was a powerful manipulator after us, and we had no way of escape.

"Wait." I put my hand on the soft fox. "Arilna said to follow this thing. I think we should trust it."

"You just said Vatius has been after us," Keegan said. "What makes you think we can trust them."

"Did you see that storm destroy our ship?" I flattened my hand towards the burning trees. "We might not be the strongest manipulators in the world. We can either trust this and maybe die, or trust ourselves and probably die."

"Was that supposed to encourage us?" Keegan said.

"I'm following Finn," Hadlee said walking towards me.

"Me too," Miller said.

"Okay, we will follow the little, creepy fox-thing," Nax said.

The nimble creature hopped over logs and in between trees, not too worried whether we could keep up. It wandered into a cave, and we followed. It continued to stretch deeper and deeper. Openings in the rocks gave us enough light to keep running. I pushed hanging plants aside and reached the end where stalactites dripped cold water into muddy puddles. A mix of lilac and emerald created a strange hue. The sound of water dropping was almost constant. It was peaceful here.

I plummeted onto a cold bed of moss, and the alokrite timidly walked up next to me. I made an embarrassing kissing sound, and the creature crept towards me and laid his head on my leg. I put my hand on its stomach - his stomach - and scratched him.

"What the hell just happened?"

"You tell us. You and Hadlee are the only ones who know anything," Keegan said.

I looked over at Hadlee; she was better at talking than I was.

"Well," she said with a confused smile. "Vatius brought us to her throne room and then Foster was there. He is a captive now because he wants to be with his family. We fought, I won, and then Vatius told us we had to give her the Libra Piece, then I was like no. And then we fought Vatius, and I took her Halo. That's right here." She held up the off white crown, took a deep breath, and continued. "Then we found out that Vatius was the beast that kept attacking us, not Kendrax. We ran and then her four scary sidekicks chased us. Arilna helped us. I didn't trust her at first, but I had to. And now we're here and Vatius and her four henchmen are after us because we have two-thirds of the Mallux, which Vatius confirmed was real." She took a couple more deep breaths.

Maybe it would've been better if I talked.

Everyone stared for a little bit. "So what you're saying is the most powerful person in Centure is after us," Miller said.

"Pretty much," Hadlee nodded.

"Okay... So, what's next?"

"We wait here for a while, until we feel safe, and then we go find that third piece," Nax said. "We only have what we brought off the plane, so we need to hunt at night and keep our clothes dry."

"I can't believe I will be stuck wearing this." Keegan pulled at her thick black jacket.

"That's the main problem you need to worry about," Hadlee grunted. "Are we not going to get Foster back?"

"It was his choice," Kira said. "If he was just in a cell we would, but he is working against us now."

It seemed like everyone was in the midst of betrayal. Arilna betrayed Vatius. Hadlee was going against the Vestrins; her people. There was no way to know who we could or could not trust. The only people left to help was ourselves. Like it or not, we were more wanted now than ever, but this time it is not our life that people are craving.

CHAPTER SIXTEEN
AS MOUNTAINS FALL

Every step I made, an unfamiliar shadow followed me. The little alokrite became one of my favorite things about this place. He had this strange attraction to me. Jin said light inside a person attracts them. Maybe Vatius was right; maybe I could be light. Maybe I was.

"I think it's time we name him," Miller said. It was just Miller, Keegan, Hadlee and I in the cave while Nax and Kira hunted. "I know we aren't supposed to name wild animals, but he is a part of our team now. I think we should name him Renn."

I couldn't look at this creature without thinking of Jin. Thinking about her gave me the emptiest of feelings. I still didn't believe it was real, but she was gone. Nothing was the same without her here. Nothing ever will be. Not the flowers, or the stars, or this little animal.

"Finn." Miller snapped in front of my face. "We can name him something else," Miller said. "It was a dumb name."

"No - no I like it," I said.

"Are you okay? You were out of your head."

"I'm fine." I wiped my eyes.

"I'm hurting too, Finn," Hadlee said. "She was my best friend. All of this is surreal."

"It isn't fair." Tears welled up in my eyes until Hadlee wrapped her arm around me.

"When we fight, we're fighting for her. All of this is for her and for people like her," Hadlee said with a strong whisper.

"We've hardly had a chance to react. We moved so quickly for Foster just to see he left all of us," Keegan said.

"It's just us four now," Miller said. Water swelled into his eyes as he looked around the room.

"We need to have each other's backs, always." Keegan grabbed Miller's hand.

"I'm sorry for anything I've done," I said looking at Keegan. I should've talked to her when it was just us, but this moment felt right.

"You don't need to apologize for anything." Keegan smiled at me for the first time since Caltus. "We're in this together. All of us."

Nax and Kira's voices echoed through the dark cave. He threw a large deer off of his shoulder and onto the ground.

"Eat up and try your best to sleep. We're leaving in a couple hours," he said.

I flipped open my clock - just about ten. "How far do you expect us to go in one night?"

"We will go to Misula first. Erra, the Keeper of Seasons, is only a few miles away," Kira said. "She might help us."

Kira pulled snow down from the open holes and created a sharp blade of ice to cut up the deer while Nax and I tried using wet wood to make a fire. It wasn't working. At most the fire would last thirty seconds. The quick glimpses of warmth made me realize how cold I was. We had to heat pieces of the raw meat over our hands while boiling blood dripped on our fingers.

"This isn't working," Nax pulled his arms back. "Just put the meat on the ground."

"I'm not putting it on the ground, that's disgusting." Kira brought down even more snow and made a thick plate of ice for the raw meat.

"Ready?" Nax asked.

"Ready." She smiled.

She stiffened her arms towards the plate of ice, and fire turned the pale meat a light brown. The ice was not melting. When the embers stopped falling, the heavy slate of ice remained. I thought fire and water were complete opposite, but I was wrong. Fire and ice were the extremes of the spectrum. Nax and Kira shouldn't work, but it does. It does because they want to make it work. Anything can happen, no matter how slim the odds are. Even this: a group of teenagers fighting against an entire world to change it was possible. And it started right now.

We laid down on the cold wet floor. I wish we could be in our little shack back at Domister right now. I folded my jacket and tried to get comfortable.

Before long, Nax shook my shoulder and told us to wake up. It felt like a blink, but five hours had gone by. It was still dark and somehow even quieter than it was earlier in the night. I stood up and squeezed my jacket around my body.

We stepped out of the cave and into a cold, starry night. Renn walked right up against my leg. I have tried to feed him every night, but he doesn't eat. I'm not sure how he would with that mask covering his face. He wasn't skinny by any means, but I didn't know how this creature functions. I wish the *Outworldly Tales* book didn't explode with the rest of our things because I'm sure they had something about alokrites.

"Why is that thing still following us?" Nax said looking back towards me.

"That's Renn," Miller said scratching Renn's ears. "A pet is long overdue."

"We can't have a pet."

"Why not?" Miller sounded like a child. "He is already well behaved."

"Do you realize how close we are to winning this? Finally ending this constant war we've been fighting?" Nax stopped. "You need to understand that you can't be like the rest of the kids your age."

Miller bent down and wrapped his arms around Renn. "But look at how cute he is," he said with a soft voice.

"Fine," Nax said. "If he makes things more difficult, you are getting rid of him or I will."

I brought my hands to my mouth and breathed a small fire to keep them from becoming numb. Nax had a similar idea. He grabbed Kira's hands and put them up to his mouth. He kept her warm before worrying about himself.

"You wanna help me out?" One of the girls said. She grabbed my hands like they were eggs.

It was only Hadlee. I nodded my head and brought her hands to my mouth. Her hands were freezing when they grazed around my face. Keegan looked back at us and smiled. She turned back around, and I realized my hands still held Hadlee's up to my mouth.

"Sorry." I pulled my hands to my side.

"Want girl advice?" She walked slower than the rest of the group.

"I don't need girl advice," I laughed. "What makes you think I need *girl* advice?"

"It's obvious." She stopped walking, and so did Renn. "You need to give Keegan some space. She can tell that you are drooling over her, and she is used to it. She gets that kind of attention from everyone. Act like she is nothing more than a friend, and I guarantee she will come around."

"I've had nothing but space from her. We haven't had a real conversation in a week."

"Maybe you have physical space, but she is smart enough to see how close you want to be. It's the stares, the little conversations, and the prolonged touches after every hug or bump."

"How do you know all of this?"

"I've been in your exact shoes," she said. I hoped that she wasn't talking about me. "For the same girl. I want to tell Keegan how I feel about her, but she doesn't. . . like the same people I do."

"I had no idea. I'm sorry, I shouldn't be talking about her-"

"I talked to you about it," she interrupted. "I will never have her, and I think you deserve her. Where you guys are from is very different. We don't care about what the person we love looks like on the outside. We choose whoever we want." She looked up and noticed the rest of our group left us behind. "We should get back to everyone."

She jogged up, and I grabbed her shoulder. "Hey."

She stopped.

"Thank you," I said.

She smiled at me and then ran again. Renn and I followed.

We left around four a.m. and it was already seven. We had not passed another town or even another person since we left. It became warmer as dawn approached us.

Through the trees, the earliest light of the sun reflected white light along the mountain range. Three massive pine trees towered in front of the summits surrounded with a dozen smaller ones. The trunks of the aligned trees made a large door rimmed to half of the palace. The two large pines to the left and right had large circular windows where it formed into its peak.

Two Vestrin guards stood at the door. We were still far enough away to run without getting caught.

"Nax," I whispered. "Do you see those guards?"

"Yeah," he replied. "Act like nothing's wrong. I doubt they already know what is happening, it's only been a couple days."

We walked through the path surrounded by white hedges and bright flowers, and I noticed a strange creature in flowers. It had the body and face of a wolf, but strong antlers extending a foot above its head.

"That's a pulurve," Keegan said. "I thought they were extinct."

"A pulurve?" The word sounded familiar.

"It's a half-creature," Hadlee said. "My book talks about a man who could manipulate life, except he couldn't make something come alive unless he had two living beings. He was mad and tried making uber-intelligent animals."

The closer we got to the green palace, the more pulurves we saw. There were large ones; like the tiger with the thick rhino body and horn, and small ones; like the meek fox with huge bunny ears and tail. Half of them slept in the beds of flowers and others still roamed the empty dirt path.

We walked closer to the pearl white doors, and the guards didn't react. They opened the doors for us with no questions asked. A woman with a light ginger color hair cut to her shoulders and a black haired man sat on opposite sides of a long table. She had a thin crown of bending branches with a few yellow leaves on her head.

"Great, a bunch of children are here," the woman said with an English accent of sorts. "First thing in the morning, what a treat." She lifted a crystal colored glass sarcastically and poured it down her throat.

If the greasy black hair wasn't enough indication, the scar on the side of the man's face was a dead giveaway it was Sylvic. It was refreshing to see him again.

"You guys decided to visit," Sylvic said standing up. He walked over to Nax. "It's good to see you again." He opened his arms wide, and they hugged each other.

"You must be the Craved. Sylvic told me *so* much about you," the woman said.

"Erra, it is such a pleasure to meet you after-"

"What do you guys want," Erra snapped.

Nax looked around and saw a few more guards circling the building. "Could we go in the throne room, or someplace quiet?"

"I suppose." She stood up. "Sylvic can you make sure the guards check the stables, I am worried about all of my little babies."

Sylvic nodded his head and walked towards the guards. A large wooden door with a tree divided into four different sections stood at the center of the back wall. We walked through the door and into a circular room with vines dangling from the ceiling. The outer ring of the room spun counter-clockwise. We stumbled through the spinning ring and headed towards the woman at the throne.

An old tree made her chair and thick braids of vine hung it from the ceiling. Two of the wolf-deers sprinted from her throne to examine us. They halted to sniff around Renn who barely reached their neck.

"Athena. Artimus. *Mahno!*"

The beasts drooped their heads down as they walked back to her throne.

Eight trees rotated around the room. One represented the start of the season and the other was the end. A bright yellow tree closed in on Erra. Next to that tree was a dead one bearing no leaves. Winter looked like it would come in the next day or two.

Nax looked all around us, but no one else was in the room. "We need to get to Umbrous. We are close to finishing the Mallux, but Vatius is trying to stop us. Her henchmen destroyed our ship, and it's too far to walk."

Erra sat back down on her large throne and rested her hand in between the antlers of her pulurve.

"I would love to help, but I cannot," she shrugged. "I am on good terms with Vatius, and I need her guards to protect my little palace. She is also allowing Sylvic to come visit which is a definite bonus."

"I don't think you understand how important this is," Nax laughed.

She clicked her long white fingernails together. "You should thank me. I won't tell Our Sovereign I saw you here." She stood back up and rolled her eyes. She walked right passed us and swung open the door. "Sylvic. Get in here," she screamed.

Sylvic walked in and shut the door behind him. She walked towards us, then opened the door again to walk out. A couple seconds later she walked back in with her crystal cup filled with a white wine.

"Did you need something from me?" Sylvic asked as she sat back on her throne.

We waited for her to finish drinking before she responded. "Oh that is delectable," she said licking her lips. "Can you take my friends to the train in Vellanon? They need to leave as soon as possible and no one can know you are with them."

"Why does it have to be a secret?" he asked.

"These kids are doing peculiar things. As they say, 'Peculiar does peculiar.'"

Sylvic spoke the phrase at the same time mocking her tone. She glared at him. "Just tell me where they are going?"

"I can't tell you that. Please do this for me." She put her bottom lip above the top. She was a little drunk no doubt. I tried keeping my mind blank of the place we were going because Erra didn't seem to trust Sylvic with that information.

"Sure, I'll do it," Sylvic laughed.

"Okay, bye now." She shrugged us away with a few flicks of her hand.

"It was a *real* pleasure to see you," Keegan said as we walked out of her throne room. "Someone woke up on the wrong side of the bed."

"She has to be like that during winter," Sylvic laughed. "If you would rather have constant hugs and giggles, come back this spring."

"I think I am fine with this," Keegan said.

"It isn't easy for her." Sylvic looked back as he led us through the field. He had a big bag hung around his shoulder. "She hates winter. She hates how she acts and feels, but she has to feel that way."

"She doesn't have to do or feel anything," Keegan said.

"You tell her that. She has to be cold. It's the only way she can keep the weather how it needs to be," he said. "But she sees it pushing everyone else away. That's why she needed to side with Vatius. I am the only person who stays with her through every season."

263

"How do you know?" I asked. He was not in the room when she told us that.

"Know what?"

"That Erra had to side with Vatius."

"I was eavesdropping," he said. "It's a bad habit, but I can hear everything you guys are saying without trying."

"So you know why we are going to Umbrous?" Hadlee asked.

"We went on a similar adventure," Sylvic laughed and wrapped his arm around Nax.

"That was not even close to what this has been like." Nax shook his head. "We actually know what we're looking for this time."

"There's no way you're having as much fun as we did," Sylvic said. "Nax saved all of us from some pulurves. Half woman-half shark. They are the nastiest things you hope you'll never see."

"How did you save them?" Hadlee asked.

"It's not a very interesting story," Nax squirmed.

"Oh please, he had them tied around his fingers. They came up to our ship and lured us towards them. They were gorgeous, except for their teeth. They surrounded us, but Nax was a charmer like usual and got them to side with us. He might have scars on his lips still."

"You didn't tell me this." Kira hit him on his bicep. "Did you think I would be jealous of some half shark freak? Was she prettier than me?"

"No, I swear it wasn't when we were dating or anything."

"I'm kidding dork," she laughed. "But I heard the story about that paralyzed girl kicking your butt."

"She was good with her branch." Nax turned red.

As we approached the small opening between the mountains, the world above us roared. An avalanche forced rocks to come tumbling down the hillside, blocking our exit. Vatius's four henchmen stood near the woods.

"We need to run," I said. I was the only one that knew what they were capable of.

They ran towards us. "Finn, go get Erra now," Sylvic yelled.

I sprinted into the palace and through the throne room door. She said something about how rude I was for barging in, but I interrupted her.

"Please help us. They're here."

As she stood, the winter tree came in front of her chair. Her colorful dress became an ice blue. The thin crown tied around her head became much larger as dead twigs grew from the two twirled vines. They twisted around each other and rose above her. Her dull, pink lips became a maroon color, and her skin even appeared lighter as small flakes of ice stuck to her cheeks. Her short ginger hair became dark brown with hints of red stretching down her shoulders. The ground below her became ice as she sprinted out of her palace. I followed her and so did the two pulurves that stood by her side.

The ground frosted over and the mountains became covered with snow. Snow did not fall from the skies, it rose from the ground.

Sylvic pulled sand out of his large bag and swung a long stream towards them. The youngest one was knocked down, but the others pushed through it as if it were nothing. The large man smiled as he noticed the fresh snow that had risen around him.

"You need to go, now," Erra said.

She created a blizzard, forcing the four henchmen to turn and advance towards her. Sylvic ran towards us too. The large man stood in the storm and created one of his own. He spun the air in front of him, ripping snow from the mountains and the trees. The vortex pulled me towards the henchmen, so that's where I went.

The freezing temperatures made it difficult to create fire, but as I came towards him, my fist held a spurring flame. As I spun around the tornado, I used his own momentum against him and shot him down with a heavy blow.

The storm seized, and he threw wild punches at me. I couldn't beat him in hand to hand combat. The blizzard slowed me down, so I expelled as much heat from my hands to get space. The flames passed through him as if it were air, but Sylvic's sand did not have the same effect.

Sand knocked the man to the ground while Erra fought off the three girls. She seemed to know who they were because she wouldn't let Aviva focus. Sylvic knocked Paragon to the ground, and I ran towards Aviva.

"Finn, go." She pushed me away and then froze the vines the ragged woman tried to tangle Erra up with. "Now!" she roared.

"Let's go. She can't control herself when she transforms," Sylvic said pushing more sand towards Paragon.

As he pulled me away, Erra sprinted on all fours. Her small hands stretched into massive paws with sharp, dagger-like nails. Her face extended into a long snout with razor-sharp teeth. A thick coat of auburn colored fur took over her body as she became a massive wolf.

We pushed through the storm, but it only became stronger as she howled. The two pulurves ran to her side and attacked the women. Erra could still manipulate when she took this form, and she seemed to be even stronger. She stood and slammed her front paws on the floor, causing massive icicles to pierce Aviva's side.

"We need to go," Sylvic said as we reached the rest of the Craved.

Lighting struck every couple of seconds, but it couldn't hit her. She knocked over the muscular man again and enclosed him in a slab of ice. The one that controlled glass spun in circles trying to pierce her as she slid along the tundra. Erra brought snow out from both sides and crushed the woman in between it. As she did this, roots buried deep underground entangled her.

The blizzard stopped, and the sky became clearer. Roots pulled Erra up to the sky as she became human again. One of the wolf-deers was on the ground, lifeless and the others cry echoed through the valley.

"We need to help her," Hadlee said again.

"She's telling us to leave," Sylvic said. A tear rolled down his scarred face. "Go!" he yelled.

He pushed me in front of him, and we ran between the mountains. They wouldn't kill her. She was a Keeper - they couldn't, but what Vatius will do with her might be worse than death. She stayed hung in the thick plants, and two of the girls ran after us again.

We didn't make it too far before glass soared towards us.

"We've got company," Keegan said.

Renn stepped in front of the group and screeched. The echoes from his voice shook everything around us. Whatever was left of this mountainside tumbled down on these two woman.

"Good boy!" Keegan kissed the top of Renn's head. We kept running.

We reached flat land, and I was about to pass out. Vapor poured from me with every deep breath I had to take. Sylvic sat on a gray rock and pulled his hair back as far as it stretched. I sat down next to him.

"She didn't tell us to leave, did she?"

He tried to speak, but he couldn't. He shook his head and buried his face in his hands. I didn't know how well he knew Erra, but it didn't matter. He loved her, but he gave her up for us. He gave her up for this. We were so close to finishing this that nothing and no one else mattered.

The snow blew harder up here, and it was much colder. My face numbed, my skin became leather, and I couldn't find any heat to warm me up with a fire. I opened the compass and thought of Vellanon. The arrow stayed stagnant in front of me, pointing to a small village I could hardly see.

Every house in the small village was forged from the earth. Kira knew where to go. She walked into the only house made of gray stone instead of brown and opened the door. It was empty. Her hands traced down a silk curtain as she sat on a wooden chair in the middle of the room.

"They already left," she sighed.

"We can come back in the spring or summer," Nax smiled. "Your parents wouldn't have left if they knew you were coming."

"It will be a full year since I saw them if we don't come back until Summer."

"I didn't know you were from Vellanon," Hadlee said.

"I tell people I'm from Misula because no one knows about this place," she laughed.

"Are you kidding? The hunters of Vellanon are legendary in Kordia," Miller exclaimed. "Is this where you learned how to fight."

"It's what we're raised for," she said. "The train will be here in an hour or two, but we can get warm and eat whatever remains."

Kira walked into the room at the end of the hall, and Nax followed her. She was upset because she won't see her family for another couple of months, but I wasn't sure if I would ever see them again. A part of me accepted that I never would, but I wondered what they thought happened.

I looked over at Sylvic, and he already stared at me, listening to the thoughts running wild through my head. I wondered what he knew and if he controlled what my family believed. I thought loud thoughts so he would hear me and hoped that he would give me an answer, but it didn't come.

Curiosity swirled inside me now. I wanted to know so much, but I didn't want to ask. He hadn't spoken since we left Erra, and he wasn't going to start now. He lost someone he loved today, and the day had only begun.

What we were doing had consequences. We lost Foster. We lost Jin. I didn't have room for curiosity. We already questioned everyone in power, and they questioned whether or not they can afford keeping us alive.

CHAPTER SEVENTEEN
MY REALITY

There wasn't much left in the icebox, but we found a skinned rabbit and some other meat to eat. We cooked it over a chimney and ate the charred meat. No one talked while we waited for the train, all we wanted to do was sleep. I sat on the couch and closed my eyes, but a loud whistle from the train told us we needed to leave.

We walked through the subtle snow and towards the gray steam trailing through the mountains. The station wasn't far from the village. Splintered wood and rusted steel contrasted the snow beneath the station. The track looked how they did back home, except here snow covered the wooden planks. Miller hopped off the platform and onto the rails. He balanced on the steel and tried to walk on them for a little.

"Hot! Hot hot!" He jumped off into the snow and put his finger in the holes the burning rails melted into his shoes.

"They heat the rails so the snow doesn't cover them," Hadlee laughed.

"You could've told me that before I burned my feet," he said sticking his bare foot in the snow.

"Come here," Hadlee laughed. She put her hand on his blistered foot and a dim light covered it.

"What are you doing?" he moaned. When she removed her hand, the blisters were gone. "Cool little trick. But there's still the other one." He took off whatever remained of his shoe and wiggled his toes in front of her.

"You're welcome," she laughed.

The train screeched as it came to a stop. This one was two stories tall, a dark black color, and stretched four cars long.

"Are ya comin' or not?" a man groaned from the front of the train. He spit into the snow, and it turned to steam.

His gray beard stretched close to ground, but his hair did not have the same luck. We stepped onto the train and in the golden door on the right. A soft red carpet with a yellow triangle pattern filled the space between the rooms. Little cubbies seating four people were on each side.

"Guys in this one." Miller slid open the door on the left. I followed him in, and Nax and Kira followed us.

"I'm crashing your guy party," Kira said sitting next to Miller. "Hope you don't mind."

Keegan and Hadlee sat in the den across from us. Keegan turned towards me while I already looked at her and waved at me with a big smile. I threw my hand up and raised my eyebrows. Sylvic walked into the cubby with them, and Keegan pretended to throw up. I laughed, but when Sylvic saw her doing it I cracked up.

"Ugh, I'm so tired." I stretched my arms across the bench.

"I should tell the captive where we are going," Nax said.

"Where are we going?" Kira asked.

"Umbrous," Nax said. "That's where the Apex is."

"Umbrous?" Kira shook her head. "There is no way we will get in and out of there with just us. We need to find help."

"Erra said she wouldn't help us, who else will?" Nax yelled. "I'm trying my best to figure everything out and no one is helping."

"Don't be like this," Kira said.

"Finn and Hadlee got Vatius's Halo pretty much on their own," he said. "We don't need anyone."

This was the first time I've seen them fight. I didn't even know if I would consider this a fight, but it was still strange to see. It almost seemed like the natural chaos that everyone and everything faced never affected them.

"We could go back to Kordia," Miller said. "There were people there. Underground. They might want to help."

"How do you know?" Nax asked.

"I felt them underground. It would make sense. That is where the war started." He looked out the window and stared at the colorless mountains around us. "They have to still be there."

"Even if they were, we don't know if they will help," Nax said. The train jolted forward. "We could find the Slate Ward."

"They could be anywhere. They left Caltus after the uprising." Kira replied. "I think we should see if anyone is in Kordia, it is not too far from here."

"Fine, let's go talk to the captive," Nax said to Miller.

He stood up and dragged towards the door. Keegan starred as Miller and Nax walked down the aisle. A reflection coming from the glass window made half of her face appear blue and her eyes look teal.

"Is Miller all right?"

"Huh?" I looked back at Kira.

"Is Miller all right?" Kira put her chin on her folded hands.

"He's from Kordia. He's hoping that his family is underground," I said. As the train moved, the tint on Keegan changed. It went from a white, to a blue, to a lilac.

"Girl trouble?" Kira tapped my leg.

"What? No," I laughed. "The view is just beautiful."

"I'm sure it's similar on this side," she said. "Can I give you some advice?"

Is it that obvious I need help? I nodded my head and looked into Kira's bright eyes.

"Be yourself. Keegan will come around, I hear her talking about you."

"She barely notices me half of the time," I said. "But I don't care because she is just a friend."

"She wants you to be happy, Finn. We talked a lot after we lost Jin and Foster. You make her feel like she's home whenever you're with her.

I couldn't help but smile. Maybe everything was in my head. Maybe we could be more than what I thought we were.

"Has she said anything else about me?"

"Yes, but that is classified," she covered her mouth.

"Please," I said. "Pretty please?" I put my hands together in front of my face.

"Oh no. Don't beg in front of me."

I grabbed her knees and pouted.

"She told me you almost kissed." She slapped her hand over her mouth again. "She is going to kill me. Don't you dare tell her I told you. I swear I am not bad at keeping secrets, you are just good at getting them out," she blurted. She took a deep breath in. "She said she did not want her first kiss with you to be like that."

"So she wanted to kiss me?" I smirked and sat back down in my chair. I rolled my fingers around each other.

"That is all I am saying, if you tell her I told you I will beat you up. I can beat you up. I beat up Nax all the time."

Nax and Miller walked in.

"Okay it will be another half-hour," Nax sat down next to Kira.

He kissed her, and she smiled at him. They were fine again. Keegan and I were too. Everything holding us back were my own delusional thoughts. Renn sprung up onto my lap and looked out the window. The snow turned into rocks. Mountains no longer occupied the sky to the right of us, only the stretched out waters. Dark black clouds spread a mile from the shore, but only blue skies covered us here.

Renn looked outside the window and growled. I looked out the window, and the platinum haired woman stood on cliff's edge. *How are they following us?*

"I have to go to the bathroom," I stood up. "Miller don't you have to go to the bathroom?"

"No I went when we talked to the captive." He smiled as he grabbed Renn.

"Miller," I glared at him, "I need you to come to the bathroom with me."

"Okay?" He said. He stood up and followed me out the door.

"We'll be right back," I laughed as I slid the door closed. "Vatius's friends are here."

"Crazy one with silver hair, big guy with huge arms those friends?"

"Yep," I said.

"This should be fun." We walked to the open space between the two carts. A ladder iced over from the blizzard led to the roof. "So we're fighting them?"

"I don't know if that's what they want." I torched the ladder until the ice thawed. "I want to see who they are."

"Finn, that guy blew up our entire ship in two seconds. I don't think they're friendly Vestrin guards."

I climbed the cold steel. "We can take them," I said. "You have rocky cliffs all around us." I pulled myself up onto the snow covered roof. I spun a fire around my body trying to get rid of all the snow. "And I always have my fire."

I reached my hand down and pulled Miller up. We walked towards the middle of the train while pushing against the strong wind. We made another wide turn over the coastline. I wish we could enjoy the view here; black sand contrasted with the teal waters. We made one more turn and approached a small tunnel. The four strangers all jumped onto the speeding train once we came out. They had vines stretching from the top of the cliff to their body.

They released the vines to drop onto the train. The black-haired one who manipulated plants held long whips in each hand. They walked across the train towards Miller and me. A black cloud followed the dark-skinned man as they walked. They cleared the gap between the trains and stood still five feet in front of us. The black cloud moved overhead and gave me an uneasy feeling.

"Who are you guys?" I asked.

Rain drizzled over us, pattering on the metal roof and sliding off the side of the train.

The one with silver hair held the smirk I've grown accustomed to seeing. She bent down towards us. "I am Paragon," her voice held eloquence. "This is Botak." She pointed to the muscular man. "And this is Zinna."

The black haired woman stared at me with a cunning smile. She licked around her mouth and bit her lip.

"We are an ancient group called the Trinity. We are here to keep order, and you are disturbing that," Paragon said.

"The Trinity," Miller said. "There's four of you."

The young girl allowed loose streaks of her brown hair to fly in front of her face.

"Oh that. . ." Botak stuttered. "That's Aviva. She's new so we aren't sure if we classify her as one of us. It's not like she isn't, but she isn't made like-"

"Botak enough!" Paragon snapped. "We aren't here to make

friends."

"I was rather enjoying our company," Miller said. "Weren't you, Finn?"

"I just love meeting new people," I laughed. "I'm Finn, this is my best friend Miller."

"We're a part of an ancient organization that constantly messes things up."

Zinna wrapped the vine around Miller and threw him off the train. Miller slammed into the rocky wall and slid down it with his eyes closed.

"Miller!" I screamed. I ran to the side of the train and was about to jump towards him until another vine constricted me.

"It was Finn that we had to keep alive, right?" Zinna released a nasty cackle that rattled my bones. "This doesn't have to be hard." She crept towards me as the drizzle turned into a pour.

The sound of grinding rocks scraped against my ears. Miller skated across the side of the cliff. A boulder broke as it crashed into Zinna's shoulder. Miller jumped back onto the train, rolling when he hit the roof. Zinna screeched and sent two different vines towards him. They moved just to the right of Miller and wrapped around Paragon.

"What are you doing?" Paragon pulled off a piece of glass from her necklace and cut the vine in half.

"Did you guys think you could do this without us?" Hadlee said crossing her arms next to Keegan. They walked towards us.

"This is Hadlee and Keegan," Miller said.

"Miller, you can't let that young one focus," I whispered. "She messes with your reality."

"I'm on it," he said. A long rock swept under his feet, and he soared above us.

"Remember," Paragon said, "we can't kill the pretty boy." She ran towards me.

Keegan fought Botak, and Hadlee tried to fight Zinna. Another piece of Paragon's necklace slid off, and she swept right past me with her shard of glass aimed at my side. I hit her hand with my forearm, and the glass shattered on the ground. I incinerated the glass shards being projected towards me. As I focused on the speeding glass, I didn't see Paragon creeping up on me. She put her left arm around my throat and stuck another shard of glass at my neck.

"You may think you and your little friends can change things, but you can't."

"Maybe," I said putting my hands on her arm, "but I know you cannot hurt me." I flipped her over my head and onto the ground.

A sharp pain plunged in the side of my stomach. Glass buried deep inside my skin. I pulled it out and watched blood drip with the rain. The cut was not that deep, but it stretched across my whole side.

"You're wrong once again, Finn," she said standing up. "I can't kill you, but I can hurt you. I can hurt you in abominable ways."

She walked towards me while her white dress blustered in the wind. All I could look at was her hollow arm. She didn't bleed like I did, she broke. She pulled another shard off her necklace and stuck it on my leg.

"We want you to still look presentable for Kendrax."

She twirled the shard around on my knee. Her hollow arm and porcelain skin looked as if she was made of glass herself. If that was true, I would be the one to shatter her. A thick plant wrapped around her stomach and pulled her off of me. Hadlee ran towards me and healed me with light.

Miller tried to hit Aviva, but wasn't able to. She was quick, and it seemed like she could change where she was in Miller's vision, but couldn't focus hard enough to change his reality.

Paragon cut Zinna out of secure vines wrapped around her arms. My side stopped bleeding, but there was still a long cut.

"Thanks." I stood up. Paragon helped Aviva, and Zinna teamed up with Botak. "We need to help them."

Keegan fought against her own branch. Botak controlled how much it rained and manipulated water. Every time Keegan would try to attack, he directed it back towards her.

I ran towards Keegan. She was soaking wet. A vine came from underneath her and gripped her foot. Zinna pulled her to the ground, but I burned the vine to a shrub and continued to fight Zinna. She was running out of plants. Every time she tried to entangle me, I would turn it into dust. Frustration welled inside her, and she came for a closer combat. I discharged a fire from my foot and burned her black hair. She pulled the burnt piece in front of her face and screamed.

She looked up and saw that the rain stopped falling. Keegan stood with her arms held wide and kept the droplets of liquid in still air. I released a flow of embers towards Botak while Keegan caught him off guard. Keegan turned towards Zinna and torrented all the water towards her.

"Nice one, Keegs," I said.

She pulled her hair out of her face and grinned. The train made another wide turn onto a long brown bridge built into the sand below. A shallow tunnel hugged the track not too far ahead.

"It's time to go," Paragon said leaving Miller.

"We weren't done yet," Miller yelled still hovering above us.

The flower beds on the cliff stretched towards the train. They each grabbed onto a section of the plant and jumped off. Aviva blew Miller a kiss as she ascended up the cliffside. He lowered the rock back onto the train and stepped off of it. Something gripped around my foot. When I tried to burn it off, it pulled me off the train.

Vines were entangling my body as I scraped against the rocky cliff. The Trinity watched me as I freed myself from the vines and dropped to the sand. I hit the rock and my vision became blurry. I could hardly keep my eyes open, but I was aware enough to see the ground approaching me.

"Finn!" I heard Miller yell.

My eyes fixed on the ground with intensity. There was no giving up for me. Not yet. Flames burst from my feet and hands. We can win this. I can be different, and I can make this world different. *My world.* My eyes sprung open, and I lifted my body. I flew through the white supports on the bridge and soared above the cliffs. The train roared in the tunnel, and I followed it, igniting the walls as I passed.

I exited the tunnel and landed back on the train. "I told you he was fine," Keegan said.

Miller had tears covering his cheeks. "I thought you were dead," he laughed.

"I'm not going anywhere just yet," I hugged him. "You jump I jump, remember? We're in this together."

I let go of him and looked at the three people around me. Through all of this, they have become the most important people in my life. I felt like this moment would last forever. We were on top of the world moving a hundred miles an hour surrounded by the storming seas and the calming tide. We were doing it together.

"Jin would've loved this," Hadlee sighed as she looked down at the coast.

No one knew what to say. We had each other, but it could've been so much more. We were missing Jin and Foster. The consequences for our actions were real, and they would plague us every day.

"We should get back down there," I said. We climbed down the ladder and walked back into the cabin.

The train slowed to a stop. Kira and Nax walked out of the room. "Where did you guys go? Me and your friend bonded." Nax said holding Renn in his arms.

I blurted out "we were in the bathroom" the same time Miller said we were "in Keegan's suite."

"We went to the bathroom in their suite," Miller said.

"It's crazy nice in there," I said.

"Okay. . ." Nax said. "You're both awful liars, but at least you tried." He walked towards us. "We're here let's go."

Miller nudged my shoulder and faked a cough. I rolled my eyes back at him. "We sorta had a run in with Vatius's henchmen; the ones who destroyed our airship. We are not sure how close they are to us."

"If you guys just fought them off, I'm sure we can again." Kira put her fist in her hand. "And we should have the people you think are underground to help us."

We walked out of the hall, hopped off the train, and circled around a burnt wooden station. The train sped past us into another long tunnel under the old village that stood on the cliffside.

"Isn't that where you said the people were?" I whispered to Miller.

He followed the moving train and nodded. "That might be how they get in and out. Through small tunnels within that one."

"Why are we here again?" Sylvic asked. "Don't we need the Apex from Kendrax?"

"We do," Hadlee said, "but there is no way we can even step foot in Umbrous without being destroyed by the darkness."

"Miller thinks there are people underground," Keegan said. "He thinks they have been there since the first raids started."

"There's only one way to find out," Sylvic said. He walked through the tall grass.

This place didn't hold the same beauty it did during sunset. I looked over at Keegan, and small drops of rain balanced on the tip of her nose. She looked up and smiled with her arms open wide. She was like the rain: never constant, always moving. Sometimes strong enough to tear down fortresses, and other times soft enough to feel with just your fingertips. She was devastating and delicate all at once.

It poured over us. "This can't be good." Keegan turned around.

I followed the slow movements she made. I snapped out of my daze and saw the Trinity walking towards us. Aviva was not with them.

"There is no way they could have found us," Kira said.

My vision twisted. Aviva was getting in my head, and I couldn't do anything to stop it. Everything moved slower. I stood in the same place with the same people, but I was not fighting with them. A shadow crept up Miller's body, and darkness covered my hands. I felt his life come out of his body and into mine. He fell to the ground, and I moved to the next. I manipulated a wave of darkness towards Kira and Keegan. It dropped hard on them, and they fell to their knees. Kira laid in the weeds, lifeless. Keegan looked up at me and somehow I was right in front of her.

"Please." Her eyes lost color as she begged. "Don't do this, Finn. I love you."

"This isn't real," I screamed and ran away from them. I looked back and all of them fell to the floor because of my darkness. "Get out of my head!" I hit the ground.

I looked up and was home. My mom kneeled in front of me. She wiped my wet eyes. I fell into her warm embrace. I knew it wasn't real, but I didn't care. It felt real. She smelt like a fresh cup of coffee.

Her brown hair was soft on my face.

"Come with me," her voice was hypnotic.

"I'm scared mom," I cried. "I don't want to be what they want me to be."

"I'm here. I'll always be." She held me close to her. She wore the gray sweater she wore whenever it got cold and we would sit by the fire. "You don't need to worry about anyone hurting you anymore, Finn."

Finn. My mother never called me Finn. No matter how good this seemed: the curl in her hair, the silky smooth voice, the smell that only she possessed. I had to let go because I will never get to experience it again.

I incinerated everything in front of me and the illusion faded back to reality. Aviva moved out of the flames way. It was just her and me. I continued to project flames towards her, but she seemed to be one step ahead. I left her to go help my friends because I knew my reality.

Renn stood in front of the group once again. He produced a loud screech that vibrated the cliffs. The three of them were backed up to the edge of the cliff. Nax blinded them with bright flames. Miller jumped to the front of the group, put his hands inside the ground and pulled it apart. He stood up and stomped his foot. The ground fissured, and then the side of cliff crumbled. They screamed as they plummeted down. We ran towards the abandoned city.

"Wait, Miller," I stopped. "Are you sure you want to do this?" I looked for Aviva, but she ran off into the woods. "We know that they will make it through that fall. We should get away while we can and keep them safe."

He looked back and forth. He looked for an answer from someone, but it was his turn to be the leader. "You're right," he said. "We should leave while we can." He ran towards the woods. He didn't look back, not even once.

He also knew the reality: we can't always make the choice we want to. Sometimes the things we don't want become what we need. Our choices in these moments determine who we are, and the fate that soon follows.

CHAPTER EIGHTEEN
STILL

I had never been so deep in a forest. We walked for a whole day with little rest. There was no snow yet, but it rained. And it kept raining all day long. Sylvic said this was the changing of the seasons. I didn't know if that was true, but it made him think Erra was safe. If it weren't for the stretching branches, the rain would've soaked us. Keegan and I were still far drier than the rest of them because she kept rain from hitting us with a dome like umbrella made of water.

It reminded us of Anador. That was one of the first places I enjoyed. We didn't get to enjoy much ever since we left Domister. So much has changed and so much will never be the same.

It's still raining, so there wouldn't be a fire tonight. We tucked ourselves in a cold, wet cave. Everyone slept, but I couldn't. I opened my necklace: 9:03 P.M.. I wanted to turn around and try to get comfortable, but I didn't want to wake up Keegan.

My arms engulfed her, and she stretched down every inch of my body. Her body burned through the freezing breeze. A part of me still believed she didn't want me like I needed her, but she needed me for her own comfort. We had been on the run for days, so I wouldn't blame her. I found a comfortable spot on my arm and drifted into sleep.

A light rose in between the trees, forcing me to wake up. I assumed the morning sun crept around the Earth, but it only came closer. I heard a multitude of distant voices, and then it sounded like an army.

"Guys," I whispered.

No one moved.

"Guys."

They all sprung up from their sleep.

"A bunch of people are walking towards us," I said.

"This can't be good." Nax stood up and walked in front of us.

"Is it Vatius's army?" Hadlee asked.

They walked closer and a familiar face formed in the shadow. Hadlee created more light. Jin's father, Bradley, came into the cave. I felt sick. He lacked the ability to care. He was numb to his own daughter's death, and he was emotionless now. Twenty members of the Slate Ward followed behind him, all of them wore some shade of gray.

"Well if it isn't the Craved," Bradley scoffed. "What are you guys doing under some moldy cave?"

It took everything in me not to hit him in the face. I didn't even want to burn him. I wanted to punch him right on his stupid looking grin.

"We're about to get the last piece of the Mallux that we need," Nax said. "We are looking for some numbers to get us into Umbrous. Do you think you can help us out?"

"I would, but we are looking for more people that want to join the Slate Ward." Bradley kept staring at Hadlee. "You branch in light?"

Hadlee didn't respond.

"Come here girl, what is your name?" he asked.

"Hadlee," she mumbled as she stepped forward.

"Hadlee?" Bradley asked. "You are one of the most powerful beings in Centure whether you like it. Not only are you a Craved, but you are a Craved that can manipulate light. Can you say your name again for me?"

"My name is Hadlee," she said again. This time louder with her shoulders stretched back.

"That is more like it young lady. Do you know what the Slate Ward is?" He put his arm around her.

I didn't know what he was doing, but I didn't like it.

"I am aware," she said. "You guys believe in equality. You will fight for it."

"That's right," Bradley said. He took his hand off of her shoulder and looked at her in the eyes. "Do you want to fight with us?"

"Absolutely not," Nax said. "She's with us. We have lost enough already."

"We need her. Someone like her could change the opinions of a hundred people just by walking with us."

"I said no! She is still a child. You aren't dragging her into these politics. This is a sick game we aren't playing."

"We don't want her in the Ward, *we want her leading it.*"

Hadlee's eyes lit up.

"We will take care of her every second of the day. We have someone that can teach her how to manipulate light to the fullest extent possible."

"Have that person lead you. Hadlee is not leaving. End of the discussion. We wish you luck on your travels now leave."

"That person is not Hadlee. That person is not a Craved. She can't lead the way Hadlee can. Hadlee can turn the tables in this never ending fight and bring peace to all of us."

Nax walked up to Bradley with a fist engulfed in flames. "Do I have to make you leave?"

"Stop." Hadlee pushed Nax back. "I am not a child. You don't control me. I want to lead the Slate Ward."

"You can't be serious," I said.

"Hadlee, come on we're almost done," Keegan said.

"You can finish without me," she said. "This is bigger than us. I want to help the Ward, and I know that I can. This won't be the last time I see you guys I'm sure."

"If you are coming, we need to go," Bradley said. "We have to be at Gemile by morning."

Bradley walked with the Slates following behind. None of them made eye contact with us as if we were a taboo they didn't want to have any relation with. Hadlee looked at us for a second.

"Sorry," she said as she walked away.

Just like that, we had half the number we started with.

Hadlee ran back to us. She peeled my bow off of her shoulders and handed it to me. "I believe this belongs to you."

I reached out to grab the bow.

"You take it," I said. "You can use it better than I can, and you might need it more than I will."

She embraced me and whispered thank you into my ear. She turned back around with my bow in her hand and ran back to her new group.

"I'm going with her," Sylvic said. "I can make sure she is being watched." He grabbed his bag and ran into the darkness.

Both of them left. No goodbyes. No remorse. The light dissipated back into darkness. I looked down at the clock again: 3:10. In less than ten minutes, two of our friends left. I didn't have the slightest knowledge of whether I would ever see them again.

"What just happened?" Miller said.

"Couldn't tell you," Nax replied. "I didn't want to lose another one. I promised that I wouldn't."

"This isn't your fault," Kira said. She put her hand on his back. "We have to let Hadlee choose her own path."

He didn't respond. He looked around for a second. "It stopped raining. We should keep walking. I doubt I will get any sleep tonight."

We walked with the little group we had left. Keegan pulled the water out of most of our clothes before we packed our bags again.

"Renn," I said.

He looked up and saw that everyone leave. He hated being alone. He whimpered a little and sprinted towards us. I knelt down, and he bulldozed into me.

"It's okay buddy." I wrapped my arms around his neck. "We wouldn't leave you."

I wish I saw his face instead of that mask. It's weird to think something as scary as a seiron possessed him. Sylvic told me that these things were dangerous, but I still can't understand why. They seek light; they can sense where it is and they follow it. That was what Jin told me. Ever since I came here, they've had a polarizing attraction to me.

Even still, after I believed I was dark, Renn followed me everywhere.

"Where are we going now?" Miller asked. "The ward is not going to help us get into Umbrous."

"We go ourselves," Nax said.

"We could go back to Kordia," he whispered.

"No. This is our problem. We're doing it ourselves."

"But they could help us if-"

"No!" Nax yelled. "If they are hiding, we won't ask them to leave. We've dragged enough people into this."

"Nax, he was trying to help," Kira said.

"I'm sorry, Miller. We're down to half the numbers we started with. I don't want to lose anyone else."

The moon bruised the sky with an off-white color, and the flowers below us emitted light all around us. They breathed out the same lavender color they had before. Months ago, this was the most beautiful thing I'd ever seen. Now they hold different memories that mixed to create a numb feeling. It reminded me of the beauty of this world, but it also reminded me of Jin. Her death and her delicateness. A warm hand weaved around mine.

"Aren't they beautiful," Keegan said.

I looked over at her and associated these flowers with another memory. With my warm hand and beating heart. Ours. Our hands. Our hearts. In our garden not contained by a fence or organized in any way, but wild.

We kept walking and our hands stayed close. The clouds created curtains in front of the moon, and the shade of purple touching the trees faded. Keegan's warm hand strayed from mine, and it became dark again. Nax held a flame and steam roamed through the air. I assumed that it came from the fire, but it surrounded us.

"What is that smell?" Kira plugged her nose.

"It smells like rotten eggs." Keegan wafted the steam away.

A slow streaming river flowed next to us and we continued to follow it upstream. It led us to a pool of water that contained a thick layer of vapor. A small waterfall poured into a crystal pool below. Granite rocks covered with small crystals surrounded the pond.

"Are you sure we're awake right now?"

"I'm honestly not sure," Kira said. "This is too perfect."

"Are you guys gonna keep talking about it or are you gonna go in?" Miller was taking off his pants and his shirt was already off. Once he was just in his underwear, he sprinted into the pool. "You guys better be coming."

Keegan looked over at me and smiled with her mouth wide open. She peeled off her clothes one by one. I threw my shoes and socks off, and then my shirt. I stumbled to the pool as I ran while taking off my jeans. The clouds moved over again and light returned around us. Flowers didn't create a surreal glow over here. No glowing trees or anything out of my world. This seemed real.

I climbed to the top of the waterfall and jumped into the warm water. Keegan stood outside of the pool, soaking wet because of my splash.

"You do not want to start with me, Finn." She jumped in on top of me and splashed my face.

"You call that a jump?" Miller made a cliff rise from underneath him and flipped right over us.

Keegan stopped the water from hitting her and all of it got pushed towards me. She laughed when she saw my angst filled expression, and then she showered more water at my face.

Nax ran in, but Kira stayed in her clothes. He crept towards her with his big arms stretching wide. "Don't make me throw you in," he said.

"Nax I will kill you if you throw me in," she said, but he kept coming closer. "Nax I mean it, you will literally be dead by morning."

He wrapped his arms around her and she screamed with laughter. He ran with her in his arms to the pool.

"Stop, I'll come in. Let me take off my clothes," she laughed.

He put her down and she pushed him in. Nax grabbed her arm and pulled her in after him. She came out with soaking wet clothes promising that he was dead meat.

We all sat in the corner of the pool. Every problem we faced stopped existing for a moment. We didn't care about the Ward, or the Mallux, or Vatius; we only cared about each other. Kira and Nax sat with their arms twisting around each other. Their bracelets gently tapped, and they changed to the beautiful silver color.

Nax looked at Kira. "Let's do it."

"Do what?" Kira laughed.

"Get married. Right now," Nax said grabbing her other arm. Nax moved Kira's hands closer to his body, as if he tried to prevent the rest of the world from seeing it. "Kira were safe. We can do it now."

Kira pulled her hands away from Nax's. "I don't want to have it wherever because we can. I want it to be beautiful. *I* want to be beautiful. And don't tell me I am because I'm soaking wet right now."

Nax sunk deeper into the water. "Okay," he said. "We need to have it soon though. We have space from the Trinity."

"We can do it first thing in the morning." She kissed him.

It rained again. We got out of the pool and Keegan pulled water off of all of us. We threw our clothes back on and laid down as soon as we found an open space. Miller created a tent from the ground up to cover us from the rain. Keegan laid with me again. This time Renn slept between us. We both had our arms around his back.

I didn't sleep as long as the rain fell because I knew what rain brought with it. It was now five in the morning. My eyes were heavy, but I wanted to stay up to make sure everyone was safe. I couldn't beat the strength of my eyelids, and I finally let them close.

As I drifted away, something touched my lips. Keegan's blonde hair fell around my head in ribbons. She smiled at me with her blue eyes. It was much easier getting lost in her eyes than being found in them. Her lip curled at the tip as if a secret was waiting to pour out. I wanted her lips. I wanted her everything. I pulled her close again, our lips grazed each other.

"Follow me," she whispered. She stood up and was gone.

I levitated off of the ground. I soared above the trees still in a laying down position. I was being held captive in midair. The tops of trees hung above me as my body rotated. My feet rose to the ground above me. I was in the woods again, and Keegan stood in front of me.

"Finn," she said. The world spun around me. "I love you."

There it was. She finally said it. She should've said it in the glowing light of the forest, but there was no light. A heavy white fog covered everything except Keegan. I looked to the sky and there was no moon.

This was not real. I wish it was. I wish I wasn't such easy prey for Aviva's sick games. "You aren't real," I yelled. Everything turned to darkness except for Keegan.

"H-how could you hurt me?" She cried.

As she told me she loved me once again, her face and even her voice transformed into my mother's. Water sat beneath us in complete stillness.

"You could've saved me," my mother cried.

She slammed her hand in the puddles of water we sat inside. She touched the side of my face and pushed my stray hairs off my forehead. *God it felt so real.* She put her hand on top of mine and smiled for a second, and then she shattered under the sound of a high-pitched screech. I fell off of Botak's broad shoulders and crashed into the ground.

"Get away from him," Kira screamed as she and Renn fought Botak and Aviva. "Finn, go get the others, quick."

I ran, but I didn't know where they were. I didn't know where I was. I flipped the sides of my compass and followed the red arrow. I didn't have to think hard to find them, it pointed to Keegan by default.

When I got back, it was not Keegan that I saw, but a hurricane of shadows spiraling around her. Her face stretched out of the fog and up to the open sky.

"Keegan." I tried to grab her out of this vortex, but I couldn't penetrate it.

The darkness pushed me to the floor. A loud cry came from Keegan as she fell back down. *This was real.*

All I saw was her blonde hair. I ran back to her. Nax and Miller watched, but kept their distance. I knew what happened. I knew she was claimed, and she was dark. I rolled her body over. Her eyes were closed, but that wasn't the first thing I noticed. The markings on her body stretched across the left side of her face. The thin veins grazed her eye and almost touched the side of her mouth. I couldn't see where they started. It dwindled down the entire left side of her body.

"Keegan," I whispered.

She opened her eyes and pressed her hands to her chest. "What happened?" she groveled.

"Nax, the Trinity came here. They were trying to take me but Kira came and is fighting them."

"Stay here, Finn. Miller come with me. Which way are they?"

"I want to help." Keegan stood up and fell back to the ground.

"You're staying here," Nax yelled. "Finn where did they go?"

"Straight through the trees." I lifted my right hand towards the woods.

They ran through the forest. "What happened?" Keegan asked. "You were claimed."

Keegan looked down at her arms and legs. "Where are they?"

"Follow me."

I took her hand and pulled her to the warm pool of water. The markings on her face looked like they were pulsing. I couldn't stop staring at them. We got to the edge of the spring, and I held out a flame so she could see. She tilted her head and touched the black veins on her face. She turned her head away from me.

"Just because you are claimed for dark doesn't mean that is what you are. You are-"

"Look at this!" She turned and had tears rolling down her face. "I don't care that I'm dark, but everyone else will. It's covering my face, Finn. I look like a monster."

I put my hand on her thigh. It was strange to realize it now while her world fell apart. Beauty was not on her smooth face. It wasn't in her white teeth or golden hair. It was her. She had magnificence stitched inside her. I thought she was just some strange infatuation I couldn't shake, but I was wrong. I loved her.

"Keegan you are so much more than what people can see."

She shook her head. "You're wrong. Growing up, what I looked like is who I was. . . for my parents at least. That is what I found my identity in, and now it's gone."

I was going to say it right there. I was going to tell her I loved her, but a storm formed in the sky. Kira came running over screaming that we needed to leave. She stopped and stared at Keegan's face for a few seconds, and then she pulled us to follow her. Rain came pouring in on us, and we ran. It was impossible to see a thing.

"Where's Renn?" I asked over the thunder.

"I don't know," Kira said. I stopped and turned, but she grabbed my arm. "Finn, no! They are after you and only you. If they get their hands on you again, they won't let you go."

I couldn't leave Renn behind, so I ran back. My eyes had adjusted to the darkness. I hopped over the raised roots and swerved around trees. The rain only became heavier. I kept running until I ran into Nax. He carried Renn in his arm. A darker liquid fell down his right paw.

"Finn we need to go this way," Nax said.

Lighting struck a tree, and it ignited into flames as it crashed in front of us. I looked over at Nax, and neither of us slowed down. I hoped over the smoldering tree and swung my hands above my body to create a pocket of air to jump through. I tripped as I jumped over and fell to the ground.

I looked back to make sure Nax made it over, but I didn't see a burning tree anymore, I saw my church being engulfed in flames. Cries of familiar voices ran rampant through my head. The stained mosaic shattered to the ground. I looked in the reflection of the shattered glass. The same markings covering Keegan now possessed my face.

"No!" I spread my hands out wide and inflamed all the trees in front of me.

A bright flame and dull smoke covered everything in sight. I kept trying to snap out of this vision, but I couldn't. This was real. The forest erupted with flames. I felt bigger than it. I was stronger than it.

I no longer needed to run, but I did anyway. We ran straight out of the rain and out of the woods. Everyone stood in the middle of an open patch of land. I looked back to dark clouds mixing with the smoke of my flames. Lighting struck over the acres of trees, but we were far away from the storm. We were safe.

"We need to keep moving," Nax said. "Finn can you take your wolf-thing."

I grabbed Renn, and he whimpered as my hand hit his side. "What happened to him," I said catching my breath. His side was cut and his blood stained my jacket.

"Paragon. And if you don't want the same thing to happen to you we should move," Nax grabbed Kira's hand, and they ran together.

We kept going, and we didn't stop. We didn't talk. We just ran. We had nowhere to go, and if we did, we couldn't even see how to get there. We ran through more trees and more flowers that all looked the same in the dark. Hard dirt became soft sand.

We stopped in the middle of a cove, and I collapsed to the ground. It was seven in the morning now, and Renn was still in my arms. We sat for about five minutes catching our breath. Keegan separated the salt from the ocean water so we could drink something. It still tasted disgusting, but it was better than nothing.

"We should fix his paw up," Keegan sat next to me and Renn.

The left side of her face captivated my view over everything. All I looked at were her new markings. She enveloped his paw with the water and drained the dry blood off of him. I ripped the bottom of my shirt off and wrapped his paw with it.

"You can look at me still, you know right?"

"I know," I said looking down at Renn.

"Then do it," she said.

I lifted my eyes up and tried to focus on hers. I'd never examined markings. It looked like they were all breathing. They stuck out almost an inch from her skin. Dull ones faded out from the main veins. I looked back down.

"Have you branched in anything else yet?"

"Not yet," she said digging her hands in the sand. "I thought I would just feel it inside me, like how water moves, but I don't feel a thing."

I put my head back down on my jacket. "It will take time." I grabbed her hand.

She let her head sink on the ground. It would take time. Everything does. It would be hard for me to look at her the same, but the only way I ever would be able to is if I tried. I turned my head towards her. Her closed eyes faced the rising sun in front of us. I stared at her new embodiment. It didn't change who she was because it didn't change how I felt about her. I wanted her, even still.

CHAPTER NINETEEN
I AM THE VALLEY

My mother and Jim's wedding was nothing special. It took place in our church and there might have been thirty people there, maybe a few more. It was both of their second weddings. They pronounced both of their previous spouses dead, so our church didn't see any problem with this marriage. This was the first wedding I ever went to, and for the most part it was boring.

My mother never told me about her and my father's wedding. I can imagine it being a spectacle though. I pictured it happening in Vatius's throne room or any other place in Emor. My mother didn't have her betrothal bracelet, at least I had never seen it. Sometimes, I wish I could see how beautiful she looked in her younger years because of how stunning she was at her second wedding.

She wore an off-white dress, and the back of the dress dragged down the entire aisle. When her and Jim met each other at the front of the church, my mother read her favorite verse; "Although I walk through the darkest valley, I will fear no evil, for you are with me."

That verse had always resonated with me. It didn't just apply to her faith, but her love for her new husband. Here, people surrounded me even as both dark and light sought our demise.

The sun had been up for hours, but we refused to get up. Last night felt like a never-ending one. We were safe here though. The Trinity had not found us yet, but we knew it was a matter of time. I hated the constant fear we had for them. I hated running away. We had seen what they can do, and it was remarkable.

The sun didn't beam on my eyes, so I moved my shirt from my face and woke up. Keegan was the first thing I saw, and her markings were harder to look at in the light. They had also seen what we could do. We were coherent together, a team.

"Finn." I jumped off the ground. Nax grabbed my shoulders. "Sorry for waking you up."

"It's fine," I yawned, "I've been up all morning. What's up?"

His eyes peeled wide. "I need to borrow your jacket." He put his lips together and kept his eyes held open.

"Why?" I asked.

"Kira and I are having the wedding," he laughed. "Like right this second. Seriously, I need your jacket like now."

I grabbed my maroon jacket from the sand and handed it to him. "Why now?"

"We're safe," he said regaining his cool. "We have wanted to have this for a month now and just look at where we are."

I sat up and looked down. The ocean water was a clear blue color. Colorful rocks ordained with a variety of different stones stood tall past the shoreline. Pinks and blues and greens covered the gray rocks. It was perfect for them.

"You need to get everyone up, we want you guys there."

"All right," I laughed. "Keegan, you have to-"

"I heard," she said. She stood up and threw her white sweater on.

I should've talked to her, but I could tell that she didn't want me to. I walked over to Miller and noticed that Renn laid with him. That was the first time he didn't sleep with me. I looked back towards Keegan. She talked to Kira while trying to hide the markings on her face. Kira grabbed the left side of her face and pulled it upwards.

"Miller. We gotta wake up."

Miller looked at me for a second then threw his face back on his sweatshirt. I looked at my watch. It was already well past noon, but the clouds kept the sun away from us all morning.

"Nax and Kira are about to get married."

"What?" he laughed.

"That's what they told me. They want to do it here while, you know, we aren't being chased by four sociopaths."

"Ugh," Miller groaned. "We better not be going anywhere tonight." He stood up and dragged his feet towards me. "Where is this thing happening?"

"I know just as much as you do," I said. "We should ask Nax if he needs anything."

Nax stood near the water, trying to fix his hair in the reflection. He licked his fingers and stretched stray hairs far back.

"Do you need any help?" I asked.

"Yeah. Miller can you make a small arch out of these rocks? Oh and Finn." He reached in the front pocket of the jacket. "This shouldn't just be sitting around in your coat." He waved the Libra Piece in the air and stuck it in his bag.

Rocks piled the sand into small mounds as it rose from underneath. An arch that stood a foot above Nax's head glistened in the light. Waves crawled to the articulate rocks and pulled the stray sand away. He looked at it and took a deep breath.

He put his hand over his golden bracelet and smiled. "Not quite the crowd I hoped for at my wedding, but I think I'm ready," he said. "Can you guys go get Kira if she's ready?"

"We're on it." Miller dragged my arm away from the beach. "How's Keegan doing?"

"I think she'll be fine," I said. "It will take some getting used to."

"For you or for her?"

I looked down at the sand underneath me.

"She needs you, Finn. We all do."

"Don't get all sappy with me," I nudged his side.

"Seriously though. Things weren't the same before you came."

He looked at me with wide green eyes. I didn't know what to say back. I don't think words expressed how much he helped me transition. "Do you think that has anything to do with us being chased around by some of the strongest people in the world?"

"You don't know how to take a compliment," Miller laughed. "I'm glad you're here, Finn. I haven't had a friend like you before."

I felt bad. I had been putting Miller on the sidelines while I chased Keegan; while I chased the light and the dark. I should have been there for him back at Kordia. His friendship was the best thing I had gained from coming here.

"Thank you. I don't know what I would've done without you."

He almost said something, but we saw Kira and became mute. She wore a short white dress, but she was ordained with ice. A light blue ice stretched around her chest and just over her shoulders. A whiter color faded into a near transparent as it stretched down to the floor. A solid white ring wrapped her hair in a bun. White and blue hues covered every inch of her except for her gold bracelet.

"We were just about to head down," Kira said. She looked ethereal.

"You look incredible," I said.

"It was all Keegan," Kira said. "I mean I manipulated all the ice, and I have to keep it from melting every second, but it was their idea."

I looked over at Keegan. She shook her head and smiled. If anyone could get through to her, it was Kira. She fixed people no matter how hard they've been shattered.

We walked over. We sat down in the sand, and then Kira floated down. Nax didn't take an eye of her for a second, not even to blink. His eyes filled to the edge with water as he grabbed her hand and pulled her under the arch. He held her other hand as they stared into each other.

"I couldn't imagine anything as different as us," Nax started. "I am fire. You are ice. You can stay organized and you keep a strong mind."

It was weird how similar this was to a wedding back home. There was an aisle, and vows, and a first kiss. I knew the two worlds lived together at some point, but how long were they intertwined.

"I have been in love with you since the first time you showed me how good a girl could be at Gimbat."

And what made them hate my world so much? What made us create a never-ending storm all around just so they could not come back?

"You love everyone you come in contact with, and that is what I love most about you," Nax said.

Kira smiled as she grabbed the back of Nax's neck. She pulled him in close and they stood still for a second. They were timeless for that one second. Nothing else seemed to matter. Not for them. Not for us. We deserved this. They kissed each other, and we all cheered once both of their bracelets emitted a bright glow. We deserved to be regular even if it was just for those few seconds.

We hopped off the ground and ran towards Kira and Nax. I wrapped my arms around the group and water drenched me. "You have no idea how hard it was keeping all of that together," Kira laughed as her ice melted all over us.

We let go of them and Nax picked up Kira, both soaking wet, and kissed her again.

A couple hours stalled between now and sunset, but we already got ready for the night. Keegan caught fish while Miller and I collected wood. Nax and Kira laid on the sand. He had a dandelion in his hand plucked from a field of them constantly blowing white petals around the beach. It was beautiful for a while, but after I swallowed a couple, they lost their charm.

I threw the small logs in a pit of sand, stacked them on top of each other, and ignited it. Miller and I sat on the sand staring at the fire, and the water, and the rocks. We didn't talk much. I would usually find this awkward, but not with him. It felt like I was alone; that was how I acted at least. Nax and Kira walked over to the pit. He wrapped his large arms around her stomach, and she couldn't stop laughing.

"Stop you're getting sand in my dress," Kira laughed and hit Nax in the arm. She grabbed the side of his face and kissed him.

"So, I'm gonna go," Miller said as he looked over at Nax and Kira kissing right next to him.

"Sorry," Nax said. He kissed Miller's cheek then laughed.

"What is wrong with you," Miller tried holding in his laughter as he wiped his cheek.

"Haven't you ever been in love?" Nax said.

"Keegan. I need food, these people are being weird." Miller inched away from Kira and Nax.

We all snickered. Kira got out of Nax's lap and sat down next to me.

"Before she comes, I want to know if you talked to Keegan?" Kira asked.

"Yeah, we talked for a little bit. Did she say something to you?"

"Not specifically, but she is not taking her claiming too well. Especially where her markings are. You of all people need to be there for her. Act like nothing has changed about her because nothing has. Make her feel beautiful."

I wouldn't want to do anything else. I shouldn't tell her how I felt, not yet. She needed a friend more than a relationship. We all did.

"I will."

She took her hand off of my thigh. I looked over at Nax who longed for his wife. He was lucky. Maybe the luckiest guy in the world. He didn't deserve Kira, and he knew that. Kira was beautiful, strong and compassionate. None of us deserved her.

"Congrats. Nax is lucky to have you."

Keegan walked up with a dozen fish. "Sorry I brought so many, I forgot how few of us there are now." Keegan sat down next to me. Renn moved to Miller once she sat down. "I'm sorry," she said. "I forgot they don't like darkness."

"No, it's not you," I said. "Miller has been taking care of Renn's foot so he has gotten more attached to him."

She didn't buy it. She pierced the cold fish with the wooden stick and put it in the fire. Renn growled, and then he wailed. He stood up and limped around in small circles. His cry was piercing and painful to listen to. I walked towards him, and his neck twisted towards me.

His eyes were not caring and filled with compassion anymore; they looked black, lacking any emotion at all. His fur rose the opposite direction as he lifted his face towards the sky and screeched. The air vibrated from the frequencies he created. My ears still buzzed once he stopped. He tried to run away from the shoreline, but he couldn't get far.

Something came towards us, I felt it. It was not the heat most people carry, but the complete opposite. It was cold. Bitterly cold. I walked up to Renn and stood there with my chin up towards the trees. I was done running.

Seirons flew right above us. It started with just a few at a time, but then they became hoards. I was too busy looking up at the sky to see the ones stuck on land. They didn't wear the same masks that the ones in the air wore. The ones without the masks looked almost human. They had long limbs, sharp claws, and a face that only comprised a large mouth.

They limped towards us, and I tried to destroy them in my flames. Their burgundy bodies caught flame, but they didn't burn. One engulfed in flames held my body down at the throat. Its sharp teeth gnawed the air just over my face. Renn howled at the face of the seiron, but the sound didn't seem to affect it. It took one of his arms off my throat and slashed the side of Renn's body. I pushed its cold body off of mine in that moment, and I held it down with my forearm.

"A little help," I screamed.

I stared at its skin-tight body. It looked like a human. This creature didn't have any idea what it was doing. It was too innocent to kill and too dangerous to keep alive. A sharp blade of ice went through the head of the creature, and it stopped fighting.

"There goes our day off," Kira said.

She pulled the ice out of the seirons body and there was no blood. It descended into a pile of ash.

I stood up and grabbed Renn. He was shaking and blood covered his body, but I couldn't do much to help him right now. I carried him towards the trees and put him in a patch of grass. He stood up and tried walking towards me.

"No," I said putting my hand out, but he crept towards me. "No!" I created a line of fire that nearly burned him. I turned around and ran back. Few seirons roamed the land, but the ones in the sky swarmed. "Where are they going?" I yelled.

"I don't know," Nax screamed. "None of them are even trying to attack us."

Nax discharged a storm of lightning towards the dark clouds that the creatures made, but only about a dozen of them crashed down on the land lifeless. The ones in the air kept flying towards the middle of the ocean.

They couldn't get far because of the storm raging between us and - "They are going towards Earth," I said. "We have to stop them now!"

I propelled my body upwards with flames under my feet. Keegan was right under me sprinting on top of the water. The seirons swirled around each other, creating their own storm. A force pulled me towards them. An enormous wave of water rose above me.

Keegan pulled the water over the seirons and caused them to crash into the sea. Fire shot from both of my hands. I had to keep my body almost horizontal to keep my balance. When they caught flame, the masks and wings burned. They fell into the storming ocean, but we couldn't stop all of them.

They tried to go through the storm once again, this time they pulled Keegan and I with them. For a second, there was a static in time. There was no sound, and I couldn't manipulate fire. I floated in an empty space, like a vacuum. The seirons couldn't get far and soared out of the storm. Once again, they took me with them.

The storm freed me, but I still couldn't control fire. I fell towards the water. Keegan yelled something at me, but the wind overpowered her voice. A pillar of water rose and caught me. Keegan stood on the water and reached her hand down towards me. I grabbed it, and she pushed us back to the land. We were right underneath the seirons, going back the way they came.

Once we landed in the sand, Keegan pulled water out of my clothes. Everyone was still fighting them, but they were not bothering to fight back. I opened my fist and could manipulate again. I shot two long streams of fire in the air, and a couple more seirons fell onto the sand.

A human body with a dark maroon mask stood at the top of the beach. A warmth the size of a match suffocated in its cold chest. Nax walked up to it.

"I know you're still in there somewhere," Nax said.

It didn't respond. I knew seirons could possess people, but it no longer looked human. Its tan skin stuck to its body. I walked closer. Its collar bone protruded inches out of its skin, and the seirons circled over its head.

"We will take it back," her voice echoed.

"Please, listen to us. You can fight this thing." Nax yelled.

"We will take it back," she repeated. She lifted her arm up and the legion of seirons dragged her away.

The piles of black ash blew around the beach. "There's someone still in there. We need to go help them." Nax screamed.

"Nax, it's too dangerous," Kira said. "That body looked like it was already far too corrupted to save."

"I don't buy that. They're still in there somewhere, and we can't just give up on them."

"We can't go follow them," Kira replied. "We have nothing fast enough."

They continued to argue while I ran to get Renn. He laid on the ground right next to the burning tree. I brought the flames to the ground and Renn continued to lay there. I walked over the smoky tree and put my hand on his back. The cut on his side was not too deep and most of the blood dried.

"Come on buddy. We have to go," I stood up and snapped my finger by my waist. He limped towards me. "You're such a baby." I picked him up and carried him to the beach.

"I swear, I saw them right here," a girl said.

"Well they aren't here anymore," said Paragon.

I ducked beneath the trees. Renn hopped out of my arms and crept towards the voices. The Trinity and Sylvic walked down towards the beach. "How did you not see where a hundred seirons went?" Sylvic yelled.

"We couldn't see anything through those trees," Paragon said. "You have no idea where they are."

The back of my shirt and right arm were pulled upwards. I looked back and Botak smiled down towards me. "Think we might've found something a little better."

He pushed me down to the ground in front of them. Renn howled towards Botak, but he kicked Renn to the ground.

I jumped up and sent countless blasts of fire towards him. "Don't hurt him!" I yelled. I drew my arms back to release a final blow, but something restricted me.

Zinna wrapped my arms with different plants and dragged me to the ground. "He has a temper this time," she laughed. "He might need a leash!"

"You should not have done that," Botak looked at his blister covered arms. I heard the crackling of lightning coming from his hands.

A wall of sand pushed him away from me. "Not him," Sylvic said. "We cannot hurt him. He has gotten strong though."

"What is going on?" I said struggling to get my hands loose. "Why are you with them?"

"You didn't think we would let you keep the Mallux? Finn, you're still a child." Sylvic bent down. His dark eyes rested solely on mine. "We needed your help. Her pureness will be so grateful for your hard work, she might even make you light."

"If he's light we don't need him anymore," Zinna laughed. She tightened the grip of the vines on my hands.

"Zinna, stop," Sylvic said. "He hasn't been claimed yet. We might still need him. Finn, where is everyone else?" He tried to be sincere.

I could see right through him. We were being used this whole time. He tainted Nax's mind to go look for this dumb thing. None of it was for us.

"You're very observant," his voice rang through my head. He stood up. "A lot of us were skeptical of you. Especially when they said you were the next Keeper of Dark. You are smart though; and cunning, and strong. We need to have all the pieces of the Mallux destroyed, but you are all fighters."

"It would have been a lot easier if we could've killed you," Zinna yelled.

"Do it. I'm done playing these games," I said. "Kill me."

Zinna stretched my arms further upwards. Another vine wrapped around my throat and began suffocating me.

"You're so brave, Finn." Paragon walked out of the shadows.

She pulled three long pieces of glass from her necklace, twisted them above me, and then brought them down towards my throat. I opened my eyes, and they hovered right above my skin.

"You can only play soldier for so long. Wait until the real fight starts. You won't be so brave then. If you keep this up a war is coming."

"Where are the others?" Sylvic asked. He finished pretending to be my friend.

"They aren't here," I said. "I left them once the seirons came."

"Aviva. Paragon. Check the beach. Don't touch them until you report back to me," Sylvic said.

"Don't hurt them," I erupted.

Fire spurred out of my mouth like lava. I was terrified, but I reveled in it. I tilted my head upward and burned the vines that kept me down. I rolled over to my feet and jumped up. I brought both of my hands together to hit Sylvic hard with fire. Then I ran towards my friends.

I ran up a rock and jumped just in front of Paragon and Aviva. Without a second to catch my breath, I unleashed everything stored inside me. All of my rage turned to flames. Paragon tucked behind a rock, but I continued to send an array of fire at her without giving her a chance to fight back. Zinna wrapped my leg with another vine, but I burned it immediately. A thicker one laced around my body, and Zinna pulled me towards her. I lit the plants on fire and whipped it back towards her face.

Two flaming whips rolled from my hands. I stretched them back and brought my arms forward towards Zinna. When I looked up, there were no more trees around us. I was at the Obrum. My whips were not wrapped around Zinna anymore, but the female guard during the revolt. I dropped my whips because I knew what happened next.

She looked at me for a second and then fell into the bathing pool. I ran towards her. Her dark hair contrasted with the clear water. Blood mixed with the water until it was the only thing left in the pool. It cracked open and the fluids poured over my feet. I laid in it now. It was cold. I put my hand inside it and lifted up. It dropped in clumps instead of how a liquid normally would. *That's because I'm not lying in blood.*

I looked over, and I laid in the sand. They searched my pockets already. I can tell because my cross necklace sat on my chest. They knew I didn't have any part of the Mallux. I let Aviva control me again.

I hopped up and heard the loud groans and wild punches from here. I ran to the group as fast as I could and dropped the burnt vines as I drew closer. I was back to being weak. My moments of courage were pushed away by the people I hurt when I had it. I took a deep breath in and ran down to help. The wind became strong and I could only imagine how much stronger it would get. Zinna whipped seaweed to block Botak while he created a storm. I snuck in from behind and knocked him down.

"You don't know when to give up," Zinna squealed.

She lifted piles of seaweed and entangled my entire body except for my face. Miller charged towards her with an arm covered with rocks. He swung towards her face, and she dodged it. Stones came out of the ground and tripped her. Miller dragged his hand back. He grunted as he lifted it back towards her with as much momentum as possible, but his hand froze halfway down. He wasn't moving at all. Zinna opened her eyes and looked back towards Sylvic. He stood up by the trees with all of his focus on Miller. Sylvic controlled him.

Miller stood up with the lack of any emotion. Gem covered rocks crawled up his other arm. Zinna crooked her head so it lined up with her smile. She put her arms to his face, and he did not flinch.

"Nice work, Sylvic," she said.

Nax had Paragon under his knee. He looked up and saw Sylvic. "What are you doing?" he screamed. The fighting stopped for a second. "Why are you helping them?"

"We need the Mallux," Sylvic walked towards Nax. "I was wrong the first time we went after it. It will only cause more fighting." He didn't break eye contact with Miller.

"No, it's not," Nax yelled. "You want exactly the same thing you did years ago. You want more power, but you can't control everyone."

"That's where you're wrong," he said.

Miller sprinted towards Nax and swung his hands towards him. I sent blasts of fire towards Sylvic. Botak was back up and kept a strong wind pushing me. Fire could not move in the empty air he created. I tried hand to hand combat but Botak was too strong. He put his forearm around my throat and kept the strong breeze.

"Look," he whispered. He jerked my body in a semi-circle. "You lost. All of your friends are going to die. All because of you."

Kira tried to get to Nax, but Paragon wouldn't stop sending hosts of glass towards her. Zinna and Miller still attacked Nax. He would've been able to beat Zinna, but he was too afraid to hurt Miller. The only one who held her ground was Keegan. Aviva was quick, but Keegan read her moves. She had Aviva wrapped in the sea, unable to change her reality.

Botak dragged me next to Nax who was wrapped in algae. Miller and Sylvic stood over him.

"You could give me the pieces you have Nax. I don't want to hurt you," Sylvic said.

"Miller, I know you're in there somewhere," Nax said. "Don't let him in your head." The plants covered his mouth until his voice became incoherent mumbling.

"You're still so naïve Nax. This world cannot live in the peace you are looking for." He took his foot off of Nax. "Finish him."

Miller held his heavy hands over Nax's head. When Miller threw his fist towards Nax, he barely missed his face, turned his entire body, and knocked Sylvic to the ground. Sylvic's hair covered his bloody face. Botak gripped my throat tighter and made the storm stronger. Miller pushed against the wind, trying to hit Sylvic again.

"I've had enough of this." Sylvic pushed his body upwards and bulldozed Miller to the ground with sand. "Give me the Mallux or the girl dies." He lifted himself high above us on a pillar of sand.

Keegan lost control of the water and walked into it. Her whole body sunk underneath the sea. She was under for a couple seconds and I expected her to come right up, but she didn't.

"Stop," I begged.

I was ready to wake up from one of Aviva's false realities, but I didn't. This was real. Her hands floated up, but they were not struggling to move. Her entire body breathed underneath the crashing waves. Rings spilt around the absence of her once her hands plummeted under water until another wave pushed the only trace of her away. She was going to die.

I kicked my foot underneath Botak's and knocked him to the ground. I covered my fist with fire and sent it straight to his face. He screamed, but I didn't care. Paragon ran between Sylvic and I and sent small pieces of glass into my body. I tried to fight back, but she was too fast. I fell to the ground and saw Keegan's blonde hair reaching the surface water. She was my breaking point.

"Enough!" I screamed.

Shadows etched their way through the earth from every direction. Beams of cold darkness stretched to my skin and never left. The darkness was inside me. I felt it.

Every last bit of energy came out of my body. There were no more final rays of golden light in the sky. There was only darkness. Not from the setting sun, but coming from me. I used to believe light existed inside me, but everything in me spilled out. And everything was dark.

Shadows expelled from my hands in waves that corrupted everything. I tried to make them stop, but the more I fought the darkness the more deliberately it came. Everything and everyone was caught in my storm, and then it all dispelled into nothingness once again.

I felt an intense burn inside of my chest twisting around. I made sense of a few things. Sylvic was on the ground after my darkness immobilized him, but he laughed hysterically, cheering that I was dark and the new Keeper of Darkness.

Keegan crawled out of the water and coughed out what filled her lungs. Paragon, Miller, and Zinna were all on the ground only able to move their eyes. Botak still screamed in agony. His face was covered with blisters already. And there was Kira. She just cut Nax loose from the plants. Now she was lifeless on the floor. I stood right over her, and she wasn't breathing.

Kira was the closest to me, darkness struck her the hardest, and she suffered the most consequences. If she was lower to the ground like Nax, she would just be paralyzed, but instead she was dead. *And I killed her.*

"What did you do?" Nax cried. "What did you do?"

He put his hand on her chest and tried to push air back into her lungs. It didn't work. I looked at everyone, and they looked right back. I was a stranger to them. I ran towards the woods.

"No. No. She's dead!" Nax screamed.

I didn't look back.

"You killed her!" Lighting stuck a couple feet from me.

I ran. The crackling of lightning created a static around us while I tried to replay what just happened. I swerved through the trees until my body couldn't move, and then I sat behind a thick tree. My chest and my back experienced an unknown amount of pain. I looked down at my chest and it was vacant. I stretched my arm back and felt cold markings pushing up on my skin.

I traced it with both of my hands. It was the sharp "c" shape of the Apex of Darkness. The bottom swerved into a "s". I closed and opened my eyes at least a dozen times trying to figure out if this was real. I took a deep breath and held both of my hands out. I focused everything I felt out in front of me and screamed. Darkness was easy to conjure right now.

Dark smoke dissipated all around me. It was strongest when you felt wicked, and I felt unbearably wicked. *I killed Kira.* My hands swirled the shadows against the sunset. I reached into my pocket, and all I found was my cross necklace.

Although I walk through the valley of darkness, I will fear no evil. That verse used to help calm me down, but this time I couldn't rely on it. I never thought I would be the evil. I never thought the thing I would fear most is myself.

I continued to dance with the shadows around me. I felt powerful, but it came from the worst place possible. It came from my guilt, my heartbreak, and my selfishness, but it was who I am. It is who I have been. I am a consuming fire and a deteriorating darkness. I can control darkness, *and this darkness will control me.*

CHAPTER TWENTY
DEAD PLACES

I should've known this would be the outcome. I saw it happening when I crossed the bridge, Vatius warned me, and my mother saw it coming ever since the first day I discovered what I was capable of.

We were alone on a beach when I was eight before she got married to Jim. The final rays of golden sun stretched over the water on the cold winter night. This was our tradition every Sunday night. My mother first became sick around this time, so cold weather wasn't something her doctors recommended.

"It's time to leave," she said. Her eyes were turquoise in this light.

"The sunsets almost done. Just five more minutes," I begged.

"Finny, we have to leave before it gets too cold."

She grabbed onto my hand and pulled me away from the crashing waves. I wasn't ready to leave. As I pushed her hand off of mine, flames came spiraling from my palm and surrounded her wrist. I was amazed at first, and then I heard her agonizing screams as blisters covered her hands and the flames became nothing.

"I'm sorry. I'm sorry. I don't know." I cried, and then I started sobbing.

"Hey. Shh." She put her other hand over my head and caressed me. "You didn't know."

She turned me towards the water, which was now fluorescent as it reflected both the sun and the moon. She pulled streams of water from the ocean until they covered her hand. It wrapped around her and then she swirled the water above our head creating a different world underneath the light the water reflected.

"I can do it too." She smiled. "We both come from a place where everyone can control something. This incredible world where we are limitless, but this isn't our world." She let the waters that soared above us plummet back into the sand while she kept a thin layer around her burnt wrist. "What we can do, what we are doesn't belong here. Finny, promise me. You won't manipulate fire in front of anyone but me."

I tried to make sense of everything in that moment, but I couldn't. There were things that my mom hid from me, an entire world she hid from me. An entire world she wanted me to keep from everyone else.

She grabbed onto my wrist and held her face close to mine. "Promise me. If they find out where I am, they will hurt both of us. Promise me."

She gripped my hand even tighter, but I didn't push her hand off of mine.

"I promise," I finally said.

"We need to go." She looked around the beach, making sure no one was around.

I didn't argue with her this time. We walked back up to the street and didn't talk about anything that happened. Every time I asked her after that day, she told me I had to wait a little longer and reminded me to never manipulate again.

I listened for the most part. I stayed calm and didn't tell anyone about what we could do, not even Jeremy. On late nights, in the comfort of my room, I would practice control. I taught myself how to hold the flames in my hands, and how to subvert them back into air. The night at the church, the night I left, proved that what I learned was never enough.

What I learned at Domister wasn't enough either. What happened just a few hours ago proved that. I didn't know what Nax or Kira could've taught me that would've prepared me for what I became.

Night came for me although the tall trees had kept most of the light out. It was comforting to be in the darkness even if I was alone. I didn't know what happened to Keegan, or Miller, or Sylvic, but I knew all too well what happened to Kira.

My mother, the people at the concert, the guard at Caltus, the Keeper of Death, Jin, Kira. The faces flashed through my mind like lightning. When I closed my eyes to sleep, the faces were all saw. I couldn't escape my mind. *I couldn't escape the truth.*

I put my jacket over a wet log and laid down on it, trying to get comfortable. It was freezing, but I couldn't use flames to keep my warm this time. I didn't know how close the Trinity and Nax were, and I didn't want to fight anymore tonight.

I counted the stars instead of sheep to get my mind off of everything. They were beautiful tonight. I'd seen the world fall apart at the hands of the stars, but they still looked beautiful.

One. Fire absorbed Kate's home so many years ago. On a night like this. On a night when I admired the small specs of light that graced the sky. I swore that I wouldn't admire them again because it would only remind me of her sister's death, but here I was.

Two. The night Sylvic took me to Centure was the same night I lost control. I've never felt anything more powerful, more overwhelming than myself. In that moment, I unleashed potential locked away for ten years, but it came with a hefty price. Most things don't exist without something else falling out of place to make room.

Three. I realized just how spectacular this world was when Jin and I laid in the luminous garden of lavender flowers. The stars were dim compared to everything that lived beneath them. She was so beautiful that night, resting in the supernatural light. It hurt so bad when she left. It still hurt, but I had no tears left to cry tonight.

Four. Hadlee brought the constellations down to earth when she was claimed. She was light, something all of us wanted, but none of us got. I wanted more than anything to be claimed for light because I hated what I felt when Aviva manipulated my reality. Now, that feeling was my reality. But was this darkness something I'd always felt?

Five. Keegan's claiming differed from anything else I'd seen. The darkness that encapsulated her body didn't blend in with the darkness of the sky. The sky was bright with the moon and stars that night, but when Keegan was claimed there was no light.

For a minute, I thought I lost her to the darkness. When the shadows settled, and I stared at an unrecognizable face, I didn't think I'd be able to look at her the same. Nothing changed. Not her beauty, or her confidence, or the feeling I had every time we were together.

Where was she now? I didn't know if she or Miller made it out all right. She had the Halo, the very thing that the Trinity wanted. I grabbed the compass from my pocket, but never clicked it open because knowing a vague direction wouldn't settle my fear. I wanted her here. I wanted her now.

Six. Miller told me Vestrin's souls become the stars once they die. I knew it wasn't true, but if it was would I be looking at Kira. Would she be staring back down at me? Is she wondering what happened, and why I did it? Does she know I couldn't stop it? Do they know I didn't want it to end this way?

My step dad always said *don't look for life in dead places.* It was based on some scripture, but he used it all the time. He didn't want me or Jeremy to pursue something that wasn't realistic. He wanted us to dream, but he knew when to be honest with us. He told this to Jeremy after his girlfriend cheated on him and he wanted to get back together with her. He told this to me when I started working to get money for my mother's medical bill. We tend to search for life in dead places, but it's a waste of time.

Seven.

Eight.

Nine. A fox walked behind me. I hoped that it was Renn, but it was just a regular fox. Renn wouldn't come find me. Light attracted them, and I was everything but. Silvic told me they were dangerous, and I needed to stay away from them. Maybe he feared that this creature could sway me into the right direction. Maybe he feared I would be light. What were his motives? Why did he want me to be dark?

I trusted Sylvic from the second he stepped onto my front porch, but he always had a plan for me. He probably had been in contact with Vatius from the beginning. He told her to come to Domister, he told us to go to Kordia, and she waited. Our demise was always his plan, but they couldn't kill me.

Why did he want me to be the next Keeper of Darkness?

Ten.

I took a deep breath in and stopped counting stars. I needed to sleep. My mother, the strangers at the concert, the guard at Caltus, the Keeper of Death, Jin, Kira. The faces flooded my mind again, but I never opened my eyes. I had to let it play out, and it did, over, and over, and over again.

The shade from the tall trees made it easier to sleep in. I woke up around ten, and I was starving when I did. I stood up and threw my wet jacket over my shoulders. My back throbbed. I traced my markings once again with a sensitive finger, assuring everything that happened yesterday was real.

The pain subsided as I walked. I had no idea where I was going or what came next. First, I needed to eat. The trees didn't bear any fruit, but some bushes had handfuls of blackberries. I ate as many as I could and stuffed my pockets with more.

I needed something with substance. There weren't many animals out here likely because of winter. There were traces of small footprints, so I scanned the trees for a squirrel or a bird, but no luck. Branches cracking echoed through the silence in the woods. It sounded like something big.

I crept towards the ridge, avoiding leaves and twigs as I made my way. I sat behind a tree and heard more crushing leaves. I peeked around the trunk and saw Nax looking for me. His eyes were bloodshot and carried by dark bags underneath. It looked like he had been up all night looking for me.

I tucked my body behind the tree and waited. I needed to get away from him fast. I could fight him now that I can manipulate darkness, but nothing in me wanted to fight. He walked up a hill, and I lost him in the overlapping branches. Once I couldn't hear his heavy footsteps, I ran.

I ran through the crowded woods, dodging trees and fallen logs. A squirrel scurrying out of my way, but I didn't stop running. I looked back to make sure he wasn't close and tripped over a rock. My body plummeted to the ground and continued to roll down a small hill until I smashed into a tree.

Now my back was in serious pain.

I laid against the tree, groaning and trying to catch my breath. I felt dizzy as I pushed myself off the ground and fell back to my knees. Shadows flooded from behind me, but I wasn't the one controlling them.

A seiron towered high above me. I jumped to my feet and ran away from the creature, shooting flames towards it but missing every time. I fell back to the ground and inched myself against another tree facing the seiron.

It didn't attack me, but it moaned. The beast seemed sad. As it walked towards me, I noticed that one of its wings was broken in half. The mask was still intact. Orange and yellow lines swirled around the eyes and a thick red bar went from the chin to the lips.

The being moved toward me and stopped a couple feet in front of me. Darkness extended from its body and grazed the side of my face. If this thing wanted to take over the darkness inside of me, it had a lot to choose from. It never did.

Eventually, the being fell onto the floor and seemed to sit down. We were eye to eye with each other. The creature never stopped moaning although it sounded more like a cry. It couldn't fly anymore, and the rest of the seirons were long gone.

A little bit of life existed in this thing. It had emotions and the capacity to understand that I was something different. I reached my hand up to the mask. I pulled on it, but shadows came from all around and kept the mask nailed to its face. I pulled just a little harder, and the seiron let out a loud screech that violently pushed me back into the tree.

The creature tried to fly out of the woods, but it crashed into the ground just a couple feet away from me. Shadows pushed its body back up and the seiron scurried down another hill. I stood up and crept towards it. My head spun as I stepped closer and closer to darkness.

I stood at the top of the hill and stared down towards the seiron.

It tried lifting itself off the ground again, but it couldn't fly. Another screech vibrated the floors. I looked behind me to make sure Nax wasn't following us, but I figured he would try to avoid the creature I'm trying to understand.

I created a living shadow that stood just as tall as I did and manipulated it towards the being. Curiosity fell hard on the beast as the shadow I casted moved around it. The seiron moved next to my darkness and circled around it. It almost looked like they were dancing together.

I slid down the hill while my shadows distracted the seiron. I dragged the darkness over the small pond and towards me. the creature followed every movement my shadows made. The shadows moved slowly as they glided closer together.

Once it was only a few feet away from me, I realized the seiron held onto the faux living shadow I crafted. *There is emotion in this being.* Both the shadows and the seiron were only a few feet away from me now. I let the shadows dissolve, but the seiron couldn't accept the fate. A shadow like hand stretched out even after my darkness became a bitter nothingness.

The beast was no longer crying, but staring at me. It watched the shadows crawl back into my hand and looked back at me. It tilted its head with confusion and brought itself back to eye level with me.

I showed it the shadows I could control. I can't imagine how strange it was to see everything that created the creature manipulated by someone else. Fountains of darkness spurred in the palm of my hand, and the lurking shadow the seiron held out stretched until it wrapped around my wrist.

It brought my hand back to the mask. I stopped manipulating the darkness, and it pushed my hand back towards my body. It stared at me once again, waiting for something. I manipulated shadows again. This time I didn't stop manipulating as it pulled my hand to the mask.

I understood. Seirons could take over someone's body, but no one told me what they looked like. This one seemed different from the ones that attacked us on the beach. It had emotions and conscious decisions. This creature wanted me to expel the darkness that held it down.

I pulled on the mask again, only this time I pushed the darkness that detained the creature. It was hard to rip off. I dug my fingernails inside the small space I made and continued casting the darkness away from me.

The beast screamed out towards the sky as the mask peeled off of it. Shadows unraveled inch by inch as I retrieved whatever life was trapped inside the long-decayed body. Through the curtains of darkness, I saw the face of a woman for only a second before everything became a pile of dust. No more screaming, no more pain.

Sometimes, life can be found in dead places.

There was a woman trapped inside absolute darkness, but my darkness freed her from the reign of the seiron. I witnessed a life overtaken by darkness, and when the shadows fade there was nothing. I was something before darkness took over, and I will always have that piece of my life.

I didn't get to decide what I was claimed as. That woman didn't dictate the seiron to corrupt her living body. We don't get to choose what happens to us, but we get to choose what happens directly after. We can be the very thing we want people to remember us for if we hold the capacity to remember ourselves.

I cannot destroy my demons. I cannot take back what I had done or what I had become, but I didn't want to. There was a part of me that existed before I even knew what I was capable of, and there will be a new part of me after everything I had been holding in was released.

I am not just dark. I am not just Craved. I am not just a manipulator. I am not just human. I am all these things existing simultaneously. This world is a battlefield and everyone has a part in this war. I won't be what they want me to be. I won't be the next Keeper. Instead, I will burn the way of this world to the ground and restore a new peace from the dark ashes.

Anthony Tacheny

ABOUT THE AUTHOR

What a ride these past few years have been. This is it. This is the physical entity of the world I have been dreaming of. There is a version of everything I love inside this fantasy – and it is just a fantasy. It is no longer mine, and I don't want it to be. My name is Anthony Tacheny. I am twenty years old as I place the last commas on the same document I started two years ago. I am twenty as I start this new chapter in my life. Yes, this is the end of the book. With time, I am hoping to complete the story of Finn Lynch and a group of unlikely heroes, but for now, hold onto the words you were given. Do the very thing you can't live without, and do it to your fullest potential. Find who you are. Strive to be who you want to be remembered as. Passion is the only thing that will keep you going when you feel like giving up. My name is Anthony Tacheny. This is not just a fantasy.

Made in the USA
San Bernardino, CA
15 January 2019